The Perils of a Literary Life

The Perils of a Literary Life

Jennifer Weeks

Matador
9 Priory Business Park,
Wistow Road, Kibworth Beauchamp,
Leicestershire. LE8 0RX
Tel: 0116 279 2299
Email: books@troubador.co.uk
Web: www.troubador.co.uk/matador
Twitter: @matadorbooks

ISBN 978 1788036 351

British Library Cataloguing in Publication Data.
A catalogue record for this book is available from the British Library.

Printed by Printed and bound by CPI Group (UK) Ltd, Croydon, CR0 4YY
Typeset in 11pt Baskerville by Troubador Publishing Ltd, Leicester, UK

Matador is an imprint of Troubador Publishing Ltd

To my lovely husband, Graham.

Prologue

Lightning flashes some distance away from us through the trees. The entire volume of river water is being funnelled into a narrow gap between two huge boulders. The distance between the two boulders is only about two metres. The river rushes downwards, hammering against the moss-covered rocks before plunging into the boiling cauldron below and its roar is deafening. The deep whirlpool at my feet churns and heaves. Its power is *terrifying*.

Cold mist sprays over me, stinging my face as he stares at me and I glance around, trembling. There's no-one else about. I'm trapped here with him. His face looks pale in the twilight. The face of a killer. Fear slices into me. It will only take one sharp shove from him …

I open my mouth to scream – but no sound comes out … I can feel how it will be – flailing in empty space, the threshing waters closing over my head, somersaulting over and over. Water flooding my nose, mouth, throat – my lungs. Writhing convulsively, lungs burning, as it drags me down into its black depths…

What a fool I've been, suffering from such delusions, from phantom conceits of the brain. Literature breeds such fatuous lies.

Chapter 1

I stare at the bubbling, boiling water.

My life isn't flashing before my eyes, as you might expect; it's more as if I've gained the long view. Detached myself for a moment from the present. This rushing water seems symbolic, its two sources intermingling to form the narrative flow of my life. I can trace the origins of my life story, one tributary springing from my desperate desire to be Me, my self, and the other driving my Romantic dreams of a rural idyll. Both have combined to shape the course of my life, precipitating me here at its disastrous climax.

'To Begin at the Beginning' to quote a famous Welsh poet – and to begin at my beginning, the origins of my life, is to begin at someone else's too. Becky, my identical twin sister. Identical yet not identical. A source of affection throughout my childhood – and of friction. I have studied those pictures on the Internet of the cells of monozygotic twins to try and fathom how the two of us came about. Our genesis. The natural phenomenon that occurs when one zygote splits and forms two identical embryos.

I've always fancied I sensed Becky's pink pulsing presence in the womb, so intimate and bound up with me as to seem a part of me. And during the first two years of our lives, the sense of my self and Becky's merged. We

1

were always together. Becky was the familiar voice, face, smell. She was forever the active blur in the corner of my eye, playing, crying, clambering over me. Becky seemed an intrinsic part of my developing self. We even had an idioglossia before we could speak – when we knew what the other meant through our babblings. Mum was amazed. Our own secret language, quite common between twins according to the Health Visitor and nothing to worry about. It would disappear as soon as we learned to speak, which was true – it did. But we still had a telepathic link – sensing somehow when the other was unhappy. That was something else that united us, another bond.

Or another manacle, chaining us together.

Becky was my mirror image – but she wasn't *me*. Definitely not. Internet pictures of the slender DNA strands in the cells of our twin bodies were, to my mind, like slivers of metal attracted by opposing polar forces, aligned totally differently. Maybe she'd had more oxygen or different amounts of nutrients in the womb, influencing the neural connections in the brain. All I know is that, as my self acquired definite edges, I felt more and more distinct from her.

I would sit, infant fingers fumbling with cardboard pages to reveal the surreal antics of an egg called Humpty Dumpty or some strange old woman with hundreds of kids who lived in a shoe. On the other hand, Becky would be leaping off the back of the sofa or swinging wildly on our rocking horse.

I lingered over my Beatrix Potter stories. The furry figures of Peter Rabbit and Tom Kitten were appealing. But I savoured the faint, dreamy landscapes of hills, valleys, ponds and lakes. I looked up from light-filled country scenes at the long line of houses across the street, cutting the sky in two. But, of course, Becky tossed 'The Tale of the Flopsy Bunnies' aside in favour of her skipping rope. But Mum did manage to read them with her too, sometimes, when she was ill or tired.

I'd inherited my mother's gentle, more passive nature whilst Becky was driven and dynamic, like Dad. Yet we looked identical to outsiders' eyes, with our fair hair, freckles and blue eyes.

Dad and Mum could tell us apart though for we were not completely identical. We spent ages comparing faces, hands and feet as we grew. My face was slightly rounder than Becky's, and more freckled, my hands a bit broader. Again I found the explanation for this on the Internet: the DNA may not be divided equally between the two cells. This was vividly illustrated by a comparison with an apple; when you cut an apple in half, the two halves do not look exactly the same.

Yet we had many of the same mannerisms. Becky's lower lip would wobble when she was about to cry, just as mine did, and we both had a childhood lisp which vanished as we approached puberty.

Mum liked to dress us in identical clothes sewn on her sewing machine with hand-knitted cardigans and jumpers and the lady in the corner shop always addressed us jointly as 'Twins'. "How are you today, twins? Hope you're not wearing your poor mother out." As if we were part of the same package, two halves of a whole.

But even then, I knew that we weren't.

A symbiosis developed between us at Nursery, one the

flipside of the other. Becky would defend me, demanding other children return toys taken from me. She was active, I passive, she the aggressor, I the comforter, hugging her when she bumped her knee on the climbing frame.

Literary images continued to seep into the stream of my consciousness. Our Nursery teacher, Mrs Tingle, in her appearance, was, to me, the embodiment of Mrs Tiggywinkle. With no neck to speak of and bright black eyes, the rounded figures of Mrs Tingle and Mrs Tiggywinkle merged one into the other. Whenever I looked at Mrs Tingle, Mum's words echoed in my head: "and her nose went sniffle, and her eyes went twinkle, twinkle."

Mum had a beautiful book of fairy tales from her childhood. The binding of the 'Treasury of Fairy Tales' was sumptuous. The soft brown vellum covers adorned with gold and vermillion lettering, the cryptic patterns of green swirls evoked mystery. I kept it tucked away under my pillow, like contraband.

Inside, translucent tissue paper unveiled another world. A world where maidens with long, Pre-Raphaelite hair drifted through green glens, where evil witches lurked in dark caves. Knights fought fire-breathing dragons outside magnificent castles with towers and turrets. A world as fantastical as a mirage. For me, though, this was a realm as real as the play park down the road – just somewhere … further away.

The first story in the Treasury was 'Cinderella', its climax vividly illustrated. Cinderella stood in a pink ball gown against a midnight blue backdrop, sparkling with stars, gazing up into her prince's eyes. What a spell was cast on me by that enchanting story! One day I would find my romantic hero. And live happily ever after.

Most fairy tales passed Becky by, for Mum had trouble getting her to sit still for any length of time. Maybe reading my books 'switched on' an epigene, as the Internet described it, and set me off down the fantasy route that Becky never followed. Food and drink are thought to cause changes to genes, so why not stories? Who knows exactly how Nature and Nurture work?

I read voraciously, devouring book after book, their images filtering through the flux of consciousness, layering the foundations of my mind. At primary school, our Year 2 teacher, Mr Asquith, was an elderly man with bulging eyes and a wide grin who wore a waistcoat and bowtie. He'd sweep into the staff car park in his bright yellow open-topped VW Beetle. As Mr Asquith gave me a wide grin, I saw Mr Toad before me, about to exclaim, 'Oh bliss! Oh poop poop!' Ridiculous, I know, but I couldn't stop myself.

I told Becky about it, showing her my copy of 'The Wind in the Willows', but she frowned. 'Well, I suppose he looks a *bit* like Mr Toad,' she conceded.

Becky and I still needed each other. A new girl joined our class called Alice. 'I'm Alice so you can't be called Alice too,' she insisted. She had sole rights to that name and she seemed to speak with such moral force that I stared helplessly at her. How could I argue with such overwhelming conviction? But as usual Becky vigorously defended me – by the simple expedient of pulling Alice's plaits till she accepted shared ownership of our name.

And when Becky broke her leg, falling off the swing

in the park, I knew straight away, even though I was in the park toilets at the time. Telepathy was still a powerful bond between us. I kissed her leg to make it better. She was stuck in hospital for a few days because the fracture was complicated and I would make up stories to entertain her. I told her about a cat named Smokey, who found a magic stick in the forest. This stick could speak and, when waved by Smokey and accompanied by a magic spell, it could rescue other cats in trouble. I blushed as I recited my rhymes to her:

'Smokey the cat was walking along one bright and sunny day,

When all at once she came across a big brown stick that lay

In front of her upon the ground, and so for quite a while,

She played with it – but the she jumped – for it gave her a great big smile! ...'

Why *are* rhymes so satisfying? I can't think of a rational explanation.

Nor can I explain my sympathetic pain the minute Becky fell off the swing; I *felt* her agony. Telepathy vibrating at a visceral level. It united us. A communion of minds, the weft of our kinship.

Unable to move because of her leg, Becky became immersed in my story. Eyes glazed, she existed for a while, as I did, in another world, a wonderful world of a cat and her magic stick. We were united by my fantasy. But only for a little while.

I suppose Becky and I both sensed our differences – but it was me who, at the age of eight, asked Mum to let us buy different clothes. We both wore jeans and t-shirts most of the time. But I loved pretty clothes. And I guess I wanted to express my unique individuality even then. Yet when I wore a floaty skirt and blouse for the first time, I couldn't look at Becky standing there in her jeans.

Becky sulked for days. She saw it as a rejection of her and retaliated by having her blonde hair cut short, like a boy. She told Mum she couldn't be bothered tying it back any more. But I knew she was angry. She didn't speak to me for a week, wanting me to suffer. And I squirmed whenever I saw her short blonde hair.

Mum wasn't very happy about this.

'They've always looked so *cute,* dressed the same,' she wailed.

'I know – but they're not a box set,' said Dad. 'You can't dress them identically forever just because you think they look cute. They're very different and Alice just wants to show that she's her own special self. Don't you, Alice?'

I nodded vigorously. Dad understood me.

My reading of books even included browsing through the dictionary. The listing of all the words in the English language. Words were like flints which struck sparks in my mind, glittering as they burst upon the brain. Yes, "Exuberance" resonated with the first thrilling glimpse of the shimmering sea when we visited Grandma and Grandpa in Weston-Super-Mare. "Luxuriance" was a word to bathe in, as it lapped around the tongue, as lush and lovely as the long grass of summer. "Nebulous" – a fumbling, bumbling word as hazy as a figure stumbling in the mist.

Mum didn't read much – apart from magazines – but she loved to hire a romantic film on a Sunday afternoon and I'd curl up with her on the sofa to watch it. Those films formed the romantic bedrock to my being.

We'd always have a bag of toffees on our laps. And Mum would be knitting something for one of her clients, her needles clicking away. Maybe a pair of mittens for Mrs Gledhill or a scarf for Stan Hazeldine, a hundred and two year old man she'd helped to look after for years. 'He feels the cold so badly, does poor old Stan.'

Mum could knit complicated patterns and still be able to watch the film, which I thought was really clever. Or she'd be working on one of the pretty tapestries she'd bought – of country cottages with a flock of geese outside the wooden latched gate or a Victorian little girl in a pinafore dress running down a country lane with a whip and top.

When Audrey Hepburn thought Gregory Peck had had his hand bitten off by the ancient stone face in 'Roman Holiday', Mum and I sat there, transfixed. It was the way the two of them gazed at each other so lovingly.

I remember the time I watched 'Brief Encounter' for the first time. I surreptitiously wiped away a tear when Alec left Laura in 'Brief Encounter', putting a hand on her shoulder. The longing, the tenderness, the sadness in that touch – it was all too much. I heard some loud sniffing coming from the settee. I looked across at Mum. Tears were pouring down her cheeks.

'Are you alright, Mum?' I asked.

'Oh, it always gets to me, this part,' she sniffed. She wiped her eyes with a tissue and blew her nose. 'Don't take any notice of me. I'm just soppy.'

Then Becky and Dad came bursting in from a game of tennis, wanting to watch the football.

'Yuk!' Becky exclaimed when she saw the credits for 'Brief Encounter' rolling down the screen. She cast a scornful eye over the tapestry Mum was weaving of kittens playing on a rug by the fire. She always thought Mum's tapestries were too chocolate boxy. 'Well, I'm glad I didn't have to sit through *that*. Why didn't you get out "Pirates of the Caribbean" instead?' She loved Johnny Depp. He was far more cool than Trevor Howard.

More differences emerged as time went on. We went to a theme park for a tenth birthday party, invited jointly by some school friends. I saw a brochure for the theme park filled with horrendous images and immediately refused to go – but somehow, Becky over-ruled me. She pointed out that, as we'd both been invited, I was obliged to go too. Becky always made the most of her seniority by birth of half an hour, as though it conferred a badge of authority over me. Mum agreed with Becks – we *always* went to parties together. We were the twins; it was expected of us. And I submitted, as usual, to their overwhelming moral pressure.

Our train crept to the top of the first slope of the roller coaster. Already I was regretting my rash decision to climb on board. We hung, suspended, at the summit, teetering precariously on the flimsy structure and viewed the immense drop before us. Then we plunged down, down, down, hurtling to the bottom. My stomach flipped. I was about to be thrown out, falling hundreds of feet to the ground! Seconds later, we were swept up to the next mountain of latticed metalwork.

Becky, of course, loved it. Sitting beside me, she flung up her arms in screaming abandon as we dropped again down to the earth. I huddled in my seat, a heap of misery, longing for it to be over. I was breathing jaggedly, in great jerks. I had to escape from this heaving monster.

Becky did sympathise, though. No, it was more than that, I could tell. She could feel my misery. She put an arm round my shoulder and helped me up from my seat. "You'll be alright in a minute,' she whispered comfortingly as I staggered away.

'Never again,' I muttered.

'Oh, come on, Alice. You'll love it if you try it a few times,' she tried to convince me.

'No!'

She didn't say anything but I could see the scorn in her eyes. Why couldn't I be a daredevil like her? But I didn't care if the whole world thought I was a coward. I was not going on that roller coaster again. I've never been the feisty heroine so popular in today's world. I much prefer the second-hand but safer world of stories.

At least, though, I had resisted Becky's forceful powers of coercion. And suddenly I knew that she couldn't always make me do things I didn't want to do. I was developing – very slowly – my will, my own sense of being.

At primary school, the teachers were always mixing us up. Becky was stopped in the corridor by the Head for my story which I'd contributed to the school magazine. Becky didn't say anything to enlighten her.

It was Becks' idea to have some fun with our twinhood, or whatever you call it.

'Wouldn't it be a laugh to see if we can get away with it?'

I looked at her, considering. Could we pull it off?

'Go on then.' So I walked into Becky's maths class, her book under my arm and she went to the bottom maths set. I sat down next to Sarah Wilkins and she returned my grin before bending her blonde head over her book. Sarah thought I was Becky. I opened my book, uneasiness creeping over me. It was as if I was cheating, lying in some strange way.

As I stared at the geometry questions in front of me, my heart sank. Why had we decided to swap identities in maths of all subjects?

'What is angle x in this right-angled triangle, where the second angle is 55 degrees?'

Hadn't a clue. I suppose I could measure the angle with a protractor.

But Mrs Jones tall figure loomed over me. 'Now you know better than that, Rebecca. It says no protractors are to be used.'

'Well, er. I'm not sure what to do.'

'Oh, come on. This isn't like you. Think, girl!'

I stared at the triangle, cheeks burning. The silence seemed an eternity.

Mrs Jones sighed in exasperation. 'So how many interior degrees in a triangle? she prompted.

'One hundred and eighty.' What had that got to do with it?

'So?'

At last I saw it. 'Oh, if you subtract the other two angles from one hundred and eighty ...'

'Exactly. About time. Work it out logically and concentrate, Rebecca. *Reason* your way to the answer. You've got a good brain.'

I was never doing this again. It was wrong – and weird. Mrs Jones wasn't seeing me at all but Becky. Somehow I'd lost myself in my sister. Where did I start and Becky end?

I found the whole event disturbing.

'Didn't it seem *wrong* to trick people like that?' I asked.

Becky shrugged. 'It was only a joke. And getting out of Mrs Jones' lesson was cool! Your Maths work was sooo easy.'

Sundays were Zoo days. We had an annual Family Pass and Dad would tell us everything he'd learned about the cute koala bear that Mum was cooing at, as it crouched on a branch, staring at us with its huge eyes.

People would often glance at Becky and me as we strolled along the paths in the zoo and then do a double take.

'Mummy, those girls are the same person!' one little boy exclaimed, dropping his ice cream when Becks and I walked side by side out of the Reptile House.

Dad hated his job selling double glazing and he would come home on weekday nights, pale and exhausted. But on Sundays, his face was lit up with enthusiasm. 'Look at that orang utan', he'd murmur as we gazed through the bars in the Ape House. 'So intelligent. Such sad, wise eyes.' I stared at the orang utan as he deftly peeled a banana with his black, leathery fingers. He suddenly looked up and stared at us.

'What do you think's he thinking now?' I whispered. ' I wonder how he's feeling inside.'

'I don't know. Maybe he's a bit bored or perhaps he's quite contented in his comfortable enclosure,' Dad said. 'It's such a pity we can't ask him … There was a programme on telly the other night about animal intelligence. Did you know there's a gorilla they've taught which can understand sign language? And a bonobo that understands more than three thousand words of English. Fascinating stuff!'

We gazed at two elephants in the enclosure next to the Ape House. They were lovingly coiling their trunks together, gazing into each other's eyes. 'They really seem to love each other, don't they,' Dad mused. 'It does make you wonder whether animals are so different from us after all.'

I nodded. 'I suppose they must feel sad, happy and frightened – just like we do.'

We set up the camera to take a photo of the four of us outside the Monkey Enclosure. I treasure that photo and I put it in the silver locket Mum and Dad gave me for Christmas. Dad is standing with his arm around Mum; both of them are beaming. Becky and I are crouched in front, a happy family group. It was the last time we were photographed united as a family.

The change began during our ballet production of 'The Snow Queen'. Becky and I had gone to ballet class since the age of five. We both loved it – but, as usual, for different reasons. Becky used to practise in front of the mirror in our bedroom, trying to master the perfect arabesque. She loved the discipline, the exercise. Me, I revelled in the romance. And our production of 'The Snow Queen' was indeed fabulous – the sumptuous palace, the tall, dark and handsome Kai, the dainty, feminine Gerte, the glorious music.

Our snowflake costumes were gorgeous. Becky and I were both snowflake guards protecting the Snow Queen's Palace. The skirts of our tutus spread out in many layers of crisp, lacy gauze. The silver filigree threads sparkled in the spotlights.

On our heads we wore little silver caps which glittered as we spun and twirled around, as light and airy as snowflakes in a snowstorm.

We both stood in front of the full-length mirror in the changing room, during the interval. Two faces with the same blue eyes, blonde hair and freckles. Mum was putting a few emergency stitches in my silver cap which had spilt at the side. Then she stood back and looked into the mirror to check the effect. She smiled. 'Well, they say that no two snowflakes are identical but, looking at you two, you'd never believe it!'

Mum had told us weeks before that Dad's work wasn't going well with his new line manager, and not to annoy him. I'd noticed Dad was silent when he came in from work, just grunting when Mum asked him how his day had been. His eyes were strangely glassy – and his breath smelled sour. A pulse would beat just above his right eyebrow.

Mum was pressing our ballet dresses for the grand performance the following day. Becky and I were finishing supper after the dress rehearsal. Dad helped himself to a great hunk of cheese out of the fridge and Mum had just made some mild remark about having to buy Dad the next size up in trousers when she went out shopping.

Dad thumped his plate of cheese and biscuits down on the table. He barked at Mum, 'I can't help it if I don't have time to exercise. Stuck in the car all day and too knackered to go to the gym when I don't get in till eight! It's alright for you, getting home at five. And then you have the bloody nerve to criticise me.' His voice didn't sound like Dad at all – it was so cold and hard, as if he hated Mum.

It was Kai's cruel rejection of Gerda all over again, the troll-mirror splinter lodged in his heart. Dad's voice was icy cold. He'd never spoken like this before to Mum. They'd always been so happy together, warm, teasing. That made it seem so much worse. Mum stared at him, nonplussed, unable to defend herself when under attack. She looked stricken, helpless. I know she hated conflict, like me.

'Come on, girls. Get up to bed. You've got a busy day tomorrow, what with school and then the performance.' She spoke firmly but there was a tremor in her voice. She was frightened of Dad, I could tell. But she wanted to protect us from the ugliness of his temper.

Becky and I lay in our beds as their voices drifted up. Dad aggrieved, irritable, Mum placatory, murmuring soothing words.

Becky was smouldering with resentment, muttering, 'He's got no right to speak to Mum like that.' But I could feel her distress too and a minute later, a tear trickled down her cheek. I climbed into her bed, wrapped my arm round her shoulders and wove us a fabulous tale to distract us about a witch, called Hecate, who didn't want to be a witch any more. She just wanted to be a nice, little old lady. Two children helped Hecate to fight the evil terrifying Sheena, leader of the witches. Sheena had a strange silvery skin and adored jewellery. The children and Hecate were taken prisoner by Sheena and almost killed. But finally the children and Hecate outwitted Sheena and Sheena was trapped forever inside the huge diamond she coveted:

'There was a wild shriek. Sheena was sinking, sinking

15

into the rays of light, disappearing into the swirling depths of the diamond. At last the shining facets of the diamond closed over her. Sheena was inside the diamond ... All that could be seen of Sheena now was a silver splinter, glinting in the very heart of the diamond.'

I took a deep breath. Becky was staring straight ahead; she was there, watching Sheena disappear into the diamond along with the children in my story.

'There was a strange noise. It began with a bubbling sort of gurgle. The children looked round, startled. It grew into a panting wheeze. Then they saw who had caused the sound – as the rest of the witches on the heath stirred, quivering. Their thin, back bodies were heaving with relief. They were cheering! At last they were free of their terrible ruler ...'

What a joyful world I could create just through words! Hecate, the nice witches and the children celebrating their success in overcoming evil. Fear and unhappiness being replaced by joy. Becky had joined me in a world far away from the misery downstairs.

But then Dad's angry, strident tones punctured our peace and Becky jumped. She rolled over and faced the wall, then spoke in a muffled voice. 'Yes, but none of it's *true*, is it?'

It was the last time Becky ever accepted my panacea of fantasy, when the threat of the Dark Wood could be defeated forever.

Chapter 2

I escaped into the joyous finale of 'The Snow Queen' as tensions continued at home; the promise of eternal happiness was so seductive. But Becky stopped her ballet lessons straight after our final performance, saying ballet was just soppy. She chose the tougher world of competitive sports, playing tennis, badminton, netball. That was, I think, the moment our paths in the wood truly diverged. She kept dragging me down to the local tennis court and, just to stop her pestering me, I went. I was useless at tennis. I think that hand- eye coordination totally by-passed me in the womb. So then she made me try badminton, in the hope I found the shuttlecock easier to return.

Mum had found a coach, Jane, to help Becky as she definitely had talent. Jane watched me with interest the first time she saw me. But I swiped at the silly bunch of feathers – and whacked at thin air. And, to be honest, I just couldn't see the point.

'Keep your eye on the shuttlecock and follow through,' Jane said. But it was no good. Again and again I would miss the shuttlecock. 'You *must* have some of Becky's ability!' Jane kept saying. I stared at the ground, my cheeks burning.

Becks was convinced that practice made perfect. She refused to believe it when I made so little progress, despite her advice and sporting tips. 'Come on, Alice. Concentrate!

Focus on the shuttlecock,' she would urge me as I swiped at nothing but I just couldn't master the technique.

The guerrilla warfare between Dad and Mum continued, although Mum rarely retaliated. He would snipe at her, criticise her for earning so little as a carer, a job Mum loved but which only paid the minimum wage. Mum wasn't really qualified for better paid work, anyway. Becky became increasingly impatient with Dad but I managed to persuade her not to intervene; Mum had asked us not to.

Looking back, I think the stresses of work distorted his true personality, driving him to lash out, however unfairly. Mum was an easy soft target and she grew thin and pale, unable to deal with the situation. She rarely retaliated, seeming frightened of precipitating a huge row, which might tip over into something worse. She would stiffen whenever Dad's key turned in the front door and my stomach would turn to liquid. The air in the tiny kitchen was always thick with tension and an uneasiness seemed to penetrate my bones. My refuge lay in literature as always. Literature and, increasingly, the countryside.

Until one day a crisis developed. Mum, Becky, and I were sitting down one evening at the kitchen table, waiting for supper. Where was Dad?

I remember Mum snapped at me for playing with my knife and fork. She shook her head, muttering to herself, 'The dinner'll be ruined. A waste of good money.'

Dad stumbled into the living room at last. He stood there, swaying on his feet and fear bit into me.

'The spaghetti bolognese is all dried up,' Mum told him bitterly, 'Totally uneatable.'

'It's not my fault,' Dad's voice was thick. The vein on his forehead pulsed faintly. 'The North Circular was terrible.'

'Well, they never mentioned it on telly,' Becky said sharply.

Dad glared at her. 'The telly isn't always right, Miss Know-it-all,' he sneered.

Mum sprang to Becky's defence. 'Don't take it out on Becks!'

My mouth was dry.

Dad's upper lip curled. 'I'll take it out on whoever I please. And I don't want any supper anyway. I'm not hungry.'

'Well, *we* are – and now there's nothing to eat because of you!' Becks couldn't resist answering back. My heart lurched. Don't wind him up when he's like this.

'Well, you'll just have to eat toast,' Dad growled.

'Toast? That's not enough!' Becky glared at Dad.

Dad's eyes blazed and the air crackled with tension. I felt sick. Dad bellowed at Becky and she yelled back, then Mum was shouting at both of them – and I – I just had to get away.

I ran upstairs, flung myself on my bed and dived into the latest copy of Mum's *Countryside* magazine. She'd been buying them for years and I loved to browse through them, especially at times like this. Tonight I could join smiling couples in green wellies, strolling along country lanes, collecting wood for their wood-burning stoves. Living another life, an open relaxed outdoor life, a life filled with peace and harmony. Miles away from the row raging downstairs.

The front door slammed and I looked out of the

window. Becky was heading for the sports club up the road, off to practise her badminton again, no doubt.

What was wrong with Dad? Was his ill-temper due just to stress – or was there something else? The way he moved and spoke ... Dry-mouthed, I crept along the landing to Mum and Dad's bedroom. Maybe in Dad's wardrobe? Yes, there they were – a carrier bag full of bottles.

He'd poured himself the odd furtive glass of scotch even when I was tiny but, now I came to think about it, the 'wee drams' had become more frequent recently.

Dad's job selling double glazing was stressful, I suppose. He was desperate to succeed. But he lacked the 'gift of the gab' needed to become a very successful salesman. I can see now he had a touch of Willy Loman from 'Death of a Salesman' about him. Dad's dreams weren't romantic dreams, like mine; years ago, he'd bought in to the American Dream. Of course, he didn't have to sell door to door any more, as Willy Loman did, but the pressures of sales targets were the same: "So many closed doors, so many rejections". Younger colleagues kept being promoted over him and Dad had become more and more morose.

And now he'd become an alcoholic.

Weekends were times to be dreaded, when Dad took himself off on binges. On Fridays, I would walk home from school, trying to avoid every crack in the grey paving slabs; if I succeeded, Dad would be sober all weekend. But I could tell every time my desperate, superstitious, efforts to safeguard the future had failed from the way his keys jangled in the front door and clanged belligerently on the hall table.

My only refuge lay in glossy pictures of emerald green

meadows filled with wildflowers, or of soaring mountains and cascading gorges.

But one Saturday night, after another blazing row downstairs, footsteps pounded up the stairs and Mum burst in; her face was pale and an ugly, purple bruise was swelling round her right eye. Becky and I were stunned. Dad had never actually hit any of us before.

We were leaving, Mum said. She'd had enough. We packed a couple of bags and left for Aunt Nora's house. Mum divorced Dad nine months later and for me, it felt like a bereavement.

As I said, once upon a time they *had* been happy. A golden age when they loved each other. I remember when I was about six and we stayed at my grandparents' house by the sea. The four of us had dared the towering waves, running away up the beach at the last second. Dad had fallen back onto the sand, tripping up Mum, who'd sprawled on top of Dad and then we'd all got the giggles. And Mum and Dad had shared an intimate smile and a kiss.

And, of course, there were those trips to the zoo. I opened the locket round my neck. There was Dad with his arm round Mum's shoulders, Mum smiling up at him. Becky and I stood in front of them, grinning at the camera.

That photo was like Keats' Grecian Urn. Keats' Urn depicting joyful nymphs and lovers, and my photo – both preserved a scene of happiness forever. Mum and Dad looked so happy …There *had* been a fire between them. Once upon a time. But that fire had now burned out.

Mum met John through a dating agency a few years later and they appeared fond of each other – but it seemed a lukewarm affection, compared to the passion my parents had once shared.

The divorce seemed to galvanise Dad into seeking help. Counselling made him realise that working in Sales was not for him. So he quit his job and moved to his parents' – Grandma and Grandpa's – old house in Weston-Super-Mare. He'd found a job as an animal technician in Bristol, not too far from Weston, so he could commute.

He came round to see us the night before he left but Becky was out playing badminton.

'I realise now that for me, it's always been a case of round pegs and square holes, Alice,' he said. He put his arm round me and drew me close to him. 'I'm so sorry it hasn't worked out for Mum and me. We've tried to get back together but I'm afraid we don't feel the same about each other as we used to. Anyway, I've finally decided to do something that really interests me and it's something useful too, as it could help lots of people. It means I'll have to go and live in Weston but, of course, you and Becky can come and stay whenever you want.'

I nodded.

'I'll be responsible for the apes' welfare in the lab. The pay isn't very good but the work sounds really interesting. The team are committed to developing our knowledge of how apes think and feel. They reckon it could help find cures for certain viruses.'

I kissed Dad and his bristly chin brushed against my skin. 'Good for you, Dad,' I said. 'It sounds an amazing job.'

I was happy for him, too, but tears pricked my eyes. This meant we wouldn't see much of him anymore. And the chances of Mum and Dad ever getting back together would be virtually nil.

I told Becky what Dad had said when she came back, and she nodded, although she stared at the floor, tight-lipped.

I yearned to return to the happiness of my early childhood when the fire between Mum and Dad blazed. Isn't that a potent word: *yearn*? Such a powerful word. There's all the longing and the need and the desperation in the world in that word.

But I still found comfort in *Countryside* – and felt drawn to literature embodying country life. And as the years drifted by, I became immersed – no, marinated – in books; they coloured my life, as Emily Bronte put it, "like wine through water." Literature permeated my mind, composing my thoughts, the trail of words leaving traces imprinted in my brain.

The land of the Hobbits in "Lord of the Rings" was a land to be revelled in. Those dreams of a rural idyll were a kind of alchemy, filled with golden promise.

At secondary school, I relished the rusticity of Thomas Hardy's Wessex, with maypole dancing on the green. Oh, to be a heath broom maker like Olly Dowden or a turf cutter like Sam. These people populated my mind, as real to me as Becky or Mum. Books had for me, as Milton claimed, "a potencie of life"; they were literally transformative.

Meanwhile, Becky was winning local badminton tournaments. Light-footed and fast, her reaction times were good. Mum had taken over from Dad in driving her to county practices and their discussions were forever centred around target serves and return serves.

'Have you just been lounging about all day,' she would

demand, as she bounded into our bedroom, 'while I've been running my socks off?'

I felt dull and passive lying on my bed, reading, in contrast to her physical vitality. But I defended myself with dignity.

'I've been as active as you actually. Except I've been working mentally rather than physically.'

Becky snorted but even so, I still felt an understanding there – the old empathy, if not a shared passion. And, I always knew, through our sixth sense, if she'd lost a match, even if she was miles away at the time. I'd make and cook her favourite home-made beef burgers to cheer her up.

Becky's prowess, meanwhile, on the badminton court was excellent but she didn't make it through the squads' selection process – so her hopes of an Olympic career were quashed. She and Mum had some serious meetings with her badminton coach, Jane. She would never, Jane felt, develop the 100% accuracy required at Olympic level to address spinning net shots. I didn't need to see Becky's downcast eyes as she and Mum walked up to the front door; I knew what had happened before they reached home and I'd made her favourite Lamb Tagine.

Both Becky and I went to university in London, me to study English Literature and Becky Sports Science. Mum was so proud of us.

'Both my girls studying for a university degree,' she said, beaming. She'd never had the chance to go to university, getting a job as soon as she left school in order to help Grandma with the bills.

For Becky, it was a choice between either Maths or Sports Science – and Sports, her first love, won. 'If I can't be an Olympic athlete, I'll help to teach one,' she said grimly. We both lived at home as a financial necessity, considering the exorbitant cost of tuition fees alone.

My literary studies at uni continued to filter ideas through my brain. I read Dickens, Thackeray, George Eliot. And I absorbed poetry … Tennyson's grief-stricken vision of the city:

'long unlovely street

Ghastly thro the drizzling rain,'

And Coleridge 'reared

In the great city …saw nought lovely but the sky and the stars'.

These poets tainted my view of London, prompting my desire to move away from the ugly city. I couldn't do so at present but one day, I promised myself, I would …

I first met my friends, Liz and Peter, when Professor Jenkins mentioned to all the Eng Lit students that there was to be a Dickens Festival during the summer of my second year at university.

I attended a planning meeting and was asked to help Liz and Peter, a friendly couple in their mid-sixties who were huge fans of Dickens, prepare a seminar on Dickens' characters, inviting leading critics to attend and contribute to the discussion.

Liz and Peter were an older version of Calamity Jane and Wild Bill Hickok. Liz was fresh-faced with a wide smile, her white hair cut in a bob, and Peter was tall and tanned, with a clean-cut, humorous face and deep blue eyes; I took to them immediately. It was clear at the planning meeting that they both knew Dickens backwards – something I had yet to achieve.

I could tell they adored Dickens as soon as I arrived at their house, bearing a big box of chocolates, for Peter greeted me, grinning: 'There is nothing better than a friend unless it is a friend with chocolate!'

'Pickwick Papers?' I hazarded.

He nodded delightedly. 'Come in. Come in. I won't be a tick. Just looking for my glasses. Liz is looking for them upstairs.'

He disappeared into a room on right hand side of the hall. Peter and Liz's house was a tiny Victorian terraced house with books piled up in heaps on the stairs.

'I've found them, Peter!' A voice floated down from upstairs. 'You'd left them on the landing cupboard,' Liz came down the stairs, carrying Peter's glasses aloft. She looked aggrieved as she glared at Peter who was coming out of his study. 'So you see – *I* didn't put them anywhere.'

Then she saw me. 'Sorry, Alice. Didn't realise you'd arrived.' She held out Peter's glasses to him with an exasperated sigh.

Peter took them, looking suitably chagrined. 'Ah, I do remember now. I was upstairs in my study, looking something up when the postman knocked on the door.'

'So *I* didn't put them anywhere,' Liz repeated emphatically, looking at me with a mocking face, half an eye on Peter. 'This happens regularly, Alice. So I've decided to found a new society.'

'Oh, what sort of society?' I asked, playing along.

'It'll be called the National Scapegoats' Society ...'

Peter sighed, rolling his eyes.

'Our motto will be: "Mea Culpa"', continued Liz. 'And I've already got the first item on the Agenda.'

She stared at Peter.

'No, it should be "Mea *Maxima* Culpa"', insisted Peter. His eyes gleamed mischievously. 'For those who deliberately hide other people's glasses.'

Liz stared at him, breathing heavily. 'I believe it was Mr Tappertit in "Barnaby Rudge" who remarked, "Something will come of this and I hope it mayn't be human gore!"'

I burst out laughing, 'I hope not, too.'

'Anyway, come into the sitting room,' said Liz. Victorian cigarette card illustrations of Dickens characters adorned the walls.

'Just as I pictured Mr Squeers,' I said, pointing at a drawing of Mr Squeers, clad all in black, a black umbrella under one arm, leering menacingly, one eye closed.

'Ah, yes,' said Liz, '"Mr Squeers had but one eye and the popular prejudice runs in favour of two."'

I felt instantly at home with Peter and Liz. I could feel the deep affection between them underlying their banter as we discussed our plans. I saw Peter glance at Liz, his eyes filled with love; Dad used to look at Mum like that when we were little. We drew up lists of literary contacts, arranging who would call whom, whilst chatting about Dickens' novels..

Liz and Peter had been married for forty five years and both possessed an amazing capacity for mirth. With them, I could indeed see the great credit that lies in being jolly. Their house seemed filled with sunlight and laughter. A perfect marriage. Something that Dad and Mum had achieved once – but lost.

At this time Mum decided to go into business with John, setting up a bed and breakfast down in Brighton. She had always loved doing most of the cooking for the three of us. When she left for Brighton, I took over the cooking completely and I enjoyed widening my culinary expertise, concocting healthy meals that Becky approved of, such as mushroom and prawn stir fry or low-fat moussaka. Becks seemed to enjoy them. Her lectures finished later than mine so it seemed only natural to make supper.

And so I took over the kitchen, stirring the beef and sweet potato stew with one hand and reading a D H Lawrence novel with the other. Becky had never been interested in cooking at all so she'd never bothered to learn. Mum was pleased I was looking after my sister and I basked in her approval, as usual. So somehow, insidiously, it became my role to cook for Becks at night.

But simmering beneath the serene surface of our life together I felt a bubbling resentment. Instead of trying to develop my sports skills, Becks had decided to focus on improving my social life. She'd become a bit of a party animal since she started uni and she kept trying to inveigle me into going clubbing with her fellow students. She seemed to think it was her duty to give me a good time.

She and her mates loved post-Dubstep kind of stuff but I hated robotic electronic music. Give me a romantic singer like John Legend any day. But if I was playing 'All of Me' in our bedroom and Becks walked in, she mimed putting her fingers down her throat. Becky took it upon herself to teach me how to party – and find me boyfriends. She changed her boyfriend – wispy bearded Kevin, muscle-bound, long-haired Adam – more often than she changed her exercise socks. She met Adam down at the gym – but his problem was that he never bothered to shower after working out, or at any other time, or so it seemed.

'He's disgusting,' Becks told me. 'Dad was telling me the other day that genetically everyone is between 1 and 4 percent Neanderthal … Well, from the whiff of Adam, I'd say he was 99 percent! His knuckles practically scrape along the floor. Cave man or what?'

Then there was Daniel, an enormous guy, with black eyes and long dark hair, a droopy moustache and beard.

'Don't you think he sooo looks like Captain Jack Straw from "Pirates of the Caribbean"?' Becky whispered to me excitedly in our bedroom as Daniel was waiting downstairs for her to change into her clubbing gear.

To me, he looked more like Hagrid from the Harry Potter books but I didn't want to dampen her enthusiasm so I nodded, shrugging my shoulders. 'Maybe a bit.'

Perhaps Becks eventually came to the same conclusion as Daniel didn't last long either. She was soon bored with him.

Most of the guys on my English Literature course seemed to be either gay or geeks and when Gareth invited me to see Chekhov's 'Three Sisters' at the National Theatre, I'm afraid I couldn't see beyond his pimply skin and beaky nose. He had shoulder-length greasy blond hair too so, of course, he was to me the Pardoner in Chaucer's 'Canterbury Tales'.

None of the guys I knew had the wit of John Donne, my favourite poet in my second year at uni.

How insufferably pretentious, using Donne or Shakespeare as a yardstick to measure up potential boyfriends! But I couldn't help it. So finally I gave up on finding a boyfriend, content to find a companion in TS Eliot or Virginia Woolf or go to the cinema with my uni friend, Alex. Alex was a sci fi fan and so we saw all the Star Trek films and watched Peter Jackson's 'Lord of the Rings' trilogy five times over. I enjoyed them, although romcoms would always be my favourite films. Not for Alex though. She rolled her eyes when I suggested we go and see 'The Proposal'. So I went on my own.

Alex lived at home and her dad had a fabulous observatory in his garden with a state of the art telescope. If you clicked on a particular star on the attached computer screen, the telescope swivelled to focus on it. We spent hours studying the heavens, cuddling the family cat, Astrocat, in the observatory. I liked to dream of wonderful galaxies far away but Alex's interest was purely scientific.

'Professor Stephen Hawking thinks there is a possibility of intelligent life out there. ' She remarked. 'Wouldn't it be amazing if, one day, they could communicate with us.'

My life wasn't exciting enough for Becks. If her idea of a great night out was clubbing, then it was mine too. So she found Steve, a huge rugby player, for me. The trouble was, Steve was Chaucer's Miller!

How could she possibly imagine I'd be interested in this thickset guy whose only interests seemed to be rugby, sex and booze?

She was offended when I only went out with him five times.

'What's wrong with him?' she demanded.

"He was short-sholded, brood, a thikke and a knave …" I quoted. "His nosethirls blake were and wyde …"

'Okay, I think I've got the gist of your objection,' she said drily. 'But will you please stop dragging characters from your books into everything. Get out there and meet real people. But I know you won't … And after all the trouble I've taken to help liven things up for you.'

'I don't need to be livened up, thank you,' I said firmly. 'He's just not my type.'

'You're such an intellectual snob, Alice. So you didn't find anyone on your Head in the Clouds mental wavelength on your Dickens Festival committee?'

I shook my head, ignoring her jibe. 'Only one possibility. Thomas. Tall. Good-looking.'

'Well?!'

I shrugged. 'As Dr Johnson said, "I don't care to speak ill of any man behind his back but I believe the gentleman was an attorney."'

'A lawyer? But surely that's great?'

'Ah, yes. But Thomas was so up himself I couldn't stand him. He thought he knew everything. No more lawyers for me.'

Becky snorted. 'That's so illogical. One lawyer is a waster, therefore all lawyers are wasters … I just want you to have some *fun*, Alice. Not stuck in books all day and all night. What sort of a life is that?'

'Actually I'm quite happy with my life.' My voice was cool. 'One day, I'm sure I'll find Mr Right. But he's not round here.'

'Mr Right! Oh, my God. This isn't the nineteenth century. I don't believe it. Who cares about getting married? Look what happened to Mum and Dad.'

'They were happy when we were little,' I said defensively.

'Yes, but it didn't last, did it? I'm never going to make Mum's mistakes, that's for sure. Stuck in a marriage with a man who hits you.'

'That only happened *once* and Dad was under terrible pressure at the time.' I felt very protective of Dad.

'Well, it's never going to happen to me. Love 'em and leave 'em, that's what I say.'

Becky and I were so *fundamentally* different – but she couldn't accept that we didn't share the same values. And she really seemed to think she had a right to control me and my life. Just because we were twins, originating from the same egg. Ludicrous really. It was the height of irony; to look exactly the same as my sister, yet to have diametrically opposed characters. Romantic versus Rational. The ultimate oxymoron. We had nothing in common except our appearance.

I was fond of Becks; I loved her as my twin, of course. And I knew she cared for me deep down. But I felt constrained, bound by family ties, loyalty, deep bonds – and inwardly I railed against them. I had to escape, flee from my sister, from London, to be me, my unique self. Becky would keep making assumptions about the future, assumptions that she had no right to make.

We'd both decided to go in for teaching. I'd decided to teach after spending ages agonizing over whether to do a higher degree. Professor Jepson had called me to see him in his study and suggested I should stay in higher education.

'You work so hard and you show original insight into the texts we study, Alice,' he told me. 'I feel you could benefit from taking a Masters – it could even lead on to PhD level.'

I felt very flattered by his words and considered my options for a few weeks. I was deeply interested in various aspects of English Literature. One angle for a possible thesis which I found fascinating was inspired by a view held by the poet, T S Eliot. He believed that a separation had developed of thought from feeling, of the intellect from emotion during the course of the last three hundred years, perhaps as a result of the division between science and the humanities as our industrial society developed.

T S Eliot thought that Victorian poets such as Tennyson and Browning lacked the fusion of thought and feeling in their poems which had been present in seventeenth century poetry. It was an enthralling point of view and one which I would have loved to explore in literature. Dad found this idea intriguing too; he'd always been interested in the brain development, both animal and human. But I told Dad how I felt that my true vocation lay in teaching, helping others share my passion. And it seemed to make economic sense to train in London.

Becky had set her heart now on making it in education. She was hugely ambitious.

'I want to be Head of Department in three years, Deputy Head in seven,' she told me confidently – and, knowing Becks, I had no doubt she would achieve it. And she was talking about job prospects being so good for us both in London schools after we qualified. She *assumed* we would be living together at home, teaching in London.

I didn't say anything, as usual, especially when Mum echoed Becky's words on the phone that night. The two of them were ganging up on me again; it was a moral maxim that twins should be united in perpetuity – a truth universally acknowledged that identical twins must stay together forever.

Inside I was seething. Why did they automatically think

that I would *always* want to be with Becks? But I didn't want to hurt Becks so I tightened my lips.

And again literature was to guide the next stage of my life's course.

It was Emily Bronte's poetry, brimming with passion for the wild Northern landscape, that first lured me to the Yorkshire moors. One night, I lay on my bed quoting Emily Bronte to Becky:

"where my own nature would be leading …

Where the wild wind blows on the mountain side."

'Sounds bloody cold and uncomfortable to me,' was Becky's impervious response as she painted her nails black with her favourite nail polish, 'Midnight Passion', before going out for another night's clubbing. So I ignored her.

I adored Emily Bronte's poems – but in her novel, 'Wuthering Heights', the passion of Catherine and Heathcliff, bound up with the Yorkshire landscape, was something else.

'Cathy tells Nelly Dean, "there is or should be an existence of yours beyond you," suggesting that Cathy and Heathcliff were soul-mates. Let's consider the origins of this concept.' Doctor Liz Docherty, my English tutor, played with the coral beads round her neck. She sat on the edge of her desk, thin legs dangling. A dead ringer for Betsy Trotwood, with her grey hair severely parted in the middle, her hard features and bright brown eyes. She could be bossy, too, like Miss Trotwood, but I always sensed a certain kindness underneath.

' Aristophanes claimed that humans had great strength and threatened to conquer the gods. So Zeus split humans in half.' Liz's brown eyes gleamed. 'Isn't that what Cathy

34

is speaking of when she talks to Nelly Dean? When she tells Nelly Dean, "Heathcliff is more myself than I am. Whatever our souls are made of, his and mine are the same; and Linton's is as different as a moonbeam from lightning or frost from fire." Look at the imagery Emily Bronte employs here. Any thoughts? Alex?'

'Imagery of light, I suppose,' ventured Alex, her high ponytail swinging from side to side as she looked up at Liz. 'Moonbeams and lightning. But moonbeams aren't as bright or powerful as lightning.'

'No, that's right – nor as dangerous.'

'And frost and fire are water and fire – two different elements,' said Kirsten slowly.

Why hadn't I thought of that?

'Yes, suggesting that Heathcliff and Catherine are made up of the same element.' Lauren suggested. 'They believe they have their being in the other.'

'Yes,' Liz's voice rose in her excitement. 'Cathy tells Nelly Dean, "Nelly, I *am* Heathcliff." Or, as C Day Lewis put it, "Heathcliff and Cathy represent two halves of a single soul – forever sundered and struggling to unite."'

I stared at Liz. Her words were … transfiguring. Imagine the existence of not just a boyfriend or partner, but a *soul-mate* – someone who is a part of your own being.

Catherine described her love for Heathcliff as being like "the eternal rocks beneath: a source of little visible delight, but necessary …" My hero would be roughly hewn, too, like Heathcliff, from the crags of the north country.

I longed to live on the rugged moors in the north of England, as Cathy and Heathcliff had done. Not quite sleeping in a cot of rushes, as Mary Webb recommended – but close to nature.

I saw a job for an English teacher advertised in the Times Education Supplement at a comprehensive school in the town of Inkley in the Yorkshire Dales, only a few miles from Haworth, where the Brontes lived! And I secretly applied for it during the first term of my teacher training course. Just before Christmas, I received a letter asking me for interview. If nothing came of it, I'd never mention it to Mum or Becky.

I did tell Alex one night as we were observing an amazing meteor shower and she knew how much Becky pissed me off. She was understanding and comforting, as always. 'If it's right for you, it'll happen,' she said. 'I've always believed in fate.'

That Christmas Becks gave me a present which forced our final parting of the ways. She handed me a big envelope, decorated with robins and holly leaves.

'It's a joint birthday and Christmas present to you.'

I tore it open. Inside was a booking made for a Beach Club 18-25 holiday in Ibiza. During the summer holidays. All- Inclusive.

'You don't need to spend a single Euro, Alice. We can sunbathe all day and party all night. Wear lots of bling. You'll love it, I promise you!'

I took a deep breath. 'Look, Becks, I know you mean well but –'

'It's got loads of good ratings on Trip Review. '

'Yes, but – '

'Otherwise you'll just spend all your summer in the library or at those dreary literary society meetings. I know it. You'll love this!"

I shook my head. 'Becks, I'm sorry but – it isn't for me. You know it isn't. I'll need to prepare texts for my lessons. And I'm helping Liz and Peter host the seminars during the Dickens Festival that week. Why don't you go with Leanne? She'd love to go with you.'

Becks looked hurt and I felt a pang of guilt.

Mum leaned forward in the armchair, a look of concern on her face. 'It was really nice of Becky to buy you such a lovely present, Alice. You can't throw it back in her face. It's so rude. Why don't you just say you can't help at the Dickens Festival? Anyway, a good holiday will help you relax and be ready for your first year of teaching.'

I wrapped my arms round my knees on the sofa. 'I don't know how to tell you this. But I'm not sure I'll be here for my first year of teaching.'

Mum looked puzzled. 'Why? What are you going to do? Don't you want to teach?'

'Yes, but not in London.'

'Well, where?'

'I've applied for a job up in the north. Yorkshire, actually. I've got a job interview in the New Year.' I tightened my arms round my knees. It was just like the time I wore a floaty skirt and blouse for the first time as a child. As though I had reneged on some unspoken pact. But this was ludicrous. I was an adult. I had a right to lead my own life.

Mum gasped.

Becky stared at the floor. 'I see.'

'I just want a change. I've always lived in London. I want to see a different part of England. Live in the countryside, not in a city.'

'But —' Beck's voice started to break. '…we belong together.'

'We do, in a way.' I was shrivelling up inside; I hated hurting anybody, let alone my sister. I had to tell her though. If I didn't escape from her now, I never would. 'But you don't – own me, Becks. I have to be my own person. And to do that, I want to live by myself for a while.'

'But you're my twins,' Mum joined in. 'I'd *never* have gone to live in Brighton if I'd thought you weren't going to be together. You two need each other.'

I took another deep breath. It was now or never. 'Mum, we're twenty-two,' I said. 'This is ridiculous. We're not your little girls anymore! We're both grown up and quite capable of looking after ourselves. We need to live our own lives … And anyway, if I do get this job, I'll be coming down to London often. It's not that far. Only two or three hours on the fast train from Leeds. And Brighton's not much further.'

'It's those bloody poems, isn't it?' Becks spoke bitterly.

'What?'

'Those poems you insisted on quoting at me. Bronte, wasn't it? Made you want to go and live up there in Yorkshire.'

'Well, they may have something to do with it,' I admitted.

'You're mad,' she said. 'I bet you actually want to live on those freezing moors.'

I shrugged. 'Look,' I said. 'I don't even know if I'll get the job yet. There's bound to be lots of competition.'

A coolness descended over our Christmas afternoon as Mum put on the romantic French film I'd bought her – Renoir's 'Une Partie do Campagne'. Mum and I sat on the sofa in silence as Henriette succumbed to a moment of passion with Henri in the long grass. Becky was pointedly sitting apart in the armchair, reading her latest edition of *Fitness Monthly*.

I was sorry this had to happen on Christmas Day – but the point was important to me; I *couldn't* let Becky dominate me. We'd be yoked together forever. I hated hurting her though. I felt as though, in some way, I had betrayed her, as though it were she and I who were soul-mates. And I was even more guilt-ridden when, a few weeks later, I was offered – and I accepted – the position at Inkley Comprehensive School, hundreds of miles away in the Yorkshire Dales.

If only I had known then, as I do now, what would happen to me as a result of this disastrous decision.

Chapter 3

I'd instantly felt a rapport on interview with Jessica Davies, the Head of English, and the interview panel seemed very impressed with the demonstration lesson which I taught. I would be starting in September.

Becky just grunted when I told her I'd accepted the job. But, as the summer holidays approached, she seemed to be coming round to the idea.

Dad had had a word with her, he told me, about the importance of following your dream.

'I tried to make her see that, just as she's set her heart on getting to the top in education, so you've set your heart on a different way of life, the country way of life. And it seemed to shut her up. She was quite thoughtful afterwards. She is open to reason, you know,' Dad said.

Then Becky found a job teaching PE in a school in northwest London so she had plenty to occupy her, preparing schemes of work. She was also determined to be super fit in readiness for the new term, spending even more hours down at the gym.

Liz invited me for afternoon tea a couple of weeks after the Dickens Festival. It had been declared a great success, she told me, attracting large audiences. We sat outside in their tiny back garden, surrounded by pots of camellias. Liz had made a beautiful chocolate cake with several layers, like strata, of strawberry jam, fresh strawberries and cream, dusted with cocoa.

'A highly *geological* home-made cake,' I said and Liz laughed. 'Sorry. Couldn't resist.'

Liz said how sad she and Peter were I was going to live up north. 'Just when we've got to know you. Why are you moving so far away?'

I chose my words carefully. I didn't mention being driven mad by my sister; that would have been a betrayal. 'I think it's mostly due to the books I've read.'

'What? Dickens?'

'No, I like Dickens but I love other literary classics, too, like Thomas Hardy novels which are based in the countryside – so I thought I'd try the country life myself. Does it sound mad to you?'

"No. I do understand. There are those programmes on all the time, aren't there. About people escaping from the busy cities to go and live in the country. Well, I do hope you like it. Very different from London … But what are we going to do without you next year?' Liz wailed. 'We've been asked to research speakers on Dicken's social criticism. You were invaluable in helping with this summer's festival – better than land ahead or a breeze astern, as Mrs Badger says!"

I smiled. 'I love the way you and Peter quote the Great Man. My sister can't stand me quoting famous writers. She thinks it just sounds pretentious. But it's their words that have formed the way I think, so it's a sort of tribute to them …' Liz nodded in agreement. 'Anyway, I'm sure I'll be able to come down and help you both during the summer holidays next year,' I reassured her, slicing up my cake with a dainty fork. 'At least there's plenty of time to prepare for it.' I said. 'I'll miss you two. It's wonderful to find friends who share my love of Dickens. But it's not just that. I enjoy coming to see you both anyway. Your house is always so welcoming. And you both seem so close, almost made for each other. Proof that marriage *can* work.'

Liz smiled. 'Yes, I suppose Pete and I are well-matched ... Somehow I knew that we belonged together the moment we met.' She paused, reflecting. 'We've certainly got the same sense of humour. And we have lots of the same ideas. We often even finish each other's sentences! They say like attracts like, don't they. We are happy together.' Then her face clouded over. 'It's not always been like that though ... A few years ago, Peter went through a very difficult time ... when his dad died. They'd always been very close, going off on fishing trips together, taking golfing holidays – that sort of thing. Anyway, when his dad died suddenly of a heart attack, Peter sank into a dreadful depression. It was hard to get him out of bed in the mornings for work.' She shook her head. 'Grief's a terrible thing.

'I tried everything to cheer him up. Took him away on holiday to the Canary Islands, the Seychelles. Nothing worked. Pete seemed a million miles away from me. He didn't seem interested in us anymore. And I felt so lonely.' Her face crumpled. 'Pete just shut me out, living in the past. He said his last memory of his dad was of him clutching his chest in agony. Whenever he thought of his dad, that was the memory that filled his mind.

'In the end, in desperation, I read as much as I could on the subject of grief. And I read an article about a form of hypnotism which had helped somebody grief-stricken. But the hypnotist didn't put the client into a trance, swinging a fob watch in front of their eyes. No, it seems that somehow he helped to restructure the client's memories of the loved one. He brought happy memories to the forefront of the client's mind, instead of the awful ones. So I spent months and months tracking down a hypnotist who could offer that service. And gradually the course of hypnotherapy started to work on Peter.'

'Well,' I said. 'Peter certainly seems okay now.'

'Yes, he is. Actually I think somehow it's strengthened the two of us. Not that I would ever have wanted something to happen like that.'

'No, of course not. But you tried really hard to help him when he needed it.'

'Well, I had to do my best for him,' Liz said simply. 'I love him.'

After saying goodbye to Liz and extracting promises from her that she and Peter would soon come and stay at the cottage I'd found for rent on Inkley Moor, I went home.

Becky had gone out for the evening. She seemed resigned now to me going up north. She'd even agreed to come and stay for a couple of days before term began. And Mum was okay with me going, when Becky accepted it. In fact, she came out with one of her classic malapropisms: 'Well, I just hope you'll be happy living in rusty city.' Mum had always had this uncanny knack for creating hilarious malapropisms; Dad used to laugh like a drain when she unwittingly uttered a malapropism.

I looked at her, grinning. 'Fingers crossed it isn't *too* rusty, although with all the rain they have in Yorkshire, I suppose it could happen.'

'Hey, what d'you mean?' Mum never realised when she'd come out with another clanger. 'I just meant I hope you won't be lonely.'

'No, don't worry, Mum. I'm sure I'll soon get to know people in the town.'

Becky raised her eyes to heaven when I told her I'd found rented accommodation in the Gamekeeper's Cottage lying in a saddle of moorland above Inkley.

'And what will you do when you run out of milk in your rustic idyll? Walk five miles through the pouring rain to buy another pint?'

I laughed. I could tell that she'd grudgingly accepted my going because she was enjoying opportunities to take the piss. 'I'll make sure I've got masses of milk in when you come up next week.'

But I did feel a pang as Becks hugged me close after we'd packed my stuff in John's car. 'Now look after yourself …' she murmured in my ear.

'I will. See you soon.'

'… And watch out for those sheep. They're renowned for their foul tempers, you know, are sheep.'

I stared at the enormous grey cliff rising above my back garden; the white splashing water of a stream tumbled down a crevasse in the rock face. It joined another stream meandering down the hillside from the moor top. Then it coursed under a narrow granite bridge that formed a part of the moorland footpath above my garden and finally gushed through my back garden and on through my neighbour's.

The millstone grit walls of my old cottage were patched with rusty lichen. There were certainly no roses round my front door – but ivy curled round the deep-set windows. And my head reeled at the open moorland that stretched away beyond my cottage up the dale. The space and the pure clean air around me was so exhilarating after a life spent in the traffic-thick fumes of London.

I went into the kitchen to get a drink of water. I'd fallen in love with this place – but the house did seem silent. No chatter filled the room tinged with Becky's caustic wit – which drove me mad but was always mentally bracing. I was truly alone for the first time ever and it was strange. Not having Becks around was like having no shadow. I sipped my water, aware of an emptiness in my world, the odd sense of an absence.

Ah, well, I thought, I'd soon get used to it. Anyway, Becky was coming to stay in a couple of days. She'd soon be driving me mad again. And I had masses of work preparation to keep me busy, as well as the garden to tackle – and my house to sort out.

My new address had thrilling connotations – the Gamekeeper's Cottage. Those words, that address – the flints were striking sparks again in my mind, glittering with passion … Mellors and Lady Chatterley!

No wonder that when William's tall, lean figure strode up the rough track leading to my picket gate a few days ago, my heart had leapt. I'd never felt anything like that before. The setting was perfect for the love of my life. His bright brown eyes crinkled at the corners as they lit his tanned smiling face and I thought – just for a second – that there was a reciprocal spark of attraction in his eyes. And why not love at first sight – when even Shakespeare himself demands we accept this in 'Romeo and Juliet'? And Liz had told me she and Peter both knew they had found 'The One' the second they met. I smiled back at William; we were destined for each other. William had arrived at my front gate through some divinity which shapes our ends.

How ridiculous it seems now. Twenty first century post- feminist literature had been part of my education, and it had largely passed me by. I preserved that kernel of idealism, of romantic yearnings, unscathed by the sceptical, cynical stories of Angela Carter. Standing before me was my long-awaited soul-mate.

But William only stopped by the gate to say, 'Hi, you must be the new tenant. I'm William, Mr Locksley's nephew.' He had a pleasant voice, gentle and low. 'Mr Locksley lives next door … Is he in, do you know? '

Immediately I returned to the real world, from the ethereal world of poetry to the mundane world of prose. Of course he hadn't come to see me. Fool.

I tucked the long strand of blonde hair which had escaped onto my shoulders back into my low bun. 'Yes, I think so. Mr Locksley and I have already met, you know. His car's here and I haven't seen him go out for a walk.' I pulled off my gardening glove and stretched out my hand across the fence. 'I'm Alice, by the way.'

William wore a sports jacket, jeans and brown brogues. He must have been in his mid-twenties at a guess, his face sensitive and intelligent. He shook my hand, eyes crinkling at the corners again as he smiled warmly at me and my heart turned over. Will Ladislaw from 'Middlemarch', with his smile a gush of inward light illuminating his eyes! Yes, he even had Will Ladislaw's abundant brown hair.

'Mr Locksley's very kind,' I said. 'A nice old gentleman.

He's invited me round for afternoon tea later on. Wants to get to know his new neighbour, he says.'

'Yes, he is kind,' William agreed. He surveyed my garden and whistled. 'You've got your work cut out here, haven't you.'

'I know. And I don't know much about gardens, I'm afraid. Having grown up in London with only a back yard. But I'm sure I'll manage.

'Of course, there's been nobody living here for several months, Uncle Joe was saying. Such a shame. George – he's the owner of your cottage – was a fantastic gardener. ' He bent down and separated the tangle of weeds with a strong tanned forearm. The air was filled with the fragrance of the velvet textured roses near the fence. 'See here – some daphne, fluellen, red-hemp nettle, comfrey, foxgloves. There's even a raised bed I remember he made over here …' He pulled away a big mass of clinging ivy leaves. 'Yes, look. You've got some vegetables still growing here.'

I looked down at the bright green crinkled leaves of some healthy-looking plants.

'Look. That's kale. A perennial. And just here are some onions and garlic.' I could see the long thin leaves of the onions and the slightly broader leaves of the garlic that he was pointing out. 'They'll be lovely in a salad. Oh, look. Some herbs, too. That's hyssop.'

Some broad green leaves sprouted near one of my apple trees. 'You can put that in your salad, too,' William said, pointing at them. 'It's got a nice minty taste. But be sparing with it.'

'Great! Free food,' I said.

He smiled. 'Uncle Joe always has loads of tomato

plants and lettuces growing. I'm sure he'd give you a few to go with this.'

'That would be nice. To have a totally fresh salad … You really know your plants, don't you.'

He nodded. 'I used to help Mum in the garden when I was a little lad so I liked helping George with his garden and George taught me all their names. He told me about Culpepper's herbal remedies too. I just found it fascinating.

'Unfortunately George had to go into a home a few months ago and it's taken some time to find a tenant …' He glanced around my garden again. Yes, it'll take you some time to clear all this.'

'Well, I've been trying to restore it to its former glory,' I surveyed the weeds and thorny patches of brambles helplessly, 'but I don't seem to have made much of an impression. It still looks a bit of a wilderness. And the back garden is just as bad … Not that I want it to look immaculate, like your uncle's garden. His garden is so symmetrical. Clipped box hedges, evenly spaced rose bushes. Everything just so. '

'Yes, Uncle Joe likes to have order in his life,' William remarked.

'Well, not for me,' I said. 'I'd prefer my garden to be left a bit wild.'

'O let them be left, wildness and wet.

Long live the weeds and the wilderness yet,' William quoted, smiling.

'You like Hopkins too!' I stared at him with renewed appreciation.

'I was in a play about Gerard Manley Hopkins at the

Edinburgh Fringe a couple of years ago. Wonderful poet.'

'You're an actor?'

He nodded. 'Just finished playing Iago with a small touring company, travelling to village halls, arts centres up and down the country. Before that I was Dracula – had several teenage girls chasing me for my autograph after that one.' He smiled. 'Great for the old ego! And before *that* I was Squire William Corder.'

'The Victorian melodrama. "Murder in the Red Barn",' I said.

He raised his eyebrows, impressed at my knowledge.

'I'm an English teacher,' I explained, '- or about to be. I read "Murder in the Red Barn" with my Year 7 class during teaching practice."

'Well, picture me seducing Maria Marten, whilst twirling my mustachios like crazy.' He grinned. 'And then ruthlessly killing her in order to marry the rich widow ... Our next production's at the Edinburgh Festival in a couple of weeks.'

'How fascinating. I've always wondered what it's like to be a professional actor.'

'It's ... amazing. To take part in someone else's existence – to misquote Keats.' He smiled wryly. 'I've always found people interesting. I love to watch them, see how they move, their facial expressions, their ways of talking. And how they feel. It's so interesting to get inside someone else's skin when you act a part ...

'Of course, as a jobbing actor, you always wonder whether there will be any more work after this season. And I admit I've had to "rest" sometimes. But I've been lucky on the whole – so far.'

He was too good to be true. Gorgeous, good-looking and an actor too. This guy was *fit*.

'Money's dire though. Not that I care about that. How about you? Are you teaching in Leeds?'

'No. I've got my first job teaching English here at the comprehensive. Starting in ten days. There's *masses* to get ready – long-term planning, mid-term planning – as well as books to prepare. But I'm so lucky to be living up *here*. I come from London so I've never lived in the country before. It's so incredibly different from the streets of London. It's absolutely beautiful.' I swept my arm at the fell before me, the moorland grass mingling with purple heather and bracken, which stretched up to the huge rocky outcrop above our heads. 'What I particularly love about this place – is seeing sheep cropping the grass yards away from my back gate! Not to mention my own moorland stream.'

William smiled. 'Yes, but be careful not to leave your back gate open. Before you know it, those plants will be eaten … I remember as a child, Uncle Joe shouting to my Aunty Annie, when she was staying here once, to chase the sheep out of his garden. Like that scene from "David Copperfield" – do you know that bit? – when the donkeys are on the green in front of her cottage and David's aunt shouts to Janet, "Janet! Donkeys!"'

I nodded, smiling. 'Yes, I know Dickens well.'

'I feel the same as you about this place,' William said. 'I love coming back here when I can. I grew up here – well, I spent most school holidays here, staying with Uncle Joe.'

I must have looked curious for he spoke slowly, gazing down at the town in the valley below. 'My parents died in a car accident when I was nine, so Uncle Joe became my guardian.'

'Oh, I am sorry,' I said.

He gave a faint smile of acknowledgement. 'I went to boarding school but I came here during many holidays – although sometimes I spent time with my Aunty.

'I've got a few days off before we start rehearsals for our next production, so I thought I'd come and see Uncle Joe. I said I'd paint his spare bedroom while I am here. And I hope to get a bit of climbing in, to keep my hand in. My friend, Matt, who lives on the moors, introduced me to rock-climbing and I love it. We're climbing Everest next May. For charity.'

I gasped.

'So I'm trying to get as fit as possible, whenever I can. You have to be totally fit for that, as you can imagine. But I enjoy it too – just me and the rock face. Climbing makes such a change from being with lots of other people all the time.'

'Sounds brilliant. Being wholly at one with nature.'

He looked at me and nodded. 'Ye-es … Would you like to have a go? I could take you up there, if you like.' He gestured towards the cluster of huge crags which rose behind the Gamekeeper's Cottage. 'I was thinking of climbing up there later on.'

I gasped. 'What, climb those great things?' I was about to shake my head. I'd have to tell him of my fear of heights; I was such a wimp.

'It'll be fun,' he said.

I looked up at the vast grey cliffs towering above our heads beyond my back garden. My heart beat faster. I could already imagine being halfway up the rock face and the dizzying drop below.

But then his warm brown eyes looked into mine – and I would have followed him anywhere. Maybe he was right and it'd actually be fun. And anyway, I'd be tied to a rope so I couldn't actually fall. 'Okay, why not? They say it does you good to try new challenges, don't they,' I said.

'Great. What time's tea with Uncle Joe?

'4 o'clock.'

'Well, we could head up there after that. See you later for afternoon tea!'

I nodded, smiling as I pulled on my gardening gloves and bent to yank out a couple of thistles. William walked over to the other front gate, a spare but muscular figure. What a hunk! I'd have to tell Becks about this.

Phone in hand, I headed for the back garden to try and tidy up the stream a bit.

I raised my voice a little over the burbling brook twisting through my garden. The ferns overhanging the water were emerald green and the rocks surrounding the stream moss-covered. I pulled out a few straggling lengths of bindweed winding amongst the ferns.

'So you're going rock-climbing with him today! I've never even managed to get you to go up to the Whispering Gallery in St Paul's! Smooth talker or what?' Becks sounded impressed. Was there any resentment in her voice at my move up north, away from her? No, she sounded fine, thank goodness. It was good to hear her voice.

'Yes, well, somehow he persuaded me … He is rather gorgeous,' I admitted. 'Very fit and tanned. An outdoor type – and intelligent too.' Tucking my mobile against my ear with my shoulder, I used both hands to dig out a particularly stubborn length of bindweed with my trowel. I stood up.

Becky sighed. 'Trouble is, Alice, guys never live up to your expectations.'

'Well, that's their fault, not mine,' I said tersely. I dropped the trails of bindweed into the green bin at the end of the garden.

'I know but your expectations are so high. You're such a literary nerd. You always expect to meet a Thackeray in a teashop – or a Dickens in Dartmouth!' I knocked the soil off the trowel against the wall of the old porch outside the kitchen, still holding the phone to my ear. 'And then you're disappointed … I still don't think you ever gave Steve a chance. I know you thought he was too into sport – but there needs to be a bit of give and take.'

I dumped the trowel and gardening gloves on top of a pile of trugs and old plant pots resting on a shelf in the porch. An old straw gardening hat belonging to my landlord still hung from a hook above on the cottage wall. 'It was all take and no give, as far as I could see,' I said. 'When I dragged him to the theatre, he fell asleep. And even when we went out for a meal, he'd be checking to see the rugby results every five minutes.'

'And this time I bet you think you've found your Heathcliff, don't you.'

I rolled my eyes. And to think I'd been missing Becky! It's amazing how quickly you forget how annoying someone can be.

'I don't know what you mean.'

'Alice, you are incurably romantic. '

'It's not a disease, Becks!'

'No, I know, but try not to be so … intense. It puts men off.'

'But I love intensity. Life is so *mundane* most of the time. Always so much boring stuff to do – cleaning, washing up, ironing – over and over and over again. Life isn't like that in books.'

'Well, don't expect too much of this William, that's all I'm saying … Anyway, what's your country cottage like?'

'Oh, Becks. There are blue and white tiles round the fireplace!'

'And I suppose there's an Aga?' Becky asked sarcastically. 'Honest country folk always have an Aga.'

'Well, no …'

'And the next thing you'll tell me is you've bought a breadmaker.'

'Well, actually -'

'Oh, I don't believe it.'

'I like to have these things,' I said defensively. I'd had enough of gardening for a bit. I loosened my hair from its bun and shook out my hair. It fell down over my shoulders as I stepped back into the sitting room through the french windows. 'You know I want to live the country life. Mum fell in love with the place too … You should see the huge expanse of moors all around me.'

'It isn't a bit – bleak?'

'No, no. It's beautiful.'

'But just think of the winds in the autumn sweeping across the open moorland …What about draughts?'

'Well, the windows are quite old,' I admitted. I glanced at the old sashed windows. Could I see daylight between their frames? And how Becky would crow if she noticed there was no central heating in the cottage – proof positive that I'd made a huge mistake moving up north.

'And dry rot. And damp. There's always damp in those old houses.'

'I haven't seen any signs of any mould or anything.' Time to change the subject. Becky was not going to wind me up. 'Anyway, how are the workouts going? Interval splits working?'

'Yep. It's really improving my cardiovascular system. Should achieve my maximum running pace in a few months if I keep this up.'

'Excellent. Well, I've found you a cool health club here in the town. The fitness equipment is Olympic standard! I've booked you in for a free trial session when you come up. You could become a member if you like it and use it whenever you come to stay.'

'Sounds good.'

'And have you tried any of those recipes I showed you?'

'I did make that vegetable and chickpea curry,' Becky admitted. 'It was quite nice actually.'

'Good ... Would you believe it – I've actually got some vegetables and herbs growing in my garden. Perennials, William says ... There's an article in this month's *Countryside* about how a Mediterranean diet is the healthiest. Now I can start eating a Mediterranean diet.'

'What, in the north of England? Well, of course, Yorkshire's famous for its olive trees and fresh tuna, isn't it,' she said.

I sighed. 'At least it reminds me to try and eat well. I'll find some delicious recipes using my herbs and vegetables on the internet as soon as it's up and running here. They say it'll take a couple of days ... Have you got to know anyone on the staff at your school yet?' I asked.

'There are a couple of young teachers in the department I really like − Vicky and Kirsty. Vicky's invited me to her birthday party tonight. Should be a blast. I've got masses of work to do for school but I don't care. I refuse to stop enjoying my life just because of work. Vicky says teaching can take over your life if you let it.

'Anyway, better go. Need to go hunter gathering at Tesco's. Haven't got a thing to eat ... Now don't forget − don't go falling off any cliffs.'

I stared up at the stone cliffs looming above my back garden. I could have said that a shiver coursed down the length of my spine at her ominous words − but I don't believe in premonitions any more. No. Premonitions, a sense of foreboding, omens − they belong only in the world of literature. And literature has created delusions in my mind. Deadly delusions.

Chapter 4

The Gamekeeper's Cottage had been divided to form two smaller cottages but Mr Locksley's half of the Gamekeeper's Cottage was so different from mine. Heavy oak furniture gleamed with the sheen of well-polished wood. Leather bound books lined the shelves of this distinctively masculine bachelor's home. A fountain pen rested on a half-filled in 'Times' crossword puzzle lying on the coffee table. On an occasional table in one corner was a wind-up gramophone next to a pile of records! Antique or what? I loved the musky smell of tobacco pervading the sitting room; a pipe rack stood on the bureau in the corner. It reminded me of Grandpa. He always had a pipe in his mouth, often unlit, as it gave him something to suck on.

Mr Locksley prised a large tortoiseshell cat off a brown leather armchair for me to sit down. He held her in his arms, stroking her thick fur. 'This is Marmalade,' he said. He smiled. 'My brimstone beast!'

I laughed. 'Oh, she's beautiful!' I exclaimed and stroked her warm, soft fur. Marmalade purred loudly in Mr Locksley's arms. 'I'd love to get a cat. Someone to greet you when you come home from work. Jumping up onto your lap.'

Mr Locksley smiled. 'Marmalade's getting a bit old for any of that. She ignores me most of the time. Except when it's lunchtime, of course. She just likes to sleep all day. It'll do her good to get some fresh air.' He carried Marmalade to the back door and put her outside.

Above the fireplace hung a fine print of Constable's 'The Haywain'. The dray-horse plodding through the ford towards the blazing golden-leaved trees, and brilliant meadows patched with shadows from the sun's straggling rays seems such a heavenly scene.

'I see you're admiring the Constable,' Mr Locksley remarked as he carried in the tray of tea cups and saucers. He walked rather hesitantly and his hands shook a little, some milk spilling over the side of the jug. He was a bit like Mr Pickwick, with a rather portly girth and silver rimmed spectacles. He had a pointed nose and deeply pitted skin, presumably due to acne in his youth. He wore a faded green corduroy jacket, elbows patched with leather.

He placed the tray carefully down in the centre of the coffee table and put the cap on his fountain pen. 'I must say I like Constable's realism. He always worked directly from nature as spontaneously as possible capturing the light and atmosphere before him. Very different to the Romanticism of Turner, though the two were, of course, contemporaries … I do apologise,' he added drily. 'I tend to lecture, I know. The result of forty years of teaching, I suppose. And it's what my sister – she's a professional artist – has told me. She tries to paint al fresco herself.'

'I find art fascinating but I can't draw for toffee,' I said. I sighed. 'That old rustic way of life looks heavenly.'

'Ah, the cult of the countryside! Of course, you're from London, aren't you, so I can see why you might think in that way.' Mr Locksley shook his head. He poured out the tea and it splashed slightly into my saucer. He handed me my cup. His knuckles were swollen with arthritis. 'Yes, it's been a commonplace since Roman times to claim that the shepherd's life is better than the courtier's, that the country is purer than the city. "Sermons in stones and good in everything". Blake and Wordsworth seriously believed in it ... No, no, I don't agree with you. I think appearances can be deceptive.' He stared at the painting. 'It's tempting to become sentimental. Farmer Gabriel Oak may have played the flute with Arcadian sweetness in Thomas Hardy's novel – but imagine how the farm workers must have *strained* to scythe that hay and load those bales. It was sheer toil – nothing more. No, I think that the benefits of mechanisation – and industry – should be given due credit.'

'I suppose you're right. I think it's just nostalgia on my part.' I paused. 'Nostalgia makes the past more ... luminous, somehow – don't you think ... A vision of a time when everything seemed settled and secure.'

Mr Locksley was looking at me quizzically over his half-moon glasses, shaking his head in incomprehension. 'Well, I suppose even Ovid had his Golden Age but I don't think such a time has ever really existed, young lady,' he remarked, making me feel foolish.

I shrugged, and returned to the subject of art. 'My stepfather's hung my print of Gauguin's 'Joyousness' above the fireplace in my sitting room, Mr Locksley. You know, the one of the two women sitting under a tree in Tahiti. It's so simple and kind of primitive, *bursting* with tropical colours.'

'Hmm. But Gauguin's behaviour was appalling, treating his wife like that. '

It was the way Mr Locksley pressed his thin lips together which suggested that he was a man with whom you couldn't really discuss things; if you tried to do so, it would just become an argument. But then I suppose he must have been in his eighties. So maybe I should have expected him to be quite old-fashioned in his ideas. He wouldn't see beyond the personal life of the artist so I knew we had reached an impasse; we couldn't discuss Gauguin's achievements at all.

Instead I praised the two oil paintings hanging above the old bookcase, one of a younger Mr Locksley with thicker greying hair, the deep lines he now had around his mouth barely visible in the picture. The other was of William, with a fresher, rounder face, although with the same firm mouth and square jaw – perhaps in his late teens. 'Ah, that's Annie, my sister's work again …'

I remembered William had spoken of his Aunty Annie – who'd chased the sheep out of the garden.

'… She painted some portraits of our family several years ago – and one of George next door. He was a great friend of mine – we had so much in common. He was an accountant before he retired but he loved history too. We used to play chess regularly together.' He paused, 'Annie painted a rather good portrait of George's niece, Cathy, too. William's girlfriend.'

My heart gave a jolt. He already had a girlfriend. I knew it was too good to be true. So going rock-climbing with William wasn't a date; he probably just thought I'd enjoy an outdoor experience, as a townie.

'Cathy lives in London now. She's hugely ambitious.'

'What does she do?' I enquired.

He shook his head in admiration. 'Financial director

of a big cosmetics company. I always knew Cathy would amount to something … By the way, she's passing through Inkley tomorrow. She has a business appointment in York so has limited time. She said she'd like to pick up a few of her belongings from your house, if you don't mind.'

I nodded. So I'd get to see this Cathy. I bet she's gorgeous-looking.

'She's meeting William for coffee tomorrow morning. And hopefully I'll see her sometime tomorrow before she goes off again.' He smiled appreciatively. 'Cathy's very clever, as well as successful. A real wit.'

She would be clever too, wouldn't she. Why do some people have all the luck?

'She and William are so well-suited. As a child, she was rather wild, a bit of a handful for her mother, who was a single parent, so sometimes she used to come and stay with George during school holidays. To give her mum a break. George had a quick brain then, too, like his niece. Cathy would wind up the watch of her wit and the two of them would chime! Very entertaining. Now, sadly, George just stares into space.' He shook his head. 'A cruel disease, dementia …'

'Anyway, Cathy and William became great friends as children, always out playing on the moors together, climbing the rocks, playing hide and seek in the bracken, damming the moor side streams …'

I stared at him. 'Just like Cathy and Heathcliff!'

He frowned. 'That's just a novel. Don't confuse fantasy with reality, my dear.' He gazed up again at the portraits again. 'Annie is an excellent artist. She's really captured William …'

I nodded, staring at the picture. Yes, she had captured the depth of William's brown eyes, his lovely thick hair, even his warmth of character.

'But she's changed the focus of her artistic interest in recent years,' Mr Locksley said.

As I sipped my tea, I gazed at the collection of old photographs in silver frames, grouped together on an occasional table near the door. They were sepia photographs of Mr Locksley's … grandparents, I suppose, and his great grandparents, with various children solemnly staring at the camera, fixed immovably by the photo flash forever. One young man stood slightly apart from the children. There was something faintly familiar about him. That tall yet well-built figure, the dark abundant hair, those intensely vital brown eyes …

William entered the room at that moment and I looked from him to the photograph. Of course. The resemblance was striking.

'I believe you and William have already met,' said Mr Locksley. 'Is something wrong, young lady?'

'No, no … it's just – haven't you ever noticed, Mr Locksley, how similar William is to that young man in the photo? With his keen eyes. He looks so – I don't know – so *alive*.'

Mr Locksley picked up the photo, stared at it and then at William. 'By Jove, you're right. I suppose that makes sense, though. That's a photograph of my great-uncle, William's great-great- grandfather. So I suppose there's a good chance of a family likeness. He must have been about the same age in that photo as William is now.' He paused. 'Actually, there is quite a story attached to that young man.'

I looked at him inquiringly, sipping my tea.

'What is it, Uncle Joe? You've never mentioned it before,' said William.

'It's something my father told me years ago ... Our family, the Locksleys, do not originate from this side of the Pennines. They lived in Manchester during the nineteenth century and were quite wealthy, having made their money in the cotton industry.

'However, the American Civil War impeded the flow of cotton to Lancashire and the family fortunes soon declined. Our family faced very hard times. The young man in the photograph possessed what you might call a 'reckless streak' and he tried to save the family from poverty. He went to Manchester Racecourse and placed what remained of the family fortunes in a bet upon a horse ... but the horse lost the race! That young man you see in the picture took a gun out of his pocket and shot himself, then and there, on Manchester Racecourse!'

He gazed at the photograph for a moment before replacing it gently on the table.

There was a shocked silence.

'How dreadful for him,' I said with feeling.

'Yes, but how foolish to risk everything like that,' said Mr Locksley.

'Well, I think he was brave, to do something so daring,' said William.

'Do you? I'm not so sure,' I said. 'Everyone knows gambling's a mug's game.'

'But there was the chance of winning a fortune – and he was ready to take one hell of a risk,' said William.

Mr Locksley shrugged. 'I think he was an idiot,' he said

bluntly. 'But then you like taking risks, don't you, William?'

Uncle and nephew stared at each other. There was a strange tension between them.

I tried to lighten the atmosphere. 'Well, I just wish I could recline on this blissful cloud of summer indolence for longer ...' Mr Locksley gave a tight smile at my Keats allusion. I drained my cup of tea. 'But, by 'eck, I need to get going. There's still all t' work in t'garden to get on with.' I paused, raising my eyebrows. 'Hey, what do you think of my Yorkshire accent? I've been listening to t'people chatting in t'shops down in Inkley. So 'ave I mastered the lingo yet?'

William chuckled at my efforts, nodding encouragingly and Mr Locksley smiled.

'Yes, it's a dreadful shame your garden's got so out of hand,' said Mr Locksley. 'Poor old George. He took such pleasure in his plants. His garden was a real picture. But he started to get so confused, he couldn't tend them much. In the end, he had to go into a home. I go and see him once a week,' he shook his head sadly, 'but he hasn't recognised me for months ... I've tried to keep the weeds down but it takes me enough time just to look after my own garden.'

'Don't worry. I'll enjoy restoring it to its former glory. I'll try and do a bit each day. I've got so much else to do, especially preparing for the term ahead too. I expect you remember that all too well, Mr Locksley, as Head of English!'

'Yes, indeed,' he said. 'The summer holidays were the only vacation in which you could really forget your work for a while but, even so, I would spend a lot of time reading new texts. What are you preparing?'

'"Macbeth", "The Strange Case of Dr Jekyll and Mr Hyde", Browning's monologues. Oh, and some Elizabeth Barrett Browning poems. I've already prepared the A Level texts, while I was on holiday in Greece a couple of weeks ago. I've started the monologues but there are one or two poems I've found tricky. I need to revise "Macbeth" too. It just takes me so long to annotate the books and then plan how to teach them.'

Mr Locksley considered. 'I should have some notes on "Macbeth" somewhere. I'll have to search my bureau,' he remarked. 'If you bring your Browning poems round some time, maybe I can give you a hand with them.'

'Oh, that's kind of you. I've bought some critical texts but it's difficult not being on the internet yet. It'll take a while to be connected. So anything would be welcome … Hopefully teaching will get easier after a few years.'

'I somehow doubt it,' said Mr Locksley, shaking his head. 'I found the pupils increasingly difficult to teach. The boys became more and more careless in their work. Too many distractions these days; computer games and television have a lot to answer for! Their writing was unoriginal, too, and cliché-ridden.'

'Yep. Uncle Joe always had a bee in his bonnet about their work being – to make no bones about it – as dull as ditchwater,' said William with a mischievous grin and I chuckled. Yes, he had Will Ladislaw's quick mind, too.

Mr Locksley smiled faintly. 'There were exceptions, of course, but they became increasingly few and far between. As far as I can see, from what I was watching in a documentary on the television the other day, so many of them are happy playing inane computer games, like 'Murder Revenge

Bloodbath' or whatever the latest violence-obsessed video game is called.'

We both laughed.

'You may laugh but I do ask myself sometimes – is this really the sum total of what we have achieved after centuries of great learning and creativity?' He shook his head gravely, pursing his thin lips. This was clearly a favourite hobby horse of his. 'After the urbanity of Horace, after Donatello's magnificent "David". Now all teenagers seem bothered about is trying to reach the next level of a computer game! Is this the pinnacle of Man's ingenuity?'

'I do know what you mean,' I said, and I could see his point. 'But not all teenagers are like that. And didn't you find that the exceptions were the ones who made teaching worthwhile? Of course, I've only had the experience of teaching practice – but – to see the spark of pleasure in just one student's eyes … as I did when I introduced my A Level class to Wordsworth's 'Prelude'. You know the bit - when he describes going skating in the Lake District :

'All shod

With steel, we hissed along the polished ice …"'

Mr Locksley shrugged. 'Personally, I prefer the wit of Oscar Wilde, the erudition of Pope,' he remarked. '"What oft was thought but ne'er so well expressed." There is a great deal to be admired in their writing.'

'That's very true - but I suppose I'm not talking about admiration or cleverness so much as joy, *rapture* …'

Mr Locksley shook his head. 'What is it Cicero states? "Qui solis in sua passion, non potest usum rationis"'

'Sorry?'

'"He only employs his passion who can make no use of his reason,"' Mr Locksley translated.

'I'm not sure I agree with that -' I said.

The phone rang in the hall and Mr Locksley eased himself out of his armchair, murmuring an apology.

'Sorry,' I said to William. 'I get carried away when I talk about poetry.'

William smiled. 'Why not? You obviously love it. I love poetry too … You've got a great memory for lines.'

'Yes, I do seem to remember stuff I've read. It's strange. The words seem to imprint themselves on my brain.'

'Most actors would give their eyeteeth for that,' remarked William. 'Learning lines is the bane of our lives. I've got a good memory but even I have to work at it. '

'Hello, Annie. How are you?' Mr Locksley's voice drifted in from the hall.

'That's Aunty Annie,' said Will. 'She's probably confirming lunch tomorrow. She always comes to Inkley for the summer Art Festival.'

'Oh, yes. Isn't she an artist? She painted those portraits of you and your uncle.' I pointed to the pictures on the wall.

'Yes, that's right. And Uncle Joe's got some of her more recent landscapes and wildlife paintings on his walls, too.'

'Where?' I asked.

'In the dining room,' said Will. 'Would you like to see them?'

'Just for two minutes,' I said. 'Then I must go.'

He showed me into the dining room, in the centre of which stood an old oak table surrounded by six chairs. In one corner stood a baby grand piano.

'Who plays the piano? Do you?' I asked William.

He shook his head. 'No, I wish I'd learned. Uncle Joe plays really well – but he hardly ever does, even though I do try to persuade him to practise.'

On the table a jigsaw lay, nearly completed. I glanced at the box lid. The scene was a series of huge electric pylons, their fretwork of struts stretching up to triangular points linked together by cables across a bleak industrial landscape. How could anyone find a picture of *pylons* attractive and want to complete a jigsaw of them?

William saw me wince and smiled. 'Uncle Joe likes the geometry of pylons. So neat and symmetrical,' he remarked drily. 'He loves an order to things. And he enjoys puzzles, too.'

I shrugged. 'Beauty is in the eye of the beholder, I suppose.'

I looked round at the paintings on the walls. In contrast to the picture of the pylons, I found them delightful. Mostly oil on canvas, although there were some pastels and watercolours too, there were some lovely Lake District scenes, one of Ben Nevis – and pictures of white limestone crags perched above velvety grassy slopes further up Wharfedale.

Another picture painted in pastels displayed a red grouse perched upon a limestone rock surrounded by a lovely vista of purple heather. Annie had stippled the brown and russet plumage of the bird, marking the distinctive red eyebrow arched above its beady eye. Another showed a female grouse with speckled brown and black plumage sitting on its eggs in a nest amongst wiry heather stems.

'These are lovely,' I breathed.

William nodded and pointed at a group of pictures next to the old dresser near the front window. 'Those were from her last collection. They're pictures of animals in danger. She's getting more and more concerned about threatened species. Wants to draw the public's attention to them.'

'Look at this dear little dormouse.' Against a backdrop of brown autumnal leaves, cracked and veined, the dormouse was deeply asleep. Its eyes were tightly screwed up and its little body covered in golden brown fur was curled up, tiny pink feet tucked under its body.

'These pictures are so meticulous. You can *feel* her love for nature in them.'

'Aunty Annie's bringing her latest paintings tomorrow,' William said as Mr Locksley joined us in the dining room.

'Oh, I hope I can buy one,' I said fervently. 'I love her natural touch. My mother would love the one of the dormouse. She's very into cute animals, like me.'

'At least she displays some craftsmanship in her work, some artistic skill; she's not all *concept*, like so many artists these days. Some of the work at the Inkley Art Exhibition!' Mr Locksley shuddered. 'All squiggles and splotches of garish colour. But full of *meaning*, of course.'

'If you like, why don't you come round for lunch tomorrow and you can have a preview?' said William. 'If that's okay with you, Uncle Joe? I've got this new recipe for us to sample. It's a quanteen from the Himalayas. There should be loads to spare.' Uncle Joe nodded, looking dubious. 'I'm always introducing Uncle Joe to new recipes whenever I come home. I *think* he enjoys it!'

'Personally I'd prefer a nice roast dinner,' Mr Locksley grumbled.

'Well, it's very kind of you to invite me. I'd love to,' I said. 'Thank you again for the tea, Mr Locksley.'

There had been a frantic buzzing near the window for several minutes. A large bumble bee was blundering about, bumping into the pane of glass but, as we watched it, it dropped onto the window sill, lying on its back. Its legs waved feebly in the air.

'It's exhausted,' said William. 'Probably been shut in here for a few days so it's had no nourishment. Poor thing.'

'Squash it with a newspaper,' said Mr Locksley. 'Put it out of its misery.'

'No,' William protested. 'It's got a right to live, as much as you do. It only needs something to give it energy. Hold on a minute.' He went into the kitchen.

'What a fuss about nothing,' Mr Locksley shook his head.

'No, I think it's lovely, trying to help a suffering creature,' I said warmly. I was touched by his action.

'Ah, here comes Saint Francis of Assisi,' muttered Mr Locksley as William returned with a drop of water on a teaspoon. He ignored Mr Locksley's comment.

'I've dissolved a bit of sugar in it,' he said. 'That should give it the energy to fly off to get some nectar.'

He tipped the drop of sugared water next to the bee and then gently helped the bee to right itself with the teaspoon. The bee buzzed faintly then it turned and pushed its proboscis into the liquid. We could see it visibly gain strength as William opened the window. Finally, the bee, gently guided by a table mat, flew waveringly out of the window.

'Well done!' William was so compassionate towards the poor bee.

'And now I *must* get back to work,' I said. 'I've still got boxes I haven't opened, as well as the garden to do. And my school preparation! Thank you so much for inviting me round, Mr Locksley.'

'Are you still on for the climb tonight?' William asked.

My heart lurched. I glanced up at the dark cliff face frowning down upon me through Mr Locksley's back window. I'd half been wishing that William had forgotten his offer to take me climbing.

'Are you sure you want to take me? Don't you need to be practising for Everest, not bothering with a novice?'

'No, I'd love to take you,' he assured me and he seemed to mean what he said ... But of course William was just being kind to a lonely newcomer. He was just filling time being a good neighbour till he saw the beautiful Cathy tomorrow.

'OK, then, if you're sure. It'll be – an experience.'

'Shall I call for you about seven?'

'Yes, fine.'

I wore a pink cotton shirt, faded jeans and a pair of trainers; William nodded in approval when I asked him if this was suitable wear. He had a helmet on his head and a coil of rope slung over his shoulder. He handed me the other helmet and helped me adjust the strap so that it fitted securely under my chin. We climbed up the steep path which wound its way to the rocky summit which soared above our heads. The gritty footpath glinted with tiny particles of quartz and mica.

The spouting water which would eventually course down to join the other stream below, bubbled and splashed its way down a granite crevice off to the left. As the rock face

71

loomed above my head, my throat tightened; it must have been at least a hundred feet high. I swallowed. The fresh breeze blew a strand of hair into my eyes and I brushed it away.

'This climb's called "Fairy Steps",' remarked William, staring up at it.

'What? They've all got names?'

William laughed. 'Of course. There's a climb further round called "Desperate Dredd" … and that one over there's called "Where Blue Tits Dare!" … ' He pointed at a totally smooth sheer rock face some metres away. It looked even worse than "Fairy Steps". I laughed, despite myself.

'I think I'll stick to "Fairy Steps". Although I wish I was a bit more fairy-like!' I said, glancing down at my rather sturdy legs. 'How in God's name do I get up there?'

'Don't worry. It's just a case of using the cracks and fissures. And the ribs. '

'The what?

'Small ridges standing out from the rock face.'

'Oh. Like – where?'

'There – and there.' As he pointed, I could see that there were some shallow ledges to be seen amongst the wide expanse of smooth cliff face.

'Always keep three limbs on a rock surface at once, 'said William. 'And don't look down. Watch me to see where the best places are.'

And before I knew it, with rope coiled round his shoulder, William had lightly scaled the first fifty feet or so, with the ease of a goat. He was high above the rocky ground without a safety rope.

'Will, what are you doing?' I shouted. 'You can't go up there without a rope!'

'Don't worry,' William called down. He stood, spread-eagled against the cliff, his fingers wedged into a hairline crack, his feet perched on a tiny jutting ledge. 'I've done this climb hundreds of times before. I know every move.'

I stared up at him, my mouth dry. I could picture it now. William slithering and scraping down the rock, his wild clawing at the air as he plunged to the stony ground below. 'But what if your foot slips? For God's sake, be *careful*.'

'Everything's fine,' William's voice drifted down to me. He had vanished above a slight overhang. 'I'll lower the rope down to you in a minute.'

Sure enough, a few minutes later a rope was writhing its way down the cliff. Well, at least he didn't expect *me* to climb without a rope. I attached the large metal clip, or, as William called it, the karabiner, to the rope, and stepped up onto the first ledge. All went well at first. I followed what I could remember of William's footsteps and handholds.

'Must keep three limbs on the rock at once,' I muttered through gritted teeth in a kind of mantra.

Then suddenly I couldn't see where to go next – sideways, up, or down. In a fever of anxiety, I clung tightly to the slightly overhanging crag jutting out from the smooth surface. Glancing down made my head spin. The rock face yawned beneath my feet to the stony ground below and I felt dizzy, sweat trickling down my back. Memories of the theme park haunted me. The terrible drop beneath me. What if I fell and the rope snapped?

A cold blast of wind swept across my face and my heart jumped in sudden panic. My cotton shirt billowed out with the gust. I looked up hastily, sick and giddy. Straddling the rock face, I clawed wildly at the narrow crack above me and wedged my fingers into the gap, as William had done. Breathing heavily, I licked my dry lips.

'Where now?' I called croakily. 'I'm completely stuck.'

'There should be a ledge – over to your left,' his voice drifted down to me, calm and reassuring. ' … See it sticking out? Step onto that and reach up to the crag on your left. Can you reach it?'

'Just about,' I muttered. 'Why in God's name did I agree to this?'

You could bet your life Cathy was the perfect climbing partner. Mr Locksley had said how she and William had played all the time on the moors as children, hadn't he. Cathy would be slim and agile, scaling the rock surfaces skilfully, her lovely hair tousled by the wind as she climbed.

The rock surface was rough and gritty and I scraped my knuckles once or twice – but I was getting there. Climbing round the overhang made me feel like a fly on the ceiling and at one point it felt as though my legs were doing the splits. One foot was stretched high and over to the right, whilst with the other foot I had jammed my toes in a narrow fissure in the rock's surface. I didn't look down again, just up at William's encouraging smile as he drew in the rope above me.

I finally heaved myself onto the top of the crag and sank onto a boulder next to William on the cliff top, unclipping the karabiner. I was amazed. I'd done it! And I hadn't been reduced to a quivering wreck.

'Yay!' I gasped. 'My sister, Becky, would be proud of me – she loves all sports.'

William unwound the rope from around his broad shoulders and patted me on the back. 'Well done,' he said. 'You did it!'

I beamed at him and he smiled back, eyes filled with admiration.

And – there it was again, I was sure – that warmth of feeling in his eyes, that spark of a response, the electric thrill of attraction between us.

The blue air was all around us. Like birds in the sky, we looked down upon the town of Inkley. We could see the pointed church steeple in the centre of the town, the open air swimming pool on the other side of the valley, the green rugby and football fields with their white goalposts and the play park by the river. The cool breeze poured across our faces and the sparkling air was as bright and heady as champagne.

'Wow. You can see for *miles* up here, I said. 'Right up the Dales. I've never seen anywhere like this before.'

'Yep, on a clear day, you can see the peak of Ingleborough.'

I gazed up the dale at the purple and russet- coloured moors, stretching away to the more hazy bloom of blue hills in the distance.

'I must say,' I shook my head. 'I thought at one point that you'd have to call the Mountain Rescue. I couldn't go up and I couldn't go down. I'd have felt such a prat ...' Then I remembered. 'But why on earth were you climbing without a rope?'

'I told you, I've done this climb without a rope lots of times before. The chances of me making a mistake are so remote – '

'The chances,' I said. 'We're not talking about the odds in a horse race here. You're risking your life every time you do that.'

'Sorry. I just enjoy the buzz,' William said. 'A bit of risk adds spice to life, don't you think? Life can be so boring otherwise. We live in such a safe, protected world nowadays … My great heroes are Scott and Shackleton.' His eyes shone. ' Imagine the driving ambition to find the Northwest passage! It must have been so *exhilarating.* Adventurous men, people who dared, whether they succeeded or not…'

'I'm sure even they didn't take unnecessary risks,' I said tartly.

He had the grace to look penitent. 'I'm sorry I frightened you. But you can see the thrill, can't you. … Go on, admit it, you've really enjoyed this climb, haven't you? Maybe it reminded you of tree climbing when you were a kid. The adventure of it.'

'Oh, no,' I confessed. 'I could never climb trees in our local park, despite my sister's best efforts. To be honest, I was terrified when I started to climb. I'm a bit of a coward really. But you're right,' I said. And I meant it. 'I'm so glad I did it. It was an amazing experience.'

'There you are. And what a way to see the glorious dales!'

The wild moorland had an uncanny beauty. The setting sun burst out from behind the flushed clouds, casting a rosy hue over the purple heather below and tingeing the lichened boulders amongst them a soft pink. Beyond the heather, a gentle breeze made the emerald grass dance.

'I always thought that Yorkshire was a drab place till

I read Emily Bronte's poetry. Then I came up here for interview. This place blew me away then and it does now – it's so *lovely*, I could look at it for hours.'

'You used to think it'd all be mill chimneys and flat caps, eeh bah gum?' William said, grinning. He was winding the rope neatly round his arm, from wrist to elbow. Then he bound the rope deftly with the karabiner. His hands were quick and strong, with square-tipped fingers. 'Lots of southerners do. A common misconception. I love this place too… Mind you, Uncle Joe would disagree.' He slipped the coiled rope over his head and across the broad muscular gap between his shoulder blades.

'He doesn't like this beautiful place?'

He shook his head. 'He says it does nothing for him. Strange, isn't it.'

'I'm sure your Uncle Joe thinks I romanticise too much. Mind you, he may be right …' I laughed. 'When my mum and stepdad were here the other day, helping me move in, we went to the market in Ripon. There was a truck there in the market square, filled with sheep. They were sticking their noses out through the slats of the truck and baa-ing loudly. And I said to Mum, 'Ah, they're so *sweet*. I wonder where they're going.'

'Then the gruff voice of the farmer came from behind the truck, "Well, they're not going on bloody 'oliday, that's for sure!"

We both laughed.

'The farmer must have thought to himself – "we've got a right soft southerner 'ere",' I said. 'And I suppose he's right. I do like to see prettiness in everything around here. But this landscape *is* glorious.'

'Ah, but you've only seen the surface of this magnificent county,' said William enigmatically.

'What do you mean?'

'Would you like to see the Yorkshire Dales – from the inside?'

'Sorry?'

'Underground.'

'What? You mean caving?'

'Yes.'

'I've never been underground at all before. There aren't many caverns you can explore in London.' I suppose at least this was going down into the ground, not up a cliff. Although enclosed spaces didn't appeal much either.

'Dad and I used to go caving when we visited Uncle Joe, and then Matt and I visited the pots later on when I was here during school holidays … Uncle Joe lets me drive his Volvo out and about when I'm here. As an actor I can't afford a car. How about I take you to Ramsgill Pot up the dales – maybe tomorrow, after lunch? It's an amazing place.'

'But I've got so much work – '

'It'll only take a couple of hours. It is fascinating, I promise you. One of my favourite haunts. You'll be amazed.' His soft brown eyes smiled into mine.

He clearly loved this area and wanted to pass on his love of the beauties of Yorkshire to me, a newcomer.

'Go on, then. If Year 11's understanding of "Macbeth" is rather vague due to insufficient preparation by their teacher, it'll be your fault!'

That evening, I sat at the old scrubbed pine table till late, trying to concentrate on "The Strange Case of Dr Jekyll and Mr Hyde". But William's smiling face kept filling my mind. He was so interesting and attractive – and the most exciting man I'd ever met. I couldn't wait till tomorrow, when I would be with him again … And I could tell he liked me. But just as a friend. After all, he had a girlfriend, Cathy. And they were very well-matched, Mr Locksley said.

But William hadn't mentioned her once. Perhaps Mr Lockley liked to imagine there was more between them than there was?

No, must concentrate. In a week's time, I'll be thrown amongst teenagers brim-full of turbulent hormones. Like being thrown to the lions. Need to prepare thoroughly in order to survive.

The tale of Jekyll and Hyde was truly eerie. When Jekyll saw that his own hand was "lean, corded, knuckly, of a dusky pallor" and he realised it was the hand of Edward Hyde, goose bumps rose on my skin. Hyde was slowly being incorporated into Jekyll. 'It is a marvellous exploration into the evil recesses of human nature', claimed one critic.

At least the gruesome description of the protagonist who, when a little girl ran into him, 'tramped calmly over the child's body and left her screaming on the ground', should satisfy a typical Year 10 student's love of horror. That would be a good lead into the novel, grabbing their attention straight away.

Yes, 'the gorier the better' was the way to engage them. Becky was the one who gave me that idea.

I also prepared some story plans for the year 8's. They'd been reading some horror stories in Year 7:

'*You have been studying different aspects of a horror story, including* creepy settings, building up tension *to a* climax *and then having an* unexpected twist *to the story, when the ending* isn't *predictable.*

Now you are going to have a go at writing your own Gothic story. Make sure you have an unexpected twist *to your story – it must* not *turn out to have all been a dream!*

Make notes on your story under the headings below … '

Before going to bed, I crammed the bunches of lavender which I'd rescued from a tangle of brambles the day we'd arrived into my yellow and blue jugs. Their lovely purple flowers started to spread their fragrance through the sitting room. My table lamps with their glazed bases of faded duck egg blue were casting a soft glow from the deep window sills upon the odd pieces of china I'd picked up in antique shops.

The Gauguin painting looked just right above the fireplace. And at least I wouldn't have to stare at Becky's boring old Mondrian print above her bed any more. She loved Mondrian because, she said, it was so clever, logically reducing the world – the three primary colours, the horizontal and vertical – to a canvas but I couldn't see anything much, apart from a load of coloured rectangles and lines.

The house still seemed strangely silent, apart from the creaking noises you hear in any old house. I suppose I'd get used to it. I'd give Becky a call in a minute, just to make sure she was okay.

I'd emptied the boxes of all my books – not a sports manual or running shoe in sight. The white shelves on either side of the fireplace were filled with my paperbacks of just about all the classics Penguin has ever brought out. I surveyed my collection. You could say I'd measured out my life so far in these wonderful books.

Some of the cottage furnishings, including an old settle

next to the fire, a rocking chair on the other side of the fire, a cottage piano and an ancient grandfather clock ticking sedately in the corner, looked as though they had been there since the cottage was built in the early nineteenth century. Mum had particularly loved the grandfather clock. The mahogany grain of its wood gleamed in the lamplight. "Things men have made with wakened hands and put soft life into," the words of D H Lawrence flowed into my mind, "are awake through years.'

An ancient, slightly musty smell pervaded the air which I found restful and strangely comforting. I felt safe and secure here, surrounded by objects that had clearly been loved for their familiarity over the years. I could never convey this feeling to Becky. Objects to her were just things to be used – useful, practical things. Ipads and exercise bikes were the only kind of things worth having.

Must remember to wind up the grandfather clock every night.

Above the piano hung two oil paintings, one of an elderly man with white hair and smiling blue-grey eyes. Presumably my landlord, George Lawson. The other was a painting of a very attractive girl with brown eyes fringed with dark lashes, and wildly curling dark hair, standing deep in purple heather on the moors. Cathy. Both paintings had the artist's squiggle in the bottom right hand corner: *Annie Locksley*. The paintings Mr Locksley had spoken of and praised.

I stretched up to straighten the painting of Cathy and, on an impulse, unhooked it to examine it more closely. Cathy was certainly beautiful, with her olive skin and heart-shaped face. I turned the picture over and, sloping across the top of the brown paper backing, was a message written in sloping black letters:

'*To Cathy, from William with all my love xxxx*'.

It was dated a few years ago.

My worst fears were confirmed. '*All my love*' … Cathy and William *were* deeply in love. Just like Cathy and Heathcliff.

As I'd suspected, William was just being a good host in showing me the delights of the Yorkshire Dales. Maybe his uncle had suggested to him he take me out, make me feel welcome? That spark between us … it had just been a figment of my imagination.

I stared into the old, mildew-spotted mirror near the door. My fair hair and blue eyes were reflected back at me; I looked so *pallid* compared to Cathy's exotic beauty. I didn't stand a chance against her.

Cathy was quite a wit, too, Mr Locksley said. Now me – Oscar Wilde, I ain't. I felt a stab of failure. I can never think of a witty riposte until ten minutes after a conversation has ended – a fat lot of use.

But what value has wordplay really got? What is it but a bit of skilful skating about on the surface of words with a neatly flipping pun or the split jump of an epigram? …

But then, on the other hand, I suppose it's highly entertaining – and very attractive too if a woman is witty.

My phone rang.

'I'm off to Vicky's party in a sec. Just wondering how you got on with Bear Grylls?'

It was good to hear Becks' cheerful, if faintly mocking tones.

'I was just about to call you … We've been rock-climbing.

It was fantastic. A bit hairy in places but when you get to the top of the rock, you get such a sense of achievement. And the view's to die for ... William climbed it without a rope.'

'Wow! That's cool. Pretty fearless.'

'To be honest, I thought it was stupid actually ... But, oh, Becks,' I burst out. 'You won't believe it. Cathy and William played together here on the moors as children!'

There was a silence. 'So?' she said.

'Well, I don't stand a chance. They're made for each other.'

There was another silence. 'Why?'

'Cathy and Heathcliff ...You know?'

'Oh. My. God.' She took a deep breath. 'I thought you'd grown out of all that. Alice,' She spoke slowly, 'Cathy and William are not characters in a novel; they are real people! You're as bad as those people who watch soaps on telly and send hate mail to the actor who plays the love rat ... Or even Mum. D'you remember that letter she sent to the BBC when Josh Simmons was wrongly convicted of murder in "South Street"? I tried to remind her it was only a soap but she didn't take any notice. I couldn't believe it!'

'Actually,' I said coldly, 'I've just found a loving message written from William to Cathy. On the back of a painting of her.'

'Ah.'

'It's true love, Becks. I mustn't interfere with the course of true love.'

She sighed. 'Well, maybe you're right this time. Still, as Shakespeare said, it's better to have loved and lost than never to have loved at all.'

'That was Tennyson actually ... Anyway, I haven't exactly loved and lost. There hasn't been any love in the first place. Not on his part, anyway?'

'No, well, I'd better go.' She paused. 'Alice?'

'Yes?'

'Just try not to get too carried away, with your flights of fancy, won't you.'

'I won't,' I said stiffly. 'Enjoy yourself.'

Flights of fancy! Was this lovely old cottage a flight of fancy? I gazed around me. There was the old desk in the corner and the grandfather clock. Becky would hate them, of course. Old relics of the past, she would call them. Irrelevant dust-gatherers. She'd throw them all out and replace them with IKEA furniture. Well, *she* wouldn't have to live with them. I loved them.

And then there were my pictures on the wall, my favourite throw which Mum had embroidered with a pattern of leaves – sycamore, beech, horse chestnut and holly – spread over the back of the old sofa. And a bright rug covered the middle of the flagstone floor.

The black grate was laid, ready for the first chilly night of autumn, beside a shining copper bucket filled with logs of seasoned pine wood. A sheepskin rug lay in front of the fire. I already adored this old cottage, with its nooks and beams. I stared through the front window. The moors outside stretched up to the cliff, dark and brooding against the night sky. When my friend, Alex, came to stay in the autumn, she should be able to use her telescope as there was little light pollution. Down in the valley, the lights of Inkley twinkled prettily.

Ah, well. Even if William and I weren't meant to be,

at least I had achieved my 'Countryside'. I would live here in a haze of contentment, with a line of pristine washing outside blowing in the breeze, a basket of apples resting against an old striped deckchair on the lawn.

Well, that's the dream the magazines sell us, isn't it?

Chapter 5

I slept till late morning the next day, awakened by the roar of a car engine. Mr Locksley's Volvo was heading down the track from the cottage towards Inkley. William going to meet Cathy for coffee, I suppose.

I stared out of my window at the sun-drenched moorland. I could see the young girl with curling dark hair racing across the heather trying to beat a young William back to the cottage first. They were laughing delightedly as each tried to elbow the other out of the way. Wild, wicked slips, they would cheek Mr Locksley when he came out into the back garden to tell them off for being back late.

Or Cathy and William were sailing paper boats down the stream coursing through my garden and Mr Locksley's garden, shouting wildly at their little crafts as they spun round in circles, before careering down the little waterfalls that rippled over the stones. William would help Cathy to streamline her boat. They would have been standing just there, by my little rockery, heads bent over their work.

Or they would be lying on the cool, mossy grass of the back lawn in the golden rays of the summer sun, telling each other wonderful stories, embellishing their tales with bright, colourful language and witty quips. They were made for each other. I could picture William as a teenager with his arm around Cathy, her dark hair curling round her lovely face. William leaning over Cathy, kissing her.

Mr Locksley greeted me with a glass of sherry when I went round for lunch. An aroma of onions, garlic and various spices drifted in from the kitchen. 'William won't be long,' he said. 'He's taken Cathy to "Betty's Café" down in Inkley for a coffee before she goes to visit her uncle.'

So right now they would be gazing into each other's eyes across their steaming lattes, totally enraptured with each other.

'The stew is simmering nicely, apparently, so I don't need to do a thing.'

There was the sound of a car horn outside.

'Oh, that'll be Annie.'

Mr Locksley went to the front door. I craned my neck round and looked out of the window.

An old camper van had pulled up outside the front gate. An elderly lady with short white hair and a long flowery skirt climbed out of the front seat. Several flowing colourful scarves flapped round her in the breeze. She went round to the back of the campervan and opened the door.

Mr Locksley made his way to the front gate and gave her a peck on the cheek. They started to carry in a number of large art folders between them.

'This is my Alice, my new neighbour. From London,' Mr Locksley introduced me. Annie had the same bright brown eyes and intensely intelligent face as William, although her face was paler. Her nose, fortunately, was not as long and pointed as Mr Locksley's and her skin was smoother. A faint smell of turps and oil paints wafted around her.

'William won't be long,' Mr Locksley told Annie. 'He's

just gone to have a coffee with Cathy. She's only here for a few hours. She has to dash off to York. So busy with her job.'

'Mmm,' said Annie, lips pursed. She didn't say any more and there seemed to be an awkward silence for a minute or two.

'Can I say that I think your pictures in the dining room are fantastic?' I said. 'Especially the miniatures.'

'Oh, thank you,' Annie responded. She spoke very precisely, like her brother. 'Yes, I must say I'm particularly fond of them myself.'

'I love the one of the red squirrel.'

'Ah, yes, that was painted in the Great Glen in Scotland … I used to paint portraits, family groups or pretty scenes of the countryside. They sold well. People thought they'd look nice on their walls. But now I feel that art should do more than that. I want to help protect some of this country's wildlife, so I've painted the pictures you've already seen and I've also brought some more pictures of animals under threat to complete my collection for the exhibition.' She spoke with feeling. 'I want to draw attention to the danger posed to them. I painted a lovely picture of the Large Blue Butterfly. It's beautiful – light blue wings with black edges. I sold it instantly; a lady thought it was lovely. The Harlequin frog and the White-clawed crayfish are under threat too. But people are so illogical, irrational – they don't care about *them* because they're ugly.' She shook her head. 'It's very frustrating.'

I nodded. Unfortunately, it's easier to feel sorry for a cute animal than a hideous looking creature.

'Now I'm working on a threatened *plant* exhibition that

I hope to show next year...' She shook her head and sighed. 'You know, I can remember when I was a girl, seeing wild flowers growing in profusion everywhere in the countryside – and now so many of them have vanished. It's largely due to intensive farming methods over the last forty years.'

'Would you like to look at the rest of Annie's exhibition pictures before lunch?' Mr Locksley asked.

I nodded. 'I'd love to.'

Annie opened an art folder and extracted a couple of miniatures. 'Before I show you the animal pictures I've got ready for this year's exhibition, just have a look at what I've already started. Work in progress. These are my rare plant pictures ... This is the Common Rock Rose – not so common any more, I'm afraid.'

She handed me a delicately painted oil miniature of a plant with bright yellow flowers, with thin grey-green leaves sprouting from between two great grey limestone slabs. Mr Locksley and I gazed at Annie's latest creations. 'But I found just the one plant a couple of months ago on the limestone pavement up at Malham Cove, between the crevices.' Her eyes shone with delight. 'I was *so* excited to find it. I'd searched and searched for this. It's so wonderful to think that at least some of these species are in existence ... '

'And this is Blue Moor Grass, spotted after *hours* of searching Mount Snowdon in Wales!' Clumps of long, slender, blue-green stems were painstakingly drawn in pastels this time, topped by fine, feathery flowers. 'That's another species under threat,' she wailed. 'What are we doing to our land? I just hope my paintings will make people aware of how rich and varied our countryside once was – and how so much of all this will disappear if we don't do something to stop it.'

'They're *exquisite*,' I said. Annie was clearly totally driven by her passion for conservation. 'Coming from London, I must admit I'd never really thought very much about the wealth of plant life we have in England. I'm sure you'll make people more aware of the threat to their existence.'

As I browsed through the exhibition paintings, the key turned in the front door. William smiled his greeting at me and hugged his Aunty Annie warmly.

'How's Cathy?' enquired Mr Locksley.

'Fine,' William said, opening the catalogue Annie had given him.

'Is she calling in sometime today?'

'Yes, probably after she's seen George. But she hasn't got long. When she gets back to London from York, she's flying to Washington, the company's Head Office."

Mr Locksley shook his head in wonder. 'I always said that girl would be going places!'

William nodded, studying the pictures inside the catalogue. 'Great pictures, Aunty Annie,' he commented. 'I think these are the best I've ever seen.'

But he looked a little preoccupied, excusing himself after a minute or two as he went off to prepare the rest of the lunch. He was probably busy reflecting how Cathy looked even more beautiful than the last time he'd seen her …

Or maybe he was distressed by the thought of not seeing Cathy for a while – she lived in London, didn't she – and he had to go to Edinburgh for some time.

There were more pictures of northern scenery to be

displayed in the exhibition. One particularly lovely view of Derwentwater in the Lake District surrounded by a rippling range of mountains caught my eye. They stretched down to the silver lake, strewn with rough crags. A beautiful rainbow arched through the cloud above them, bathing the air in brilliance.

There were also more animal pictures, including a toad. 'That's a Natterjack Toad. I spotted him in the sand dunes in Merseyside,' said Annie proudly.

Another one that particularly took my fancy was a lovely illustration of a pine marten. It crouched in a pine forest, its brown furry triangular face staring into the distance. Annie had captured its faun-coloured body and clawed feet to perfection. 'Could I buy this one – and the scene of the rainbow over Derwentwater? It's *beautiful*. I'd like to go over to the Lake District and explore the area before the winter closes in. It's not too far from here, is it? … The pine marten would look lovely just beside the stairs in my sitting room. And Derwentwater could hang on my bedroom wall … And if I could buy the cute dormouse picture for my mother. I know she'd love it.'

'Certainly,' said Annie, pleased. The cost of the paintings was very reasonable. Annie clearly painted for the sheer love of it. I propped the pictures by the door to take home later.

'Luncheon is served,' William announced.

'It smells delicious,' I said. 'What is it?'

'It's an example of the superb Nepalese cuisine that I discovered when I was climbing in the Himalayas. Basically it's a Quanteen – or a meat stew and sprouted beans with garlic, ginger, black pepper, and turmeric in it. I'm afraid I couldn't get hold of any Yak butter to go with it though.'

'Thank goodness for small mercies,' Mr Locksley muttered as we went into the dining room – but at least he had the courtesy to keep quiet after that. As we ate, we discussed Annie's paintings on the walls. One painting, titled 'Sheep in Rain' caught my eye. The rain was lashing down on the moorland sheep who cropped the slippery, sopping grass, their eyes roving glassily for the next sodden tussock. Their wool hung lank, clagged in sodden clumps like old grey ropes.

'It's so realistic,' I said, laughing. 'It reminds me of when we arrived here a couple of days ago. The sky was black as Mum, John – that's my stepfather – and I drove up to the cottage a couple of days ago with all my stuff. Then the heavens opened. We felt so sorry for the poor, bedraggled sheep outside my back gate … You're not at all sentimental in your pictures of north country life, are you?'

'Well, I like to capture nature in all its aspects,' said Annie.

'Aunty Annie travels round the country in her campervan all the time,' William told me. 'She's always lived like that. She just paints, sells her pictures and travels.'

'Yes. Another one with an unconventional lifestyle,' muttered Mr Locksley. He pursed his thin lips.

Annie stiffened slightly and William's jaw tightened. This was an old argument. I could sense it. Some unresolved dispute.

Annie sighed. 'There's nothing wrong with that, Joe,' she said. 'Each to his own.'

'Absolutely,' William joined in, defending his aunt. 'We all have to make our own decisions as to how we live our lives.'

Mr Locksley grunted in disgust. Again there was that tension in the air. He was silent as Annie asked William about the ingredients he had used for his tasty stew. William and his uncle avoided eye contact with each other.

Mr Locksley and William brought in a large apple pie and a jug of cream for dessert. Mr Locksley was tight-lipped, still brooding over his spat with William presumably. The atmosphere was still rather strained.

'So you don't have a house?' I asked Annie, intrigued.

Annie shook her head. 'My campervan is my home. I'm like a snail – carry my home with me,' she said, smiling. 'I've got everything I need in there. My paints, canvases and my brushes, of course.'

'What a lovely way to live. You must feel so *free*,' I said.

'Yes, I do. And I can focus on what's important to me. I don't get distracted by running a house or maintaining a garden.'

'I do know what you mean,' I said, as I poured the cream over my apple pie. 'Art's important to me too. I've this fantastic painting of the sea, which I bought in St Ives a few years ago. A narrow lane, green hedges and high-banked, studded with wild yellow primroses, winds down to the blue sea – the painting's as bright as stained glass. And the waves are swelling and swaying about the base of the stacked rocks – and when I look at it, I can smell the salty air, hear the screeching gulls!

'I hung it on the wall in my bedroom at home,' I shook my head. '– and boy, did it cheer me up after a hellish day during teaching practice! It helped to remind me that there is a colourful natural world out there beyond the grey concrete walls of school.'

Annie nodded her understanding. She finished her pie. 'Well, as the wonderful artist, Renoir, said, "Why shouldn't art be pretty? There are enough unpleasant things in the world." So if a painting helps to make life easier for people, then I suppose it's been useful … Please excuse me,' she added, getting up from the dining table. 'I need to gather my pictures together.'

'I'll give you a hand,' said Mr Locksley and he followed her into the hall.

'That was a delicious lunch,' I told William. 'Your uncle's very lucky to have such lovely food made for him.'

'Hmm,' said William drily. 'He'd better make the most of it. I'll be off again soon.'

'What's your next production?'

'I'm with a company called 'The Wandering Bards' at present. We're doing a number of one act plays by a contemporary playwright. Sam Steele. For the Edinburgh Festival.'

I considered. 'Sam Steele. I've not heard of him. What are they about?'

'They focus on family crises … one's about a woman who is secretly addicted to pain-killing drugs and the devastating effect it has on her family – '

Mr Locksley came into the dining room. 'Sorry to interrupt, William, but would you mind helping your aunt set up at the Town Hall? The lifting and carrying's getting beyond me.'

'Sure. No worries.' William left the room.

'You said you wanted a hand with the monologues, Alice,' said Mr Locksley. 'Shall we look at them now?'

'Oh, yes, please. I'll just go and get them.'

The fragrant smell of coffee wafted in from the kitchen as I came back, carrying my folders and sat down on Mr Locksley's leather sofa. I opened my file on Browning and started to browse through the poems. Mr Locksley brought in a tray of two coffee cups, a milk jug and sugar. Then he took a pipe from the pipe rack.

'Do you mind?' He enquired politely, waving his pipe in the air. I shook my head, smiling and he tamped down the tobacco into his pipe. He settled himself beside me on the sofa and drew a box of matches from the bulging pocket of his green corduroy jacket.

'I think I'm okay now on Bishop Bloughram.' I sipped my coffee. 'I found some useful notes on him last night. But I did have problems with getting my head around this one – "My Last Duchess". Am I right in thinking that the Duke has his wife killed when he says …' I found the line: '"I gave commands; then all smiles stopped together…"?'

Mr Locksley nodded, lighting his pipe and sucking at the stem. 'Just because she is a sweet-natured girl who appreciates everything in her life,' he said. 'As the Duke puts it: "She had a heart too soon made glad."'

'But that's terrible.'

'It is,' Mr Locksley nodded. The air filled with faint blue smoke. 'But being a dramatic monologue, we have to suspend judgement to some extent – and enter the mind of a murderer. Empathy blurs our moral judgement.'

'So he has her murdered,' I said, 'just because she

appeared too appreciative and friendly – but, in his view, flirtatious.'

Mr Locksley nodded. 'The Duke is an unreliable narrator –'

'And your definition of an unreliable narrator is – ?'

'Someone whose perception of a situation is distorted by an obsession or delusion. The Duke's perception of his last duchess is twisted by the delusion that she is a flirt.'

'Ah, yes,' I nodded. I made some more notes.

'Any other poems?' said Mr Locksley.

'Well, do you mind just going over the key points of Elizabeth Barrett Browning's Sonnet 43? You know the one –' I pointed out the page and read out the opening lines

"How do I love thee?

Let me count the ways!

I love thee to the depth and breadth and height

My soul can reach …'

I looked up – only to glimpse some powerful emotion reflected in Mr Locksley's eyes. Was it a flash of pain? But in an instant it had vanished and once more his face was set. He nodded. 'Very well,' he said evenly, holding his hand out for the poem. I passed it to him. Had I imagined it? But then Mr Locksley shifted uncomfortably in his chair as he stared at the poem. I away, rather embarrassed. This poem clearly meant something to him.

There was a pause and I cleared my throat. 'Well, I love it, of course,' I said. 'Anyone would. Such a passionate declaration of love. But what can I say about it?'

'What, do you mean technically?'

I nodded, pen poised in the air.

'Well, it's a Petrarchan sonnet, of course, employing

96

the iambic beat,' he said. He spoke dispassionately in his analysis, as though dissecting a body part. 'And there is, of course, the use of anaphora.' He scratched his head. 'To stress her love for him, of course.'

He looked at me, his eyes firmly shuttered now, his feelings veiled. As he spoke of Elizabeth Barrett's father was so domineering, how Elizabeth and Robert Browning had eloped and lived at the Casa Guida in Florence, relating events to lines in the poems, he seemed more comfortable. Because he was just dealing with impersonal autobiographical facts, I suppose. He was so knowledgeable. It would have taken me days to read up all this stuff.

'Thank you so much, Mr Locksley. It'll save me hours of research, especially as school starts soon and it'll be a while before I'm connected to the internet … The poems are wonderful, aren't they. I'm sure the students will enjoy them.'

He shrugged. 'Maybe. It just seems like sentimental tosh to me.'

'Oh, how can you say that?' I said hotly, stung into protest. 'It's lovely!'

He shook his head dismissively.

'Well, what do you think is good writing?' I asked in frustration.

He reflected for a moment, puffing his pipe pensively.

'As I said before, the wit of Pope, with his lucid, polished style. Saint Augustine now, he said: "Intellectum valda amat." Faint blue clouds of smoke filled the air around him. "Love the intellect strongly" is its translation. Yes, Pope wrote wonderfully. Or there are the writings of the great classical writers, celebrating the heroes of the epic poems. There is such dignity in Latinate words, don't you think? And they described an age of real heroism with extraordinary feats of courage and skill.'

'Which do you like especially?'

'Homer's Iliad,' he said, after some thought. 'There's a magnificent description in The Iliad of Achilles' advance towards Troy to destroy his adversary. When he engages in his fateful spar with Hector, the writing is magnificent.' His voice became hushed, reverential and his eyes gleamed. 'A wonderful celebration of military heroism, not to mention the splendid ode addressed to the losses of battle.'

I gazed at Mr Locksley. Here was surely a man whose blood was the very snow-broth, an Angelo if ever there was one.

The works he admired so much left me cold. But Mr Lockley clearly valued them. There must be something of worth in them. I hate thoughtless prejudice. I shouldn't just be blindly biased against them.

'I will try to read them – when I have some free time – probably next summer holidays,' I promised.

The key turned in the front door as Will returned from the art exhibition. His footsteps could be heard in the passage. Mr Locksley scraped out the bowl of his pipe into the empty grate.

William came in. 'Have you finished your poems?' he asked. I nodded. 'Better get on some old things,' he said, smiling. 'You don't want to wreck good clothes.'

William and I headed up the dale, with me wearing my oldest clothes, as instructed – my scruffy jeans and a baggy jumper, one knitted by Mum several years ago.

'I like to dress to impress,' I said, and William smiled.

But he still seemed a little distracted, his mouth set as he drove along. What was he brooding about? Maybe he was more Mr Rochester than Will Ladislaw? Yes, he did have a touch of the brooding Byronic hero about him.

But as we climbed up the open moorland towards Ramsgill Pot, the brunt wind blew across our faces and he grinned at me, his spirits seeming to lift a little. We approached a dense, black hole beneath a grassy mound and I realised that this was the cave entrance. We entered the dark, musty cavern. I felt a twinge of fear. It seemed quite a small cave entrance, not much taller than me. I'd imagined wandering through huge great caves, staring up at their high roofs.

The raucous wind was instantly hushed and all was dank and still. Daylight dimmed to a soft glow as the jagged walls narrowed. The rock formed an archway over our heads. Will shifted the slim metal ladder coiled over his shoulder and the muscles moved under his shirt. We switched on the lamps attached to our helmets, then bent down to enter a low tunnel. Soon we were on our hands and knees as the tunnel curved downwards deep under the ground. The tunnel went down and down, becoming only a metre or so high. I tried not to think of the hundreds of tons of earth and rock above me – but I suppose it had been resting there for hundreds of years. No reason why it should all collapse on me at this particular moment.

'Further along this tunnel it will be filled with quite a bit of water, after the rain we've been having,' William told me as we crawled along a crevice. A sharp stone on the hard rock floor dug into my knee and I winced. 'But if you lift your chin, there should be plenty of air.'

Coolock Branch Tel: 8477781

I wasn't expecting this. 'But it'll be *freezing*.'

'You'll be fine, honestly. It's worth it, to see what's further in. It's amazing.'

I bit my lip. 'Okay'. As the tunnel sloped steeply down, the black water glittered in the torchlight. It filled up three quarters of the tunnel! There was only half a metre or so of air between the water and the roof.

'I can't go into that,' I said. 'How do we know it isn't flooded further along?'

'It shouldn't be,' William spoke reassuringly. 'It's not been raining that much in the last couple of days. I know this pot very well.'

He looked at me, his brown eyes filled with certainty. Well, I suppose he was the expert. I nodded, took a deep breath and slithered into the black water.

Once the chilly water had seeped into my clothes, I found I gradually warmed up. We crawled along, chins uplifted to cram the scanty air from the pockets of the roof into our lungs. But at one point William slid forward too quickly. The cold backwash of water from his slithering body splashed into my face, making me splutter.

'Slow down. I can't breathe,' I gasped. I couldn't see for a minute, water trickling down my face. I rubbed my eyes.

'Sorry.'

'Can we stop for a minute?' I just couldn't get my breath. My heart was skittering in my chest. It was so enclosed, this space. No air. The rough stone walls seemed to be pressing in on me.

William looked back at me, a little concerned. 'It's okay. You're fine,' he reassured me. 'There's masses of air. Just breathe calmly like me.'

He spoke slowly, rhythmically, 'Breathe in, breathe out.'

I tried to copy him, struggling to control myself. I couldn't stop looking at the roof almost touching the top of my head. I was heaving for breath still, turning faint. There was so little space. 'I want to go back. Get out,' I whispered.

'But it'll take longer to crawl backwards than it will to go on to the next cave which is bigger. It's not much further now.' He spoke reassuringly.

'Oh, God. How far is that?'

'Only a couple of minutes,' he promised, gazing at me, his face creased with anxiety. 'I'm sorry. I should have thought. '

'I'll be alright in a minute,' I gasped.

'I'm sorry,' he said again. He shook his head in self-reproach. 'I'm so used to this kind of thing. I forgot that you're not. Just a minute.'

William turned round awkwardly in such a tiny space, drawing his legs up to his chest, and he took my hand. He looked really worried.

'Keep on breathing like this.' He kept up his demonstration of regular breathing, which I duly copied over and over again, and very gradually I relaxed. Although maybe gazing into his warm brown eyes and holding his hand helped even more.

'Are you ready to go on in a minute?'

I nodded, feeling stupid. William seemed fearless. He must think I was such a wimp, first suffering from vertigo, and now this claustrophobia. I was *useless*, going into raptures about the wonders of the countryside and then having panic attacks, unable to handle simple country pursuits.

I bet Cathy and William have explored these caves together and, of course, she would have loved it; they would have been in their element, in their natural environment.

'Don't worry. I'll take you back out a different way.'

'Thank God,' I said fervently. I smiled wryly. 'Well, at least I'm truly now at one with nature, so close to the earth I'm *part* of it,' I rubbed away the water that was still trickling into my eyes. 'There's something distinctly *elemental* about this experience. Jacquetta Hawkes would be proud of me.'

'Jacquetta Hawkes?'

' Wife of J.B.Priestley, the playwright?'

'Oh, yes,' William nodded in recognition. 'Are you ready to carry on in a sec?'

'Yes. Sorry, I just found it a bit claustrophobic.'

William turned himself round again, facing forward. He looked back at me. Was that a smile playing round the edges of his mouth? 'So why would Jacquetta Hawkes be proud of you?'

'Jacquetta Hawkes felt that we'd lost our connection with the land, through industrialisation.' I looked at him through blurred eyes and rubbed them again. Yes, William was surveying me with some amusement. 'Rather like D.H.Lawrence. She would lie in her garden, press her flesh against the hard ground and let her eyes "stray among the stars". "Riding the back of the world," as Virginia Woolf put it.'

'But what about Caliban?' asked William as he set off, crawling ahead of me far more slowly and carefully this time. I bumped my elbow on a pointed rock to the left of me. The pain jolted and zigzagged up my arm. Must watch out for sharp edges. 'He was close to nature – "of the earth, earthy", but Shakespeare portrayed him as crass and deformed!'

'Ah, yes, but he was oppressed by Prospero,' I said.

'By Prospero … Prospero … Prospero.' My words were echoing as the stony passage opened out a little. What a relief! My spirits started to rise. I love this kind of verbal sparring. 'He had no future promise of freedom – unlike Ariel – so he had an excuse.'

As we crawled down the passage, other tunnels and caves opened off to our left and right; this was an underground labyrinth.

'Some of them stretch for miles,' William said. 'I know this route like the back of my hand. But I wouldn't recommend this place to novices. You need an experienced guide. Otherwise, if you got lost, it could take weeks to find you.'

The stone roof was rising now and we could walk, crouching still to avoid sharp overhangs. The walls were widening, too, thank God. In a minute I could stand fully upright. Relief flooded through me. Wet, beige – coloured rock walls revealed veins of rust red swirls as they bulged out right and left, cascading to the ground, knobbly and glistening. Our footsteps echoed in the wider expanse and finally William was able to stand upright, too. He stopped and stretched, looking round at me. We were in a cave as big as a large hall.

'Literature really is your bible, isn't it?'

'I can't help it.' I shrugged. 'For me, literature holds the legacy of great thoughts … Sorry, I know I sound pompous! But, for me, it's true.'

'Well, I guess it's my bible too.' He smiled at me in the

warm glow of his lamplight and I looked at him. Definitely the marriage of true minds. Oh, if *only* Cathy wasn't the love of his life. 'I try to write poetry myself, you know.'

'You do?' He was definitely like Mr Rochester, with his original, vigorous, and – what was it? – and his expanded mind.

He smiled wryly. 'Only mediocre stuff – but I enjoy it.'

'Go on then. Recite me one of your poems!'

'What now?'

'Why not? This is a great auditorium.'

'Alright, I will … 'He took a deep breath. 'Okay. Now this is a fantasy role that I dream of performing one day, maybe.'

I nodded encouragingly and sat down on a smooth, flat rock in a corner of this great cave. Despite being damp, I wasn't cold because there was no chilling wind underground.

'Right. Imagine me wearing a man of the world air … and a Savile Row suit.'

He stepped forward in his muddy sweater and jeans to take centre stage in this hollowed out stone amphitheatre.

'Okay,' I grinned, gazing at his mud-spattered face, 'but watch that stalactite above your head.'

He looked up and nodded, ducking to his left.

Then he cocked his head to one side and raised a quizzical eyebrow; he was an actor through and through. He spoke in a deep resonant voice:

'The name's Bond. James Bond.

Often seen with a tall leggy blonde …'

I chuckled.

'My mission in life is to live and let die;

For my fabled role is that of a spy.
With fists or with bombs, my foes will I slay
To make perfectly sure I will die another day.
I fight against evil but am never deterred,
As long as my cocktail is shaken, not stirred.
I can't count the times I have leapt from a plane
Or raced to catch up with a runaway train.
As I find out the threat, when the plot is unfurled,
That a terrible brute plans to rule all the world,
I work out the code with the greatest aplomb
To stop us from being blown up with a bomb.
But though you may think that my life sounds quite tough,
Be heartened I take all the smooth with the rough!
So, even though England I'll strive to defend,
I'm cheered by the thought – I get the girl in the end!'

He adopted a suitably smug expression, his mouth twitching, and then we both burst out laughing, like a couple of kids. The vast cave echoed our laughter. This guy was such *fun*.

As the lamplight gleamed in his hair, I felt a rush of longing for him, to smell and touch his warm skin. But Cathy was his true love. *Must* keep my distance. I took a deep breath.

'Brilliant,' I said. 'Yes, I can definitely see you as the next James Bond ... What's your favourite role you've played so far?'

'Iago in "Othello", most definitely.'

'Perform a bit of it,' I said on impulse.

He nodded and then his sensitive, smiling face hardened. The muscles tensed in his jaw and his features became convulsed, as grotesque as a gargoyle. Breathing raggedly, his eyes were charged with malice. I stared at him, wracked with unease. Not a trace remained of the old Will. He whipped round, glaring at me:

"Divinity of hell!

When devils will their blackest sins put on,

They do suggest at first with heavenly shows

As I do now; for whilst this honest fool

Plies Desdemona to repair his fortunes,

And she for him pleads strongly to the moor

I'll pour this pestilence into his ear –'

Even his voice had changed – thin, reedy, strident with contempt and malice. The shrill sound rang around the walls of the cave and he was shaking with rage. I'd seen 'Othello' performed before but had never felt so unnerved as I was now by this Iago, with his crazed hatred. The blood was pulsing in my ears.

Could this be the same kind, gentle man I'd set out from Inkley with?

He had slipped into this persona with disturbing ease. He was grotesque, sardonic, terrifying. And I was trapped here in this sunken cave with him, hundreds of feet underground. My skin went into goose bumps and I wanted to get away. But this place was riddled with tunnels and caves. I'd never find my way out. What was it William had said? If you got lost here, it could take weeks to be found.

But even as I stared at him, his features relaxed, widening into a smile. 'What we actors call – "being in the moment",' he remarked casually. Relief flooded over me. The old Will was back. It was just an act, not real.

His countenance, etched with ugly evil, had just been a distortion of his true self. What an idiot I was.

'Mind you, it was a role that *consumed* me at the time,' he commented. 'An incredible character. The ultimate in evil.'

I struggled to establish a matter-of-fact tone, 'Why *is* Iago so evil?'

He shrugged. 'What Coleridge called a "motiveless malignity",' he commented.

'Well, you certainly have acting talent.' I said fervently, laughing a little. 'For a minute then, you really had me terrified.'

'Ah, yes – but how do you know that wasn't the real me?' He said in a mockingly sinister voice, raising his eyebrows.

I stared at him. 'What do you mean?'

'When we were at Drama College, we learnt that we are all capable of kindness, or pride or vanity ... or evil. Acting isn't merely emulative; we inhabit the character. We *are* the character. It all comes from within. We can all love or be jealous or vengeful.' His brown eyes glittered in the lamplight. 'In fact, we all of us have it in us to kill.'

Sweat prickled the back of my neck.

William grinned. 'Sorry. Got a bit carried away ... Aunty Annie says I've got a vivid imagination and that's what helps me to act.'

I shook my head. 'No, I suppose you're right. We've all got it in us to commit evil, if the circumstances were right. If we were driven to it. Your aunt's right too. You do make that imaginative leap brilliantly ... So what role would you really fancy playing in the future?'

'Falstaff,' he said promptly. 'I'm a bit young for it at the moment – and too thin – but one day ...' Again his

107

face changed, his cheeks seeming to fill out and widen as he lolled against the cave wall. The plasticity of his features was amazing. Even his body seemed heavier, slacker. He pretended to turn out his empty pockets with a doleful expression and then shrugged. '"I can get no remedy against this consumption of the purse,"' he said ruefully. His voice was slightly thick, his speech a little slurred, as though the tiniest bit drunk. "Borrowing only lingers it out, but the disease is incurable …"

I laughed, clapping. 'Fan-tas-tic … How about films? Mum and I *love* romantic films.' I tried my best whiny, simpering Southern Belle accent: '"Oh, Ashley. Ashley … Tomorrow is another day". Sorry,' I giggled and William's eyes crinkled in amusement. 'A very Geordie-sounding Scarlett O'Hara! Now I am reminded of why I could never be an actress …

'But don't you just love it in "Pretty Woman" when Richard Gere leaps out of his white limousine and then he climbs the outside ladder, greeting Julia Roberts with a kiss and red roses? Just like a knight on his white steed rescuing the princess from the tower! Mum and I thought it was brilliant.'

William nodded. 'Wonderful stuff,' he agreed.

'Becky always says I'm much too Merchant Ivory,' I said ruefully, 'and she thinks Mum's just as bad. Becks prefers films with lots of swash being buckled."

William chuckled.

'How about being the next Edward Cullen? In the Twilight series?'

He shook his head. 'My skin's not flawless enough.'

'It looks good to me …'

He smiled modestly.

'I still can't get over what a creative family you all are!' I shook my head. 'What with your acting abilities and your aunt's paintings. Not to mention your poems … Have you got any more poems tucked away?'

'Annie's got some which she illustrated,' he said. 'We worked together on a few nature poems – she's got them pinned up in her campervan. We were going to make a whole collection and send them off to a publisher but we've never got around to it.'

'I'd love to see them,' I said.

'When we get back, I'll ask her if you can have a look at them. But don't expect great things, please … Her paintings are excellent but I know my poems are just mediocre.'

I tried to protest but he shook his head. 'No, no. I hope I might achieve some degree of imitative genius with my acting but I know I could never achieve *creative* genius …'

He glanced at me. 'You know it's strange,' he said and then he paused, looking almost shamefaced. 'I can't normally admit to feeling a failure. But it's not like that with you.' He looked at me earnestly in the lamplight. 'With you, I can say what I really feel.' His face was so open and honest now. There was none of that masculine pretence of toughness here, the macho bravado of the rugby playing guys I've been out with in the past.

I so longed to put my arms round him. Press my cheek against his chest … But Cathy's beautiful face as she stood amongst the purple heather filled my mind. Cathy and William were meant to be and don't you forget it. Two people with one pulse – Louis Macneice's phrase, I believe.

Must keep the conversation matter-of-fact. I gave him a

bright smile. 'Well, I think your poetry's great and I'd like to see the campervan poems.' William nodded. Did he look faintly hurt at my briskness? No, I was imagining things, as usual.

We wandered on through more stone passages. The sea had made an impression millennia ago of ancient coral beds and ridges. The fine indentations of rows of coral stems could be seen marked on the stratified cave walls. We traced a stream wandering through this labyrinth until it poured faster and faster, gliding swiftly over a shining stony edge, plunging down, dropping away into a yawning chasm. William unfurled the slender coiled metal ladder hooked over his shoulder and it snaked away, tumbling into the abyss. I took a deep breath. Don't look down. This was far worse than climbing the crags behind the house – but somehow William had given me the confidence to tackle heights – and depths – that I'd never ever had before.

'Keep your body close to the ladder,' William shouted above the noise of the waterfall. 'And put your arms round the back of the rungs.'

'Why do I always seem to be climbing *up* something, or struggling *down* something whenever I'm with you? ' I asked in mock exasperation. 'We never just *chill.*'

William grinned. I clambered down over the lip of stone, then swaying from side to side on the ladder, whilst being drenched by the cascading waterfall. Soaked, deafened and half-blinded, I spun in mid- air as my foot felt for the next rung down. This was certainly a date with a difference!

Gasping for breath, I dragged myself away from the waterfall and rubbed my dripping, messy hair away from my eyes.

Water was trickling down William's face as he joined me.

'What are these, so withered and so wild in their attire?' he demanded, staring at me with my soaking, tangled hair and then down at his filthy attire in mock horror.

'Speak for yourself!' I said hotly. 'God, which way's up?!!'

He laughed. 'And now for the climax,' he said, leading the way down another passage. A small underground stream running along the floor of our tunnel slipped away down a small sinkhole to the right. It made me think of the stream running through my garden. I mentioned it to Will.

'What do you think? Could I try to dig a pool in my garden so I can bathe in it when it's scorching hot during the summer,' I said.

William shook his head. 'You'll never shift all that granite under the topsoil. It's probably solid rock only a foot or so down.'

'I suppose you're right. Oh, well,' I shrugged. 'You win some, you lose some.'

The muted clump of our boots grew sonorous as we entered a huge vaulted cave. This dome-shaped cavern was vast. Adorned with huge limestone organ pipes spilling to the ground, it arched like a colossal cathedral soaring heavenwards. A place of immense beauty and grace.

'Impressed?' William asked, his eyes shining. 'Dad and I practically fell over backwards when we first saw this place.'

'Wow!' I gazed up at the arched stone roof glimmered faintly. 'It's magnificent.'

A rugged alcove off to our left revealed a bright grotto where polished stalactites gleamed in the torchlight. Fluted pillars of glowing marble rose up towards them from pearly cascades of rock, rucked and scrolled. And down in one corner william shone his torch on a bowl of stone in which appeared to rest several creamy glowing pearls.

'This is a pretty rare find. The limestone from a drip of water forms around a grain of sand in the same way as an oyster pearl,' William explained. 'The water falling into the rock hollow agitates and revolves the pearls to give them a high polish.'

'Who would have thought there was this – incredible treasure trove – hidden away from the world above!'

We returned a different, easier route, as William had promised, although there was still some crouching and crawling through some of the smaller, narrower caverns. As we emerged onto the moor side once again in dazzling sunshine, we gazed at the rough, granite-pocked landscape, as secretive as an oyster.

'Thanks for showing me all this, William. Not to mention the dramatic performances! Very entertaining. It's been *fantastic.*' I said. And I meant it.

He smiled. 'There's so much more to see of Yorkshire,' he said. 'Other places you'd love round here. I could show you them tomorrow. Before I have to leave …'

His last words made me feel empty inside. 'Yes, please,' I said. 'I'd love to see them.'

He seemed to withdraw into himself again as we headed back, shutting me out, his mouth set in a straight line. His hands gripped the steering wheel tightly. I suppose he was thinking of Cathy's brief visit. He must miss her so much when she jetted off around the world.

As we turned off the moor road in order to drive up the

rough track to the Gamekeeper's Cottage, we saw Annie's campervan stopping outside Mr Locksley's gate just ahead of us.

We pulled up behind her. Annie climbed out of the driver's seat and smiled when she saw us. 'I've had such interest in my Rare Species theme down at the Town Hall,' she said, her eyes shining. 'People seemed to really *care*. They were so concerned about the threat to such beautiful creatures.'

'Well done,' said William warmly. He hugged his aunt. 'Could Alice see our joint artistic creations in your van, do you think? She's expressed an interest in seeing my poems.'

'Of course,' Annie beamed at me. 'I'll put the kettle on in the van and we can have a cup of tea as you look at them.'

'Well, I'll shower and change, then I'll come and join you,' I said.

I had just put my muddy trainers on a sheet of newspaper in the kitchen, when there was a knock at my front door. As soon as I opened the door, I recognised her – although the cast of her countenance had subtly changed since the time her portrait had been painted. Cathy looked older too, but she still had the olive skin and heart-shaped face – now, though, her wildly curling dark hair was tamed into a smart bob. No smile curved her full lips now; her mouth was set in a straight line as she stared coldly at me.

Her clothes were very chic – well-cut trousers, high-heeled boots and a cashmere cardigan over a pure silk blouse. She was beautifully made up and her lipsticked mouth opened in disdain at the sight of me, standing there in my torn, baggy jumper and filthy jeans.

'I'm sorry to disturb you.' She spoke in a cold, clipped manner, as though to a servant. 'You must be Alice ...' She gave me a sharp look. 'So you're the one William took potholing.'

'Yes, that's right,' I said. I tried to smooth out my tangled hair. 'And you're Cathy! I recognise you from your portrait.' I gestured back towards the living room.

'Oh, yes. Annie painted that when I was young and foolish,' she said dismissively. She gave a harsh laugh. 'Before I realised that the best things in life are ... expensive.'

'Mr Locksley mentioned that you wanted to pick up some of your things,' I said.

'Yes, well, I won't be coming to Inkley again. Uncle George barely recognises me now.' A sheep baaed loudly on the moor, outside my garden. 'And Joe's so *dyed in the wool*,' she smiled sardonically at her own wit, 'well, to be frank, we have little in common.'

'I like him,' I said. 'He's been very welcoming, inviting me round for tea and things – and helping me with my work. He's very knowledgeable. And I like Inkley. It's lovely. The people are so friendly. And William's been really kind, showing me the amazing places round here.'

Cathy stared at me. 'Mmmm. Well, there's nothing here for me anymore.' There was a bitter note in her voice.

I couldn't stop staring at her in her sophisticated clothes; this wasn't the wild Cathy who played on the moors with Heathcliff – I mean William.

'Anyway, I won't take a minute,' she said dismissively. 'My things are in a cupboard in the spare room. So if you don't mind ...?'

'Of course. No problem.'

She started to climb the old wooden stairs, her high heels tapping as she went.

My head was spinning. She definitely wasn't Cathy Earnshaw. She wasn't William's type, I just knew it. She was as hard as nails. William was making a big mistake, going out with her.

A minute later, she came downstairs, carrying a small bag. She muttered some grudging words of thanks.

But, as she was about to go, she turned. Her eyes narrowed as she stared at me. Waves of hostility seemed to emanate from her. 'A word of warning.' Her voice was hard and cold. 'I wouldn't believe a word William says. Don't trust him, Alice.'

And with these enigmatic words she was gone.

Stunned, I showered and changed into a pretty red cotton summer dress splashed with white daisies. I heard Cathy's Range Rover revving loudly as it reversed away from the gate and roared off down the track.

I made my way outside to Annie's camper van. William was still taking a shower, Annie told me as I climbed inside.

The interior was a riot of colour, with striped blankets covering Annie's bed in the roof, and curtains of zigzagging red, yellow and orange stripes on either side of the windows. The smell of turps and linseed oil pervaded the camper van. A long wooden shelf hung above the side door which held her jars of brushes, stained with violet, burnt umber and ultramarine, as well as her paint palettes and jars of linseed oil.

A kettle was whistling on the little gas stove and Annie lifted it off and filled a teapot.

I sat down on a seat amongst heaps of multi-coloured

cushions. I had to find out what was going on with Cathy.

'Pretty dress,' Annie said admiringly. 'Fancy a cuppa?'

'Thanks … Cathy's just been round to collect her things,' I said. 'She didn't seem very happy.'

'Yes, well.' Annie shrugged. 'She and Will finally split up this morning.'

I stared at her.

Cathy wasn't destined to be with William!

'I think they made some kind of silly pact when they were kids – to be together forever,' Annie said. 'But people change, don't they … Cathy certainly has. I think William's been wanting to make the break for years. He had to steel himself to do it. Cathy isn't the easiest person to deal with …'

She took some brilliantly coloured mugs out of a cupboard. 'She went to university all set to study countryside conservation, you know – I was so pleased. But then she got in with a high-living crowd – and she loved that kind of lifestyle. She started to realise that there was very little money in a career in conservation work, so she changed course to study finance. And has gone on to become a very successful businesswoman as, no doubt, you noticed. Joe thinks she's wonderful, of course.'

She sighed. 'But I don't feel the same. Cathy's changed. She seems to have become so – hard-nosed. I saw a difference in her last summer when she came up to do some conservation work with the Dales Preservation Society. The Society has helped to preserve the footpaths around here for years; they get badly eroded by all the walkers. And then walkers damage the ground around the footpaths. And that affects local plant life … Anyway, Cathy and I – and

116

William – have helped the Society when we've been here.

'But, last summer, Cathy kept moaning about how she couldn't afford the time, that she needed to get back to London as soon as possible to seal some business deal. She's totally lost interest in conservation.' Annie gave a wry smile. 'I decided not to remind her about the conservation project this summer. I knew she wouldn't be interested.'

Annie opened the little fridge door and took out a small blue jug filled with milk.

'William and Cathy have only managed to meet up every so often in recent months; they've both been so busy. I saw her in June and all she could talk about was the penthouse flat – with three bedrooms – that she was buying in South Kensington. I think they've just drifted apart. I suppose she and William haven't got much in common any more. William's a real romantic, just like his dad used to be. Impetuous too, like his dad … Anyway, William is footloose and fancy free again.'

My heart suddenly felt light. 'But you'd have thought Cathy would have been ready to part from William amicably.'

'Yes, but having a handsome, professional actor on your arm in London is considered pretty cool in business circles, you know. He would have looked good amongst the Kensington set.'

'I suppose so.'

'Don't worry. Cathy'll get over William in time.'

Annie poured out the tea into the mugs.

Cathy definitely wasn't Cathy Earnshaw. More like Eustacia Vye from 'Return of the Native', with her hard, worldly materialism. No wonder William had looked preoccupied when he came back from taking Cathy for coffee; it must have been tough breaking up with someone as forceful as her. The way she tried to frighten me off him! *Don't believe a word William says* … Cathy must have decided that if she couldn't have William, neither would I!

I gazed out of the campervan window and surveyed my Gamekeeper's Cottage and garden basking in the sunshine, surrounded by glowing heather and a couple of flaming gorse bushes. This was the natural place to live. Above, the bright sky was rippled with fluffy clouds. The town nestled down in the valley; it all looked so idyllic.

There was my dream country cottage in front of me. And William wasn't in love with Cathy. There *had* been a spark of attraction between William and me; I was sure I hadn't imagined it. And in the cave he'd said how close he felt to me. That was lovely. We were meant to be. I was convinced I'd found my dream man.

I was living the dream.

But it was a dream that was about to turn into a nightmare.

Chapter 6

Pinned to the wardrobe next to the back door of Annie's campervan were several paintings of animals – one of seals lying on rocks out at sea, another of pink and yellow jellyfish floating through the seawater – accompanied by poems written in William's sloping hand. The poem I particularly liked was one about Marmalade.

'I recognise her!' I said, pointing at a smaller, kittenish Marmalade lying sprawled amongst June high grass, eyes closed, enjoying the blissful warmth of a golden summer's day. The thick white fur of her belly and chest mingled with the long hairs of her luxuriant coat. 'I love your painting.'

'It was a real challenge to capture all the glorious colours of her fur,' said Annie, pouring out the tea into the mugs. 'I used loads of different oil paints – burnt sienna, graphite grey, green … cadmium red. And I piled on the paint with my palette knife to convey her fluffiness.'

Beside the picture was William's poem. I read it out loud:

Cat

"… if a sparrow come before my Window I take part in its existence and peck about the gravel." (from a letter by John Keats)

Driven solely by desires
in a chain-reaction of impulses,
her glassy eyes glitter, galvanized to fill the aching void
of hunger.
But contemplation seems short-circuited,
in her feline mental wiring;
although she sees the shape and sway of flowers,
she seems blind to any visionary dream.

Yet surely *not* a mere machine.
She must melt to the tender throb of nurture
and thrill to the pulse of passion.
And so such sensual delights

kindle in me a sense of kinship.'

'Wow!' I exclaimed.

'Ah, yes,' said Annie, nodding. 'I remember William telling me how, at drama college, he had to carry out a particular activity as an animal might do it. As a way into a character. He tried to imagine actually being a cat, avoiding the temptation to give her human attributes but instead attempting to feel as she might feel … trying to empathise. Focusing on what an animal thinks and feels, exploring the similarities and differences between us and animals. It's always interested him and that's what inspired him to write this poem.'

I stared at Annie. 'But that's something my Dad and I have often discussed. We used to go to London Zoo every week when I was a child and Dad and I used to wonder what the animals in their enclosures were thinking and feeling … These poems aren't mediocre at all. I'd love to see any more he's written.'

'Really? I'll tell him to bring them round in the morning.'

'What made William so interested in acting in the first place?' I asked, intrigued. I sipped my tea.

'Well, I know that he enjoyed being in school productions. And when he came to stay with Uncle Joe during the long summer holidays, there were some excellent summer workshops held at the fantastic amateur Playhouse here in the town.'

'Ah, yes. I've heard about that. The theatre is a big old converted Victorian house, isn't it? The librarian was telling me. She said they've got a huge membership.'

'Yes, the standard of their productions is excellent,' said Annie. 'Joe and I used to be in some of their plays many years ago. When we were young.' She smiled. 'I know it must be hard for you to picture Joe young but he was once.'

'He does seem very set in his ways,' I said. 'Very old-fashioned.'

'I know. He is old-fashioned …' She smiled. 'If he wrote e-mails – and that'll never happen as he doesn't approve of computers – but if he did, I'm sure he'd round off his e-mails with "Your honourable and obedient servant, Joseph Locksley!"'

I laughed. 'Still, his heart's in the right place,' Annie said. She drank her tea from her mug.

'Yes, and I do think some of what he says is true,' I said. '… So you were in Playhouse productions. I didn't know you'd lived here in Inkley too,' I said.

'Yes. Before I decided to go off and do my own thing,

Joe and I shared this house. I was a teacher of art at a school in Bradford. We both enjoyed acting. Joe was very good. He played the part of Antony, you know, in Shakespeare's "Antony and Cleopatra" in 1970.'

'Really? Antony?' I said, stunned. Mr Locksley seemed so dry and unemotional. I couldn't visualise him ever playing a passionate lover. The heyday in his blood must *surely* be tamed.

'Yes. That was the last role he played. I stopped, of course, when I went off on my travels – ' She paused. 'And Joe. Well, he lost interest …

'I had always tended to get small roles but Joe – he was very good. He had quite a few romantic roles.' She smiled at me, reading my mind. 'It's hard to believe but Joe was very romantic once, you know. He used to sing too. He was the lead in quite a few musicals – "Annie Get Your Gun", "Oklahoma" … "Oliver" and some modern drama, as well as Shakespeare -' She broke off.

'Which Shakespeare play?' I asked curiously.

'Well, "Julius Caesar" was one. He loved that because it was about the Romans, of course. He's always liked anything classical. And then, as I said, he played Antony in "Antony and Cleopatra." That was the last play he was ever in.'

She paused.

'Why?'

'Well, I was away on my travels by then. I didn't know why at first when I got back. He just told me that he didn't have time for acting, with all his work as Head of Department … But then I bumped into the chairman of the Playhouse in the High Street one day when I was out shopping, and I found out that Joe had fallen head over heels in love with Cleopatra. A lovely lady called Jane. About Joe's age too. She'd never married either. She had deep, dark eyes and a beautiful face. Very sultry and exotic. Perfect for Cleopatra. Joe had never fallen for anyone else. She was the one for him. The love of his life. He bought her flowers, chocolates, gifts. He was so romantic in those days. They went for walks together on the moors – Joe loved the moors in those days.'

So not a man with snow-broth for blood after all. I tried to picture a gangly, pimply Joe Locksley passionately in love; it was so difficult, as the vision of a dry, detached elderly man kept intruding into my mind.

'Sounds like Richard Burton and Elizabeth Taylor all over again,' I said.

Annie shook her head. 'Unfortunately Jane simply wasn't attracted to him,' she said. 'I met her at the Playhouse one evening. Joe wasn't there; he had flu. She told me how he had started to read her love poems – Robert Burns, Elizabeth Barrett Browning -'

I started.

'She tried to tell Joe as gently as she could,' says Annie. 'But how do you tell someone something like that? She just wanted to be friends. But Joe never really got over it, I think. He became very disillusioned and bitter. Clamped down on his feelings. He really changed.'

'Anyway, Jane moved away to Scotland, I believe. Since then, especially since he retired, Joe's become more and more immersed in the classics. And in his crossword puzzles, and Sudoku. He likes the mental challenge ...'

'His jigsaw puzzles?'

'Yes, that kind of thing ... He used to have a great sense

of humour, very funny and entertaining. But since that time he's become more sardonic and cynical about everything.' She trailed off, lost in thought.

'I'd like to join the Playhouse this autumn,' I said. '– if I've got time. Maybe have a small part in a play. I think it's a good way of getting to know people.'

Annie nodded. 'Good idea,' she said.

That night, I speared my supper with a fork as I finished my notes on Jekyll and Hyde. I'd bought some really fine ham at the farm shop in Inkley high street – and it was gorgeous with my home-grown salad! Mr Locksley had given me a couple of tomatoes and a crunchy lettuce from his vegetable plot and I'd added a bit of chopped garlic and hyssop, as William had recommended. The crunchy lettuce tasted of the light of the summer sun, complementing the minty-flavoured hyssop.

Becky phoned as I was eating.

'Oh, Alice. I must tell you about last night. At the party.' Her voice was filled with laughter. 'Vicky only chose to play "YMCA" – and we all had to dance to it! Talk about cringe!'

I laughed.

'But Vicky's good fun. Mind you, I had one hell of a hangover this morning … Still got a bit of a headache.'

'Well, if you will go out drinking like your life depended on it.'

'I know.' She paused. 'It is strange here without you.'

I felt a pang of conscience. 'I know. I've felt the same.'

'Still, I'll see you tomorrow night – at your new abode! Should get in to Inkley train station about seven in the evening.'

'I'll meet you there and we can walk up to my cottage.

124

We can explore the shops when you're here. There are some lovely boutiques I've spotted which I know you'll love.'

'Oh, maybe I'll find something for when Vicky and I go clubbing next weekend ... Still enjoying the good life?'

'Would you believe it, I've also uncovered beneath the brambles, some rather delicious radishes, as well as garlic and a herb called hyssop. I've sliced and chopped them, added a dollop of wine vinegar and olive oil and, boy, it's so tasty with ham!'

'It does sound delicious,' Becky admitted.

'And I've bought a lovely painting of Ullswater with a rainbow arching over it, painted by Annie. It's *heavenly*, Becks.'

'It's just a prism, you know.'

'What?'

'A rainbow. It's just a prism.'

'Well, I know that.' I sighed in exasperation. I spiked a radish with my fork. 'But science can't explain everything – like why it's so beautiful!'

'Mmm. Maybe ...So what's happening with Ray Mears? Given you any survival tips for the classroom?'

I laughed. 'No. Although I could have done with some tips for surviving caving ...We went potholing up the Dales this afternoon. William used to go caving with his dad as a little lad. It was a bit frightening at first. Actually, I got a bit of claustrophobia; we were crawling through a tunnel only about a metre high. And it was filled with water which splashed into my face, which didn't help. Had a bit of a panic attack.'

'My God, this William really knows how to give a girl a

good time, doesn't he! Dragging you up cliffs and practically drowning you underground.'

'Ah, yes, but we *did* have an amazing time. He's helped me overcome my fear of enclosed spaces … Then we saw the most spectacular rock formations that you've ever seen. There were some stone pearls, would you believe! It was wonderful. William and I get on so well.'

I crossed over to the window to close the curtains.

'What a shame he and Cathy are made for each other, then.'

'Ah, but you won't believe this, Becks! It turns out Cathy and William *were* an item but Cathy's changed – and Will's just split up with her. Cathy's become all worldly and sophisticated, and Annie reckons William doesn't feel he's got anything in common with her anymore. Mind you, Cathy wasn't very happy about it. I think she may have suspected that William likes me.'

I came back and sat down by the fire.

'Oh, no. William's not got a bunny she can boil, has he?!'

I laughed. 'No, thank God. But you were right – they're nothing like Heathcliff and Cathy.'

'Well, that's a relief then … Although, hang on. We had to read "Wuthering Heights" in Year 9. And if my memory's correct, didn't Cathy Earnshaw become all worldly herself in "Wuthering Heights", wanting all those luxuries at Thrushcross Grange?'

'You're right!' I exclaimed. 'So they're still destined for each other – '

'Er, no!' Becky's voice was concerned. 'Please, Alice. No more fantasies.'

'It's all right,' I said. 'Only joking. Will's so kind and funny and – *interesting.*'

'And can you see he's a real person?'

'Yes, I'm starting to realise that now.'

'Good … Just spend time getting to know him. I wouldn't push it. He probably won't want to start a new relationship anyway so soon after finishing this one.'

'I suppose so,' I agreed reluctantly.

'Just enjoy his company and don't think about things too much. Try to relax and take things easy. He'll run a mile if you start getting all predatory.'

She was right, I knew. Becky's was the voice of reason – and reason did have its uses. I must try to be more relaxed about things with William.

But I couldn't sleep that night. I adored the old grandfather clock and I loved to imagine its sonorous toll ringing in the ears of the gamekeeper many years ago as he climbed my creaking oak stairs to bed, concerned for his clutch of newly hatched eggs out in the lean-to. But I wished I knew how to turn off its chimes. Every hour, its relentless striking reminded me of the slipping away of time, of the vanishing golden hours before William's departure.

The next morning, William came round clutching a fat folder. As I opened the front door, the poignant, regular, finely proportioned notes of Haydn's Trumpet Concerto floated through the air from next door.

'Hope it's not disturbing you. Uncle Joe's playing one of his favourite orchestral pieces at full blast on the old gramophone,' William said. 'Haydn himself said it was his favourite, according to Uncle Joe. He's given me these for you. Notes, as promised, on "Macbeth".'

He paused awkwardly.

'How kind,' I said. 'That'll save me hours of time, I'm sure. Do thank him, won't you?'

'Aunty Annie told me you said you'd like to see my other poems as you enjoyed the ones in the campervan so much. So I've also brought some more of my poems for you to have a look at, as requested,' he added a little self-consciously. He handed me a bunch of hand-written sheets of paper. 'Some are entertaining, I hope. Others are thoughts and feelings I've had.' He looked at me and said seriously, 'I'd love to know what you think of them.'

I glanced at the sheaf of poems on the top of Mr Locksley's notes, then slid the notes on "Macbeth" out from underneath and put them on the little hall table. In doing so, William's sheaf of poems slipped out of my fingers and scattered all over the floor. 'Sorry.' I picked them up as best I could and William helped me. He handed me the sheets he had collected, looking a little disconcerted. 'I'll really enjoy reading these.'

We roamed over the moors around my cottage, exploring the rocky gullies, the broad expanses of heather. He was so interested and attentive I could have talked to him forever. I told him about my Mum and Dad and their love, which had seemed to possess, for me, a spark of divinity when I was a child.

'So what went wrong – between your mum and dad?'

I told him about Dad's vitality which had been dissipated in drink as I grew up. And I told him about the gradual erosion of my parents' love. And how books had given me a refuge when Dad became violent.

'Dad was a salesman – but I don't think his heart was ever in it. It's a tough job and you have to be totally convinced of the product's worth to be convincing. Dad wasn't. He wasn't really interested in what he was selling. So he struggled for years. Like Willy Loman. You know, in "Death of a Salesman".'

William's eyes widened. 'What? … He didn't kill himself?'

'Oh, no.' I looked at William horrified. 'I just meant he felt a failure like Willy. No, Dad tried to find some relief in drink, I suppose. If Dad had had a drugs problem, there would have been so much more support for us. But alcohol – the social services weren't interested. So we put up with it for years.'

'It must have been very hard for you,' William said gently. He looked at me in sympathy.

I nodded, watching a butterfly drift from one clump of heather to another. The peaty scent of the wind blew in my face. 'You said that literature was my bible … And I suppose it was, in a way. Reading, especially books involving the countryside, gave me,' I tried to find the words, 'yes, a sort of … faith, I suppose, a promise of escape from terrible conflict and tension into a happier world. And so I've grown to love literature. And now I can pass on that love to my students – how lucky is that?'

William smiled. 'Does your sister love reading like you do?'

I shook my head, laughing. 'God, no. Mum used to read to me and Becky when we were little, and Becks enjoyed stories then, when she wasn't bouncing on our trampoline in the backyard or sliding down the bannisters. But she lost interest after Dad left. … I've always felt that that was the point when she and I took divergent paths in Robert Frost's yellow wood. You know the poem?' He nodded. 'Now she only reads non-fiction – and the odd detective novel. But mostly she's channelled her energies into sport and fitness. She's coming to stay tonight – just for a couple of days. I've booked her into the fantastic new gym they've just opened here. She'll love it.'

I told William about my friends, Liz and Peter, and our shared love of Dickens who were coming to visit me. And I mentioned Alex who planned to stay in the autumn.

'Alex is a uni friend who's mad keen on astronomy and has a superb portable telescope which we plan to use. Fingers crossed, the light pollution will be far less bad in my garden than it is in London and we can see the stars more clearly. Al is the loveliest person – would do anything for anybody. I know we'll have some fun.'

William nodded, staring down at the paved footpath which went all the way round a shining lake; this was called a 'tarn', according to William – a Norwegian word brought over by the Vikings. This footpath was popular apparently with the Victorian visitors who had come to stay at the spa hotel half a mile away. This walk was their 'constitutional' for the day. The water in the tarn gently plashed against the banks.

'So Becky doesn't seem at all like you.' William returned to the subject of my family.

'No. We're diametrically opposite in so many ways. She thinks I'm weird reading so much. I live in my head; she lives for sport. If I quote something I've been reading, she just thinks I'm showing off. She doesn't really understand that other people's words are an intrinsic part of me.'

'What a shame.' William's voice was sympathetic. 'She doesn't seem to understand you very well. And yet you say you're close.'

'Yes, there is a bond between us even though Becky can be a bit insensitive. But we do care for each other, deep down.' I paused. ' Becky can be lovely. Like when Grandpa – my Dad's dad – died. I never knew Mum's mum or dad. Mum's dad left her mum – he just walked out – when she was a little girl and her mum died of cancer just before Mum and Dad married. But I remember Grandpa well. He taught Becks to swim when we stayed with him at Weston-Super-Mare. I was desperate to swim too – but I didn't dare take my foot off the bottom. I felt such a wuss. But Grandpa kept holding me patiently in the water practising my strokes – until suddenly I could swim on my own! I was thrilled …

'A year later, a neighbour called to tell me the news that Grandpa had suffered a heart attack whilst out in his fishing boat. ' My voice cracked. 'Becks knew straight away – we have a sort of telepathy between us – and she came in from the Sports Hall, put her arms round me and just hugged me for ages.'

We were silent as we started to climb up beside a stream – or a beck as William had told me they call it in Yorkshire – to the moor top. It was quite shallow; there were only trickles of water coursing down peaty crannies between the granite boulders, flowing down to the Wharfe in the valley below. Then William stopped.

'Aunty Annie was like that when I heard of Mum and Dad's accident,' he said. He was staring down at the stream beside us. 'She was staying with us in Manchester when the police came round. She held me in her arms, comforting me all night.' His voice was hoarse and he took a deep breath. My chest ached as I saw a desolate little boy of nine standing there. 'She helped me get through the funeral, too. And I loved her for it.'

'You're lucky to have such a lovely aunty,' I said and touched him on the shoulder in a gesture of sympathy.

He nodded, 'She's wonderful. I don't know what I'd have done without her. We had some great holidays in her campervan as I was growing up.'

We continued walking up the path beside the beck.

'How about your mum and John?' William asked. 'Do they like books?'

'Not really. They both prefer films. They run a bed and breakfast down in Brighton. I was staying there last week, sunning myself on the beach, trying to read books I want to read for pleasure as well as all the books I've got to teach. It was really sunny down on the beach.'

'Ah' I wondered where you got your lovely suntan from. Makes your eyes look startlingly blue.'

He stopped, turning to look at me.

I felt my cheeks warm as I smiled up at him. I was useless at taking compliments.

'Thanks … It was lovely just lying there in the sunshine, immersed in literature.'

I surveyed the town lying below, the cars on the roads and the houses so small they looked like toys. Overhead a plane hummed faintly, crossing the blue sky.

'You obviously adore books,' William said suddenly. 'Have you ever thought of writing yourself?'

I grinned at him. 'If I wrote a novel, it would be so soppy, I'd have to call it "Fifty Shades of Cheese"!'

His eyes crinkled in amusement.

'What sort of novel would you write?'

He considered. 'I'd like to write a spy thriller,' he said at last.

We climbed up through a small clump of pine trees, the smell of pine resin wafting round our nostrils. The ground was spongy here, cushioned by masses of brown needles.

'I'd set it during the Cold War,' William mused. 'I've always been interested in double agents, people who deceive others totally convincingly. How they hold their nerve and maintain a totally believable front. Pretending to be what they're not, month after month under the most unbelievable pressure. Rather knocks acting for a couple of hours on stage into a cocked hat. Fascinating stuff.'

I nodded, gazing up at the sweep of moorland above us. Long blades of rough grass nearby rustled in the gentle breeze. The sunlight fell around us like a cape.

'What degree did you get at uni?'

'A first.'

He raised his eyebrows. 'You could really go places with that. Take a PhD? University lecturing? Academic research?' After passing through the clump of trees, we climbed up another gully, stepping from one tussock of turfy grass to another.

'Yes, I did think about that quite seriously – but I think you can get so caught up in abstract concepts, if you take higher degrees – like ... obsessing about the mood of pessimism pervading Thomas Hardy novels or analysing in infinite detail traces of incipient feminism in 'Jane Eyre'. You know the kind of thing? It seems rather removed from the real world. I do find it fascinating, I admit. But, like Dad said, what actual *use* is it ultimately?'

He nodded in agreement.

'I'd rather enable kids to express their feelings and ideas, help them appreciate the power of words. Teaching can be tough sometimes, I have to admit. But I know that by learning new words – and new concepts – at school and university, my mind was opened to ideas. And I want to do that for my students. And introduce them to some great literature, of course. Do some good with it. Even though 'doing good' has become a negative phrase nowadays.' I smiled wryly, warm with exertion. 'Precisely when did the term a "do gooder" become a term of abuse?'

'I don't know.' William shook his head. 'My parents were both "do gooders".'

'My Mum was a carer till recently. A sort of "do gooder", too. She really loved her clients, knitting gloves for them so that they wouldn't feel the cold. Or scarves. Like Peggotty in "David Copperfield"'.

William's mouth twitched. 'So you had Willy Loman married to Peggotty in your house as you grew up!'

I blushed. 'Well, when you put it like that, it sounds ridiculous,' I said laughing. 'I suppose I mean they had some of the characteristics of Willy Loman and Peggotty.'

'Only joking,' William said. 'No, your mum sounds like a lovely lady.'

'She is. She's so kind. She always cooked for Becks and me before she went to live in Brighton, what she called nursery food – shepherd's pie, sausages and mash, cheese on toast. A real home-maker.' I smiled. 'She's also well-known for her brilliant malapropisms. She comes out with them without meaning to – and they're hilarious. I was telling her on the phone yesterday about my neighbour's nephew being an actor. I said I'd met you and she commented, "Oh, he must be a real affectionato of the acting world – maybe even Hollywood!" She meant "aficionado". So sweet.'

William's eyes crinkled in amusement. 'Well, I'll have to tell my best mate, Leonardo Di Cappuccino, out in Hollywood, what your Mum said.'

I burst out laughing. 'Well done! ... Yes, Mum's a sweetie. A real "do gooder", as I said ... So how were your parents "do gooders?"'

'They were both social workers. My Dad – Uncle Joe's younger brother – worked in Manchester where we lived, and my Mum commuted to Preston. They both got so fed up with the press forever criticising their profession. If social workers took children into care, they said they were interfering. If they didn't manage to prevent a case of abuse, they said they should have intervened. And they only went in for the job because they wanted to help people – certainly not for the modest salary they were paid. It's so unfair.'

He looked round, frowning. I stopped too, trying to catch my breath. 'You're right. People have become so cynical. It's understandable, of course, when you think of the bankers' behaviour ... and politicians fiddling expense accounts and so on.

'But I think cynicism can sometimes destroy any genuine idealism, which is a real shame.'

'You're right,' I said. 'Down with cynicism!'

'Down with cynicism!'

We raised our arms in gestures of protest as we strode along the crest of the moor.

A sheep was lowing somewhere below us amongst the bracken. Some blackberries were ripening on a thicket of brambles in a hollowed out grassy area, their glossy black fruits gleaming in the sun. A kind of magic lay over this place. I'd come up here one autumn evening and pick them. I could cook them with apples from my apple trees. Make a blackberry and apple crumble.

'Now what do you make of these?' William asked as we headed down from the tops. Large millstone grit boulders lay before us, set into the ground, with deeply etched symbols on the sides and the top. Each symbol consisted of a smaller circle inside a larger one.

'They're called Cup and Ring stones, prehistoric in origin,' William remarked. He sat down in a hollow of cushioned heather and I joined him. We both surveyed the large stones. 'Probably about twelve thousand years old. Nobody knows why they have these mysterious markings. They may possess some kind of religious significance, although other theories include their being maps of springs or receptacles for offerings of milk – or blood.'

'What? Some kind of sacrifice?'

He shrugged. 'Maybe.'

I shuddered, staring at the stones. 'Twelve thousand years old!' I looked at the deeply etched markings before us.

'Do you ever try to put yourself into the minds of people from the past?' William asked. 'Tried to feel what they felt? Imagine actually working away at this stone, the effort, the skill required. And for what reason?' He shook his head. 'The more distant the past is, the harder it seems to do so, to connect with the people obscured by the mists of that time ...'

I stared at William. Again he was echoing my thoughts! Again that tingle of connection with this man.

This would test him. '"The dark backward and abysm of time" – from which play?' I rapped out.

'The Tempest,' William responded instantly.

I nodded, laughing. 'Tick. V.G. An "A" grade for you.'

'"The dark backward and abysm of time," he repeated. A bee zigzagged across the heather, busily seeking nectar from the heather flowers. 'Strange, haunting words, aren't they. ... You know, I've felt exactly the same as you about the past ... As a student, I used to go on archaeological digs during my holidays and one summer I went to York. It was the site of a mediaeval monastery inside the walls of York. I must admit that before then, museums didn't mean much to me – just glass cabinets of dusty old fossils, cave age flints, cannon balls – that sort of thing. They didn't *say* anything to me.'

I nodded and leant back against a huge boulder in the heather, gazing up at the bright sky, rippled with fluffy clouds. The bracken a couple of metres away rustled and two hikers strode past, grunting, 'Afternoon'. A tent and pans swung from the backs of their enormous rucksacks. Their legs were covered in mud above their gaiters. They must have splashed through a deep bog somewhere on the moors.

'Afternoon,' both William and I replied. I love the way people always greet each other on the moors. You don't get people doing that in the parks of London.

William continued, 'During the week and when we weren't at the pub – archaeology students can drink for England! – we were digging. And every single layer is recorded, drawings made, incredible attention to detail. I didn't find much for the first few days – just bits of pottery – earthenware, that sort of thing.

Then, one day, I found a pin.' William's voice changed. 'A cloak pin of beautifully wrought and knotted metal. It was a cloak pin, apparently, that a monk would have used to fasten his cloak against the cold. And, all of a sudden, six hundred years ago – was yesterday! The last time that pin was touched before I touched it was by a man struggling to fasten his cloak with freezing fingers! I felt like Howard Carter opening the tomb of Tutankhamen – without the curse. Tangible evidence.'

'"I see beautiful things…" '

He nodded.

I knew exactly what he meant. I know it's impossible but I've always longed to be able to see into the misty reaches of the past … to visualise life in prehistoric times … or during the Roman era … William seemed to think like me in so many ways. This *must* be a marriage of true minds.

'Anyway,' William concluded. 'I took the cloak pin to the archaeologist, full of excitement at my unbelievable discovery – and do you know what he said?'

I shook my head.

'He just said casually, "Oh, put it in Small Finds." Then he turned away to do something else!'

I laughed at his look of disgust but he went on seriously, 'Somehow that pin leapt the gulf of time for me. It was an amazing experience.'

I stared at him, framed by the golden bracken with the bright sky behind him. I felt such a profound connection with this man. We *were* made for each other, I didn't care what Becky said.

And suddenly I knew something else and my heart leapt. Of course, I knew William was a real person – he wasn't Heathcliff or Will Ladislaw or Mr Rochester. But I knew something infinitely better than that. William was *fascinatingly* himself. Full of interesting thoughts, ideas, humour, feelings. An amazing human being. Characters from novels were poor imitations of life, not the other way round. Here was a real man, truly infinite in faculties.

He smiled at me with his deep brown eyes, and I smiled back. We seemed to hold each other for a moment. I sat up and kissed him gently on the mouth and he responded warmly. My heart flipped over.

But then his mobile rang and I jumped. With a muffled groan, William reached into his pocket.

'Hi, Uncle Joe … Sorry, I lost track of the time. I'll be back in ten minutes.' I looked at my watch. It was after two. I thought it was only about twelve o'clock! The time had flown by.

William put his mobile back into his pocket, making a face. 'Apparently his roast potatoes are practically burnt to a crisp,' he said apologetically. 'I'd better get back.' I stared at him, my heart sinking. I wanted this time to go on forever. 'But listen.' He pulled me to my feet with a tanned muscular forearm. 'Before I go to Edinburgh, I'm going to take you to White Wells.' We picked our way across a scree slope below the cup and Ring Stones, down to a peat path leading down the moor.

'Okay … What on earth is White Wells?'

'White Wells is a little eighteenth century bath house which was built on the moors for ailing Victorians when Inkley was a spa town. The spring there was supposed to cure their illnesses. Now it's a little café and it sells the most delicious Yorkshire delicacies. An old mate of mine, Matt, runs it. I told you I wanted you to meet him. He and I are planning to climb Everest next spring, you know.'

I stared at him in amazement. 'Oh, yes, you said. Do you really mean – Everest?'

'Yes. Seriously, we're going to do it for charity. Matt's such a great guy. I've known him for years. We both share the same hunger for adventure. We've already tackled fourteen thousand feet high Mount Rainier and handled the cold in Alaska on Mount Mckinley so we know what to expect. Anyway, he asked me if I wanted to join him and I said yes, straight away. Matt loves the challenge – and so do I. But I also want to do it because, well, Dad and Mum always believed in trying to help other people …' I nodded. 'We can't go in the summer because of the monsoon season. I've already got sponsors from several acting agencies and theatres. It's to raise money to help the charity UNICEF – you know. They provide immunisation for children, to give them a chance in life – or buy mosquito nets to prevent malaria in the Third World.'

'Well, that's wonderful, what you're planning.' I looked at him, concerned. 'But are you sure it's safe to go up *Everest*?'

'We're joining a commercial company. With guides and sherpas, you know. Not on our own. It'll be amazing. Via the South East route on the Nepal side. The closest frontier to the universe, they say. And the view when we reach the summit will be mind-blowing.'

'But isn't it still very dangerous?'

'Yes, we have to be very careful. The land changes as we climb, varying from dangerously slippery ice surfaces and crevasses, to a moonscape. And I think I can cope with the shortage of oxygen. But we both love a spot of danger, as you know, and we're both fit. Matt's mad about the Great Outdoors, too. Anyway, I'd like you to meet him. He makes all his own Yorkshire food … My favourite is his parkin.'

'Parkin being?'

'A true Yorkshire delicacy, a cake made of oatmeal and black treacle.'

I looked down at the black sludgy peat under our feet. 'I bet they just cut out a slab of that stuff and serve it on a plate!'

He laughed. 'If you don't fancy parkin, there are loads of other delicious Yorkshire goodies. Uncle Joe and I are visiting George this afternoon. Could you come with me to White Wells tomorrow afternoon?'

'Well, my sister's coming down tonight. I thought I'd show her the shops tomorrow morning … in the afternoon, she's going to the Gym. But I'll be free.' I didn't need much persuading. 'Yes, I'd love to meet Matt.'

'That's great,' said William. 'But I'm afraid the cafe has two rules for its customers.'

'Which are …?'

'Their food is disgustingly calorie-laden. So the first rule is – you have to *run* everywhere from now on to use up in advance the calories you'll consume. And the second rule is …,' he looked at me, grinning '… last one back to the Gamekeeper's Cottage pays for it! Come on.'

With that he bounded off through the bracken, his tall, lean figure as light as a gazelle.

'Better bring some money with you then!' I yelled and chased after him through the tall, scratchy bracken and down round the side of the crags above my home. The wind was electric fresh in my face as we ran down to my lovely old Yorkshire cottage on the moors.

Chapter 7

It was weird seeing Becks beside me, climbing up the track to my house, overnight bag slung over her shoulder, the moors behind her softly glowing in the sunset. Becky inhabited places like the busy, bustling streets of London, or hot, noisy nightclubs. Not the utter peace of the lovely dales. She just grunted at the beautiful view around her – Becky doesn't do rustic.

As she brushed her windswept hair, gazing into the old, mildewed mirror in my sitting room, she sighed. But she limited her criticism of the furnishings to a suggestion that I bought a carpet to cover my lovely flagstones. 'It'll be freezing enough here anyway, in January, without a cold stone floor to make it worse.'

She thoroughly enjoyed my latest culinary creation of brussel sprouts and egg hash which I sauteed for our supper.

'Mr Locksley gave me the brussel sprouts from his vegetable patch,' I said. 'The recipe is dead easy and quick to make. And it's incredibly healthy.'

I didn't tell her about the the kiss William and I had shared yesterday. She'd only criticise me for rushing things. I did mention that William had invited me to walk over the moors to meet his friend, Matt, the following afternoon – which was when she was at the health club.

'I'd like to meet William some time,' she remarked, 'to

give him my seal of approval. But it's probably best I can't come with you tomorrow afternoon, with you two making puppy dog's eyes at each other all the time. I'd feel a right gooseberry,'

'Don't be silly,' I said. 'Of course you wouldn't. Maybe we could invite William round the day after tomorrow or something.'

Becky was very excited about the new health club when she read the brochure I'd picked up.

'Wow! It's got eighty cardiovascular and resistance machines, as well as the latest in cycling fitness equipment. And apparently I can try them all out.'

'Good. And in the morning we'll explore the shops. I've not had much chance to do that yet.'

Becky beamed at this, although she looked less keen on my suggestion that we visit the Manor House museum too. History is not a subject which appeals to Becky – yet another difference between us.

The next morning we were halfway down the track, when my mobile rang. Dad was interested and warm, as always.

'Hi, sweetheart. So how are you getting on? Do you like your new home? What does Becks think of it?'

'Oh, I think she likes my cottage.' Becky nodded agreement. I turned round and gazed at the purple moorland stretching away into the distance behind me. 'Oh, Dad. Wait till you come up and see it for yourself. It's so wild and different to London. As soon as the internet is up and running, I'll send you some photo's. Shouldn't be long now.'

'I'll look forward to that. Yes, your Mum said it's a very

beautiful place. Well, listen. I hope to come up and see you for the weekend at the beginning of October. Only a few weeks away.'

'Oh, brilliant. We can go off in your car and explore the whole area – I think you'll love it.'

'Great. Mum said you're trying to get all your lesson plans sorted for the first half term.'

'Yes, and I'm getting there, bit by bit. I need to be totally organised, otherwise the kids at school will eat me alive … How's your work going?'

'Oh, the project's really interesting. We're exploring nerve cells in the brain and their deterioration due to age or disease.'

'Sounds amazing. I'm so glad you're doing something that really interests you, Dad.'

There was a pause, then Dad said, 'Well, keep it under your hat but – there's a possibility that I could start a degree course next September – in Zoology with Animal Behaviour. A BSc. I've been discussing it with our project manager, Keith Tynsdale.'

'Wow, Dad. How wonderful!'

'I know. Keith seems to think I'm so dedicated to this work, he's going to propose it to the department. '

'Well, I think you deserve the chance to further your knowledge. It sounds fascinating.'

'It is …We're looking at neurofibrillary tangles and loss of neurons. We even have hopes that this could help earlier detection of Alzheimer's disease. It's a very slow process but if we succeed, then the progress of the disease could be treated even earlier. It's fascinating work.'

Dad sounded so happy, so fulfilled.

'My landlord's got Alzheimer's, you know,' I said. ' He's pretty bad apparently; he's in a Home now ... Even if your research centre does have a breakthrough, it'll sadly be too late for him. What a shame. It's such a horrible disease.'

I told him about sorting out my cottage.

'I've got a lovely garden, too, Dad. But it's so overgrown. I've started to make some inroads into it but there's still a long way to go. It's been a real cottage garden in the past, you can tell, but I need to clear away the weeds which have taken over.' Then I added facetiously, 'But I'm sure Becky'll give me a hand. Born with a trowel in her hand, weren't you, Becks?'

Becky shouted, 'In your dreams!' and Dad chuckled.

'Hey, listen. There's a very unusual garden centre just down the road from my flat. It sells really old-fashioned, olde worlde plants and flowers. I could bring you up a traditional old rose bush, say, for your garden?'

'Dad, that'd be lovely.' I thought for a minute. 'I know what you could look out for ... In 'Lark Rise to Candleford'. You know? The autobiography of Flora Thompson?'

'Oh, yes. It was on telly, wasn't it?'

'Yes, that's right. Well, do you remember Old Sally in it? She had all these lovely roses which are described in the book. Old Sally could remember back to the time of Cobbett's Merry England. Her roses had wonderfully enchanting names, like Maiden's Blush.'

I ignored Becky beside me miming being sick at the rose's name.

' Apparently they're all wonderfully sweet-scented. I'd *love* one of those.'

146

Dad promised to investigate his olde worlde garden centre as I walked into the town centre.

'Look after yourself, love. Don't work too hard when school starts.'

Dad had a brief chat with Becky before ringing off.

Becky did enjoy exploring some of the boutiques we found tucked away in the back streets. She finally found a little black silk dress which she adored.

'It's sleek, sexy and sooo sophisticated,' she enthused. 'And a lot less than London prices too.'

I was glad she was happy and had got something useful out of her visit.

The Manor House dated from the seventeenth century with small mullioned windows, its millstone grit walls were still blackened by the soot from the woollen mills of the past. It now housed a museum, portraying the history of Inkley over the centuries.

Apparently Inkley had been the crossroads for ancient trading routes and the Manor House was built on the remains of the Roman fort of Olicana. There was a funerary stone leaning against one wall in the museum, decorated in bas relief with the figures of a Roman family. The father, mother and child stood there in a row, their features worn away by the passage of time, although you could still see the folds of their togas carved in the sandstone.

Becky stared at the exhibits, eyes glazed. She kept glancing at her watch.

'How fascinating to think of that family living here thousands of years ago,' I said. 'I wonder what they were thinking and feeling as they looked up at the moors on either side of this valley. What was daily life like for them?

Did they hate the cold weather, being used to warmer climes?'

'Mmmm.' Becky was obviously bored stiff – so different to William's fascination with finding that medieval cloak pin. 'What time did you say I was due at the health club?'

My phone rang again.

'Hi, Mum. Everything okay?'

'Yes, dear. Just wanted to check that Becky had got there alright?'

'Yes, she's fine. We're just exploring Inkley. In the Manor House at the moment.'

'Oh, lovely. Sorry we couldn't stay long enough to help you unpack all your boxes. Only we can't close the bed and breakfast for too many nights at this time of year.'

'Oh, don't worry. I've got loads done since you left. I've just about got the inside of the house as I want it but I still need to finish tidying the garden.'

'Well, I'm not surprised you've not finished clearing away all those weeds in the garden. It was a jungle when we saw it. Anyway, I don't suppose you've had time. Becky was telling me about your gallivanting about the Dales, climbing up cliffs and getting soaked underground with that young nephew of Mr Locksley. I'm amazed. I thought you'd be terrified. You've always been frightened of heights.'

'Well, I was – but somehow William gave me the confidence to do it – and it was amazing. The rock formations underground – some of them are *beautiful*.'

'I'm glad you enjoyed it, dear. Do you good to get away for a bit from all that reading and thinking you're always doing.'

I smiled. It was true; so much of my life was spent thinking, reflecting, wondering ...

'Yes,' I said. 'I've still got masses of schoolwork to do – and the garden, of course – and I plan to paint the French windows as they're peeling.'

'Yes, I noticed they needed painting … Oh, it's such a lovely cottage, dear. Mind you, John was saying he thinks your windows need draught-proofing. He reckons it could be quite chilly in your sitting room when an easterly wind blows, straight over those moors with no trees for protection. He'll fit draught excluders next time we come up. But I'm knitting you a lovely warm jumper, dear, at the moment. I should finish it by the end of the week so I'll send it up by post. It's a lovely cream-coloured angora, patterned with sprigs of roses. Angora wool's really warm.'

'That sounds lovely, Mum. Thank you so much.'

'Well, it'll keep you nice and cosy till John sorts out the draught excluders.'

I could picture Mum sitting knitting away in the tiny lounge down in Brighton as she watched telly in the evening. A comfortable, plump figure, fingers flashing. She'd regained her old weight again since marrying John so now she was apple-cheeked again – and kindly. Yes, just like Pegotty.

'I've got some lovely fabric to make some drapes to go under your sink, too. It's a lovely soft blue material, with red swirls. I thought it'd look so pretty in your kitchen – hide all those battered old saucepans Mr Lawson's left you to cook with.'

'Thanks, Mum.'

'I also thought I'd crochet you some cushion covers, love. I thought gold wool over the cream background would look nice. But only if you like, Alice.'

'No, that sounds great.'

'Tell Becky I could do the same for her when she finally has a place of her own.'

I repeated her words to Becks, who looked horrified. 'No way!' she muttered to me, shaking her head. Then loudly to Mum, 'Thanks but no thanks. Everything's going to be chrome and black leather in my house.'

Becky couldn't stand the 'homespun look', as she disdainfully called it.

'I do envy you your Aga,' Mum went on. 'And that freestanding bath is to die for! Fancy having the original slipper bath with claw feet.'

'I know. It's real vintage stuff, isn't it.'

'You can say that again … Roll top, as well. I've *always* wanted a bath like that … And what views you've got! … I've been chatting to a lovely American couple who are staying with us for a few days. They wanted to know about places that they must see in little ol' England before they go back to America. So, of course, I said that they mustn't miss the Yorkshire Dales. I told them it's a bubonic paradise …'

My mouth twitched but I didn't say anything.

'They were amazed. I showed them some pictures of your cottage and of the moors – and they were amazed. They *loved* the photo of the Cow and Calf rocks -'

'Ah, now as it happens,' I said, 'I've just been reading about the Cow and Calf rocks. Did you know that, according to legend, the Calf was split from the Cow when the giant, Rombould, was fleeing an enemy? He stamped on the rock as he leapt across the valley!'

'Is that so? Well, would you believe it! … I'll tell the Americans all about what you've just told me.'

'Only according to legend, remember,' I reminded her. 'I suppose what really happened was – the frosts expanded, cracking the rock over millennia, and eventually it rolled away fifty feet from the main crag.'

'Oh, yes, of course.' But for a minute, Mum had really seemed to believe the legend. I remembered how, years ago, Mum, Becky and I had visited 221B, Baker Street, and Mum had asked the guide where Sherlock Holmes was buried! She had mixed up what was real and what wasn't, much to Becks' disgust.

… Maybe Mum was the original source of all my fanciful notions, my tendency to mix fantasy and reality. The delusion gene.

'Mum told some American tourists that the Yorkshire Dales are a bubonic paradise,' I told Becky after lunch, as we headed for the health club and she burst out laughing. 'Good old Mum. Classic.' Then she gasped in amazement as we entered the state of the art building. 'This is something else!' she exclaimed.

There were pictures up displaying all the facilities at the health club. It looked just like a medieval torture chamber to me – bleak, bare rooms filled with black machines covered in levers and pulleys. Mind you, the health club also had a superb looking swimming pool. 'I might come here myself to swim in the future, if it's not too pricey,' I said.

'I love the indoor cycling they offer too,' breathed Becky. 'This is going to be amazing.'

I left Becky at reception, totally in her element, and headed home. I was determined to clear away the rest of the weeds in my garden if it killed me. Once term started, I wouldn't have a second to call my own.

I pulled on my gardening gloves, picked up the secateurs from the old porch shelf and went out into the back garden to start cutting. Small heated winds blew over my face. I breathed in the warm scents of the flowers, mingled with the smell of the creosote of the garden fence. The stream gurgled and splashed a few metres away. The sunlight glittered on the French windows, catching my eye. The moorland and towering crags beyond were reflected in the glass.

A thrush ran across the grass next to me in quick, jerky rushes and stabbed at the ground. It seized a wriggling worm from out of the earth and flew away with it. Ugh. Such casual violence. Nature red in tooth and claw.

The more I cleared the jungle, the more flowers, hidden for months, emerged. The mingling scents were dizzying. There were roses, pinks, the stars of geranium flower petals amongst the green leaves, and a pretty plant with red berries and leaves like spears, which I think William had said was a daphne plant. Next to the fence which separated the two back gardens were some tall leafy foxgloves. I've always loved these self-seeders, with their beautiful purple bell-like flowers. I crouched beside a particularly stubborn dandelion near my back door and pulled at its leaves. But the roots only half came out, filling the air with its acrid smell. I brushed off the soil and picked up the trowel. As I dug at the roots of the dandelion, the sound of raised voices next door woke me out of my reverie.

William and his uncle had come to sit out in the garden after their lunch. Their voices sounded very heated, loud and clear over the bubbling stream.

'No, I won't,' Mr Locksley was protesting. 'I'm not

made of money, you know. I've bailed you out so many times. And this time I've made up my mind. You're on your own from now on. If you choose to keep gambling your earnings away, then on your own head be it. You must suffer the consequences. It's so *irresponsible*.' His voice was as cold as ice. 'You won't get a penny more till I die.'

'But I've racked up thousands this time.' William sounded desperate. 'I can't get any more money on my credit cards. They're maxed out ... It's like an illness. I can't help it. You must understand ... Please help me.' William was begging now, a note of urgency entering his voice.

'Never,' Mr Locksley spoke harshly.

There was silence. I found myself frozen to stillness, clutching the trowel, bent double.

'I *hate* you.' William's voice was full of loathing, icy cold. 'You've never really cared anything for me.' I caught my breath. There was a hard edge to his words, filled with contempt. I recognised that thin, reedy voice. My heart beat uncomfortably fast. I was kneeling in a sweat of anxiety. The sunlight suddenly seemed harsher, more austere. 'You'd better help me now or – '

At last I could move. I half stood up and scuttled into the kitchen. I mustn't listen in on a private conversation. My mind was whirling. William's voice was high-pitched with malice. He really seemed to detest his uncle ... Was there even a hint of a threat in his words? Surely not. William was such a gentle person. But the conversation between him and his uncle sounded deadly serious.

So *that* was the cause of the friction I'd sensed between them. William had a gambling problem ... No wonder Mr Locksley made those cutting remarks about risk-taking.

And William certainly seemed to enjoy taking risks when rock-climbing. And what about his great-great grandfather, who gambled away all the family money on the Manchester Racecourse? It all fitted. It must be a family streak. A gambling gene.

I'd read in the paper only the other day about professional acting. How, unless you were a 'star', the money was pretty much the minimum wage. William had said that he couldn't afford a car. It must be so difficult to stay in the black as an actor. The overdraft would accumulate year after year, the credit card would be refused. Maybe William put money on the horses, like his great-great grandfather, in a desperate effort to pay his debts. I could visualise William sloping into the bookies, watching the races, studying each horse's form, trying to assess its possible performance.

Or perhaps he bought hundreds of Lottery Tickets at the newsagents, hoping against hope that his would be the winning ticket. Like I said, it was a mug's game. There was always that perpetual lure of the faint possibility of riches, a permanent relief to his financial worries.

Or maybe he had been seduced by the glittering lights and glamour of the Casino, the spinning roulette table; perhaps Cathy had lured him there, with her sophisticated ways.

Perhaps it was just the thrill of winning that attracted him. He'd said it was like an illness. Yes, that must be it. He admitted to me he loved excitement in this dull, safe world. He was addicted to the excitement of the Big Win – a pathological gambler.

And now William was in real trouble. He'd hidden

his worries from me so well, appearing so relaxed – but I suppose that was the actor in him coming out.

After such a serious row, I half expected that William would cancel his invitation to take me to White Wells. But he appeared at my back door at the time we'd agreed, smiling as usual. I was nonplussed. His face reflected no inner turbulence of anger or bitterness – nor shame at finding himself in this terrible situation. He must be in denial.

As I stared at William standing at my door, I decided that it wasn't really any of my business. I would say nothing. I didn't want to seem nosey. And maybe William didn't want to burden me with his troubles. But if he did want to open up and discuss it, that would be okay. Although, perhaps a bit selfishly, I didn't really want our last few hours together to be ruined by discussing money worries.

We walked up over the moor ridge towards White Wells, William chatting casually and easily. But my mind was still churning with questions. How had William got into such a state? Would Mr Locksley give him the money he needed? It didn't sound like it. And how did this affect us?

But then there wasn't really an 'us', was there? William liked me – he'd kissed me back with real feeling – but did he feel the same towards me as I did towards him? All I knew was that, for me – gambler or not – he had brought the world to wonderful life.

Chapter 8

Inside White Wells, next to the cafe, the old stone bath was set in the ground of the chilly bath house. It was filled with the spring water trickling out of the ground just above the building. Moss-covered steps lead down into the bath and slimy green weeds hung down the cold stone walls. I knelt down and dipped my hand in the icy moorland water.

'Imagine immersing yourself in that,' said William. He grinned. 'More likely to give you pneumonia than cure you!'

I looked at him. How he could feign such a carefree demeanour when only an hour ago…? But then he was a brilliant actor.

We went into the café to meet Matt who was busy serving an elderly couple two mugs of steaming hot chocolate with thick cream floating on the top. The thick stone walls were whitewashed on the inside too and the floor was slate-flagged. Some paintings hung on the walls. Two farmers sat in one corner, wearing tweed jackets and cloth caps. They were the only people sitting indoors on such a lovely day. Both were silently focussed upon chewing the pile of ham and eggs on their plates. Their sheepdogs lay curled up beside their muddy boots firmly planted on the floor.

Matt was a well-built young man, about William's age,

with a broad, ruddy complexion, fair curly hair and bulging pale blue eyes. Maybe a touch of Joe Gargery about him, with his pleasant, good-natured face? No! Mustn't pigeonhole people into their literary equivalents any more. Trouble is, it's a difficult habit to break.

Matt greeted William with a slap on the back. 'Ey up, lad. 'ow's tha doing?'

He beamed at me as William introduced me.

'So tha's Joe Locksley's new neighbour. Tha's practically me neighbour too – give or take half a mile and sixty odd sheep.'

I laughed. 'How did you and William meet?'

'At t' Playhouse,' he said.

'Oh, do you act, too?'

Matt looked horrified. 'Oh, God, no. Couldn't stand being in front of folk. No, but I do like 'elping backstage-like. They allus need carpenters to build scenery and that.'

'Matt and I met a few years ago,' said William. 'We were doing the "Sound of Music", I think. Wasn't it, Matt?'

'Ay,' said Matt. 'Them mountains were buggers to cut out wi' t' fretsaw. All pointed like.'

We laughed.

'And Matt introduced me to climbing – Matt's in the Yorkshire Climbing Club.'

'Oh, right.'

'So what are you doing up 'ere in Yorkshire?' Matt asked me. 'Coming all t'way from London.'

I explained about coming to teach at the comprehensive school.

'Well, I 'ope tha learns them kids to behave theirsens and speak proper,' Matt commented.

'I'll do my best,' I said, my mouth twitching.

'Some of them are reet little buggers, jumping t'queue when I'm trying to catch t' bus to Leeds …' Matt turned to William. 'And 'ow's Cathy?' From his tone, it was clear that Matt thought Cathy was gorgeous. Only a couple of days ago I would have felt a pang of jealousy. Not any more though.

'Cathy's fine,' William said shortly. 'Doing very well for herself down in London.'

Matt nodded.

'Anyway, Alice is here to try some of your fantastic cooking, Matt,' William went on. 'What have you got on offer today? Some parkin, I hope.'

'Yep. Right 'ere.' Matt pointed out some ginger coloured cake on the counter which looked delicious. 'But this young lady might prefer to try some curd tarts- what all t'farmers used to 'ave as a snack during sheepshearing.' He pointed out some bright yellow tarts. 'Or I 'ave some delicious bilberry pie. I picked t'bilberries mesen on t'moors,' he added proudly. He indicated a latticed pie filled with small black berries. 'There's apples in there too. And I added sugar – they can be a bit acidic wi' out sugar. Make t'most of me food now,' he said to William. 'Next May, it'll be buffalo meat on Everest!"

'I think you're both incredibly brave to do something like that,' I told Matt. 'I found climbing Fairy Steps in the old quarry here terrifying enough for me.'

'Aye, we're either brave or mad!' he commented. 'I hope tha's getting fit, William, lad. I'm running over t' moors every day.'

'Yep, I'll be climbing in the Cairngorms after the

Edinburgh Festival. And I'll keep up the fitness routine wherever I am after that,' said William.

'But no more risk-taking,' Matt said firmly. He stared at William. 'We're 'aving none of that free-climbing tha's so fond of when we're on Everest.'

'Okay,' said William, laughing.

So climbing up cliffs without a rope was clearly a regular event with William.

I chose a slice of bilberry tart and William decided to have his usual slice of parkin. Matt insisted on us drinking his ginger beer – 'Yorkshire were t'birthplace of ginger beer'.

Behind Matt on a shelf were some glass jars of sweets and I bought some Pomfret cakes, the soft black lozenges gleaming.

In a another old-fashioned glass jar were a colourful mixture of pear drops, humbugs and other boiled sweets, some glistening and granular, others smooth like polished pebbles, veined with green and orange stripes – a traditional Yorkshire selection, called Yorkshire Mix, according to Matt. I resisted the sticky-looking slabs of Bonfire Toffee.

As Matt filled a couple of paper bags, two walkers came in, wearing huge hiking boots and with plastic map carriers dangling from their necks. They dumped their rucksacks in the corner of the café and stood behind us, forming a queue.

'Lovely to meet thee,' Matt said beaming at me. 'Tha must come again soon and try me curd tarts. Or next Friday, I'm doing a Pie 'n' Mushy Peas night. Come along to that if tha fancies it.'

'I'll try to,' I said. 'Or maybe I'll see you at the Playhouse.

I hope to join. It'll be a good way of making new friends. Maybe have a small part in something – if I'm lucky.'

He nodded, smiling, and turned to serve the walkers.

William picked up the tray. 'Come and have a quick look at some of Aunty Annie's paintings which she gave to Matt, before we go and sit outside,' said William, jerking his head towards the café walls.

William put the tray down on a table and we had a look round at the pictures on the walls. A peat fire burned in the old fireplace. The two farmers had finished silently eating their ham and eggs by now and were sipping their steaming mugs of tea, stolidly gazing out of the windows. My boots seemed to clomp loudly on the flagstones in the silence as I moved from painting to painting.

The paintings on the walls were different again to what I'd seen of the rest of Annie Locksley's work. Lovely pictures again though. There were scenes of Yorkshire life – but not the plants or the animals. This time the paintings displayed a fantastic view of Yorkshire places, such as the Rose Window at York Minster, the stained glass sparkling, as the sunlight filtered through, with all the jewelled brilliance of a rainbow.

Finally, one of the farmers in the corner spoke, breaking the silence. 'Muck's pilin' up,' he remarked gruffly to the other.

'Aye, muck's pilin' up,' the other replied. And he shook his head, gazing meditatively into the bottom of his mug.

Silence fell again. Then they drained their mugs and stood up, pulling their sheepdogs to their feet by their leads. That was the sum total of their conversation! William caught my eye and grinned. I continued to study the pictures on the wall closely as the farmers, closely followed by their sheepdogs, stumped out of the café. William watched them shut the door behind them.

'"Well, they don't say much,'" he squawked in his best Adelaide falsetto from 'Guys and Dolls', '"but what they do say is awful *pithy*.'"

I burst out laughing.

Another picture, hanging above the fireplace, was titled 'Brimham Rocks'. Brimham Rocks was only a few miles away from Inkley. according to William. The painting showed some huge old rocks, set amongst bright green spring bracken, carved by the wind into weird, twisted formations, nature's own abstract sculptures. Some had stones piled on top in unlikely shapes, appearing living in some monstrous form. They even had names. There was The Bear, in which a stone bear, mottled with whitened lichen, could be seen lifting its huge granite paws in the air, its long snout pointed upwards into the sky. Another rock formation painted by Annie was titled The Eagle, a great bird's head from which stretched a long curved beak. The rock formations looked strangely primitive, seeming to possess an almost pagan power in their distorted shapes. Like the megalithic idols of some pre-Christian religion.

Near to 'Brimham Rocks' was a painting of Whitby Abbey, spotlights highlighting its stark arches against a dark sky. The macabre haunt of bats and of Dracula.

Other pictures were of families, children with buckets and spades playing in the sand at a river's edge, against a Yorkshire Dales background, with a young man skimming a stone across the surface of the river. One that attracted my eye was of a grandfather and grandchild crossing the stepping stones across the river together, the old man's huge hand dwarfing the little boy's as he bent, helping him step across from one stone to another. The figures were quite dark, almost in silhouette, against the silvery shining river, the scene seemed almost biblical in its power. An image that seemed timeless and universal.

'It's great to have these on display here,' I said. 'The perfect place for them.'

'Annie got very fond of Matt when he and I became friends at Inkley Playhouse,' William said. 'Matt didn't know what he wanted to do when he left school. He wasn't academic but he really loved cooking so we persuaded him to set up his own café. He donates some of his profits to UNICEF. Aunty Annie was so impressed, she gave him these pictures to add to the Yorkshire feel to the place.'

'Well, it certainly does that.'

We carried the tea tray to one of the wooden picnic tables outside, and surveyed the little town of Inkley down in the valley. There came the clatter of plates from inside the café. I poured the little jug of cream over my bilberry pie.

'Can I just try a tiny bit of parkin?' I asked William. He cut me a sliver with his knife. It was very moist, bursting with a gingery tang.

As I ate the bilberry pie, my eyes followed the river towards its source, amongst the hazy purple moors further up the dale. This place had a haunting beauty that I could never tire of.

'Hey, look at this, Alice.' William's words broke into my thoughts. 'A miracle of nature is about to unfold before your eyes.'

I followed William's pointing finger, drinking my fizzy ginger beer. Hanging suspended from the underside of a small bush near the table was a blackish brown chrysalis swaying in the breeze. But was it the breeze? No, the chrysalis was shaking its leathery crust. Not dormant but turbulent, it was wriggling as it half slid, half crawled out of its torpid husk. The whole process took less than a minute, then it rested as its wings unfurled and expanded – a cabbage white butterfly!

The wings billowed out, drying and stiffening to the crispness of starch. The wings were white, fringed with black and with a dark spot in the centre of each wing. Clinging to the leaf, it quivered to the novel rush of the drifting air. A few seconds later it fluttered into the air and flew away to forage for food, craving nectar from nearby flowers.

'Just think of the … evolutionary convulsions of … *geological ages* that creature has gone through – shrunken to a nutshell!' William said. My attention was riveted. 'What does it *feel* like as your body's tingling buds peak inside the chrysalis and – erupt into tightly folded wings?'

I looked at him. Here was a mind original, spare, strange, encompassing.

I nodded eagerly. 'Can you imagine? It makes me think of Keats. I think you quoted him in at the beginning of your cat poem. "If a sparrow comes before my Window …"'

'" … I take part in its existence and peck about the gravel." In his letters, wasn't it? Negative capability.' His eyes crinkled, faintly amused as I smiled at him. 'Don't forget, you're not the only one who loves poetry, you know.'

'Oh, I know – but it's so nice not to feel like some kind of freaky geek. Especially being blonde; people don't expect you to be intelligent. Maybe they find it intimidating or something … Some guys I've been out with, they look at you as if you're mad if you use words of more than one sy-ll-able. Oh, no.' I clapped my hand to my mouth in mock horror. 'I've just used one!'

He laughed. 'I know what you mean … 'He surveyed the town below us. 'So what are your plans for the next couple of days?'

I thought hard. 'Well, I thought I'd go to Haworth – you know, the village where the Brontes lived? I'm teaching "Wuthering Heights" next week for A level, and I'd like to get some postcards, photo's of the surrounding moors, replicas of the tiny books the Bronte children made, you know? That sort of thing. I think it'll help to introduce the story and bring it to life for the students. Might even try to take them on a trip to Haworth later in the year. Any idea which bus I need to catch?'

'Well, you'd have to change buses at Keighley, you know …' William said slowly.

'Oh, that's a bit of a pain … I'm definitely going to buy a cheap car as soon as I've saved a month or two of my salary.'

'… But I could take you there tomorrow morning, if you like,' William suggested. 'I've got a day left before I need to go to Edinburgh.'

'Are you sure?' I asked. 'I wasn't angling for a lift, you know. I don't want to take up all the time you've got to be with your uncle.'

Becky could come with us, perhaps – although she

wouldn't be very interested in finding out about the Brontes. But it would give her a chance to meet William.

I studied his face. Did he want to be with Mr Locksley at all after their blazing row? Would he admit his gambling problem to me now?

William paused and he seemed to choose his words carefully. 'My uncle and I are very different,' he said. 'To be honest, it suits us to spend a limited amount of time together. I'd rather spend most of my time here with you.'

I smiled up into his eyes, warmed by his words. 'That would be great,' I said. 'I've always wanted to visit Haworth; it's so important to me … it's one of the main reasons I decided to apply for a job here. It seems silly, doesn't it – choosing where to live based solely upon a fantasy. "Wuthering Heights" is just a story.'

'I'm sure there have been worse reasons for choosing where to live,' he said.

'I could bring a delicious picnic to say thank you for taking me.'

As we walked back over the moors, some grouse suddenly exploded out of the heather in front of us, whirring their wings frenziedly and cackling loudly 'Chut! Chut! Chut!' I gasped in shock, twisting awkwardly away from them. A pain darted up the inside of my knee and I cried out, sitting down heavily in the heather. I heard William gasp. The world seemed to recede away from me, becoming hazy, and I felt a bit sick. I closed my eyes, clutching my knee.

'Are you alright, Alice?' William's voice drifted through the haze. He sounded really worried. He knelt down beside me in the heather. 'Where does it hurt?'

I rubbed my knee tentatively and winced. 'Just twisted,

I think.' I rolled up the leg of my jeans to look at it. Sure enough, my knee was swelling up.

'Just rest it for a minute. You poor thing.' William stared at my knee, his face filled with concern. He put his arm round my shoulders and hugged me. He was so comforting and caring.

As I sat there, gradually the pain lessened slightly. 'Stupid thing to do,' I muttered. 'I think it's a bit better now.'

'Do you think you can walk on it? If we go slowly and carefully?'

I nodded. 'I think so.'

'It's not far and I think I can help you when we get you home.'

Slowly I rose to my feet, fearful of putting weight on my swollen knee. William put his hand under my arm and supported me. I limped across the heather, leaning on William. I winced when I trod on uneven, bumpy ground but when we reached the footpath, it was much easier.

'I'm so sorry. We were having such a lovely time,' William said. He seemed really distressed for me.

'It's really not too bad,' I tried to reassure him. 'Honestly.'

'Well, we'll have a closer look at it in your house and I'll see what I can do.'

I looked at him curiously. What could he do?

William helped me into my house and I sat down on the kitchen chair. Then he headed out of the back door. 'Won't be a minute,' he said.

A few minutes later, he reappeared clutching a bunch of broad-leafed green weeds.

'What on earth are you going to do with that?' I said, amused.

'These are comfrey leaves,' he said. 'A brilliant herbal remedy.' Then I remembered. My landlord, Mr Lawson, had taught him all about herbal remedies.

'Good old Culpepper. He knew a thing or two about injuries,' said William. He busied himself filling a saucepan with water and putting it on the stove. He put on the kettle too. 'Should do the trick. I remember George putting a poultice of comfrey leaves on my ankle when I twisted it years ago out walking on the moors. It worked a treat. I was so impressed, I read the whole of Culpepper's book which he lent me … Now have you got a bandage?'

'I think there's a first aid kit upstairs in the bathroom.'

William bustled about finding a bandage, dropping the green leaves into the saucepan of boiling water and then he made me a cup of tea. After a couple of minutes, he lifted the soggy leaves out of saucepan with a fork and spoon and wrapped them in a clean tea towel. This he placed on my knee. As he bandaged the poultice to my knee, the warmth was soothing, easing the aching joint. He bandaged my knee so carefully and tenderly. Then he stood up.

'Now you wear that all night – no baths tonight, please. Keep your feet up tonight. And tomorrow the swelling should have gone down.'

'Alright, doctor.' I smiled up at him and he smiled back.

'Be careful tonight. No sudden moves,' he said in a mock strict way. He touched my cheek affectionately, looking at me with such tenderness I just melted. 'You need to be careful walking for the next few days, young lady. Watch where you put your feet on the moors around Haworth tomorrow.'

'I'm sure it'll be fine. I think it's feeling better already.'

'Well, we'll see how it in the morning. I suppose at least I can take you in the car, instead of you going on buses.'

'Yes, that's true.' He was leaving soon and my stomach tightened at the thought. He was so sweet and caring.

He nodded. 'Now rest that knee!'

When Becky came back from the health club, hot and sweaty after climbing up the track, she was stunned to find me with my leg propped up.

'You poor thing. Listen, I'll make dinner if you shout me instructions from the sitting room.' So Becky followed directions from me on how to make low fat moussaka as she cooked in the kitchen. I told her about the plan to go to Haworth with William the following day.

'Maybe you'd like to come too? Although I know you have absolutely no interest in the Brontes.'

'Hmm. Might be nice to see another Yorkshire town.' She was noncommittal. 'And what was Matt like – and White Wells?'

'Oh, it's a dear little white cottage on the moors. Matt makes all these Yorkshire delicacies – they delicious.'

'What did you have?'

'Some bilberry pie. They're these tiny black berries that grow round here on the moors. Quite sour but lovely with cream.'

'And how is our William? You two seem to be getting on very well.'

'Oh, we *are*, Becks,' I burst out. I couldn't stop myself. 'We've got so much in common. It's amazing … I kissed him yesterday,' I confided. 'My heart was racing like crazy.'

'Oh, yes. That'll be the dopamine and testosterone,' she said.

'The what?'

The biochemicals that give you butterflies, falling in love. I was reading about it in the papers the other day. It's all been researched.'

I stared at her. Why did she have to be so matter-of-fact, so clinical, so *forensic* about everything?

I leant forward, forgetting my injured knee, to give the fire a poke. A twinge of pain shot up my leg. 'Oh, Becks. It's not just a chemical reaction ... It's a marriage of true minds.'

Becky sighed, 'Do you have to be so *poetic* all the time? And why do you quote so much? It's just showing off.'

'Well, if that's true, it's just the kind of person I am,' I said briskly. 'I'm not going to apologise for it.'

'I'm afraid you've got it really bad this time. Starry-eyed or what?'

'Why on earth is it bad?' I was exasperated. 'I thought that love was a good thing.'

It hadn't taken long for Becks to start winding me up, as usual. Thank god she was only here for a little while. Becky shrugged her shoulders but she did have the grace to shut up.

As we ate our moussaka on our laps on the sofa, it was getting quite chilly.

'It's definitely colder here than London. It's only early September but I think you need to put the central heating on already,' said Becky, looking round for the radiators.

'Ah, well, that was one of the reasons why this cottage is so cheap,' I said reluctantly.

'What? You mean – there's no central heating?'

I shook my head. Becky looked aghast.

'My landlord didn't believe in such mod cons, according to Mr Locksley,' I said. 'He thought a good fire was enough for anyone.'

'Well, I think I'd better light the fire then,' Becky said briskly. 'Before we freeze to death ... I just hope you'll be alright here when it snows.' I could tell from the way she shook her head, as she knelt down to blow on the pieces of tinder she'd lit, that she thought I was mad living here. But she didn't take the chance to criticise me for once.

We both had work to do in readiness for the term approaching so we got out our files, me working on the sofa and Becky at the table in the corner. The sharp whiff of smoke filled the room as the fire smouldered, then burst into life.

I entered the dark, brooding world of twelfth century Scotland, rereading "Macbeth" and browsing through Mr Locksley's notes. His notes were very formal and structured but they helped me understand the play.

Could get the students to study the ways in which Lady Macbeth persuades Macbeth to carry out the murder of Duncan when he comes to stay at Macbeth's castle. Yes – *'Explore how Lady Macbeth attempts to fill Macbeth with "direst cruelty" so that he can perform the horrific act of murder.'*

'I'm going to focus on all the gore in "Macbeth". The stabbing of King Duncan! The ruthless, cruel butchery of Macduff's wife and little child ... Do you remember Wayne and the trouble I had with him on teaching practice?' I asked Becky as she brought me a cup of tea after we'd worked for an hour. 'Wayne – the terror of 10B! And I had to teach him Shakespeare.'

'Oh, yes. "The Merchant of Venice" wasn't it? You were in floods of tears about him and about 10B,' said Becky.

'Yes, I got Wayne to start reading the opening to the play as Antonio. Then he just stopped and loudly demanded why he had to read such crap! And the rest of the class joined in, moaning about having to read Shakespeare. It was terrible. They couldn't see how wonderful Shakespeare is. I was all ready to pack in teaching, you know ... Then, when I came home that night, you helped me.'

'Yes, I said – focus on all the gore of Shylock having his heart cut out!' Becky grinned at the memory.

'And it worked, thank God. Wayne even said he'd enjoyed my lessons – thought Shakespeare was *cool*! Thanks to you.'

Becky smiled. 'Glad I could help.'

I opened the paper bag of Pomfret cakes from Matt's café and offered Becky some. Each black lozenge was stamped like a wax seal with the three towers of Pomfret Castle.

The soft black licorice coated my teeth. Bet I had a black tongue too.

'So did you manage to get all the gardening you wanted to do before you went to White Wells?' Becky asked, chomping on her Pomfret cake.

'Yes. I found roses, pinks – all sorts under that jungle of weeds. And I pulled up loads of dandelions – but then -'

I stopped.

'What's up, Alice?'

I tried to make light of it. 'Well … I think William may have a bit of a gambling problem.' Maybe Becky would have a strategy for dealing with this problem, with her cool, clear –headed logic. I told her of the row between William and Mr Locksley. 'I thought he might confide in me, Becks. But – nothing.'

'What do you mean, nothing?'

'He seems absolutely fine. Normal. I think he must be in denial or something.'

'Alice.' Becky looked at me, concerned. 'You must be careful. There's all this in-game betting available everywhere online. And gambling's an addiction. Just like alcoholism. It's the same thing. A compulsion to do something that's self-harming – and *devastating* to those around him.'

'I know,' I said. 'But William can't help it. I think it could even be genetic. Gambling runs in the family.'

Becky's eyes widened. 'You should *avoid* him, Alice. Seriously. Remember the misery Dad's addiction caused us? He couldn't help it, I know. But it broke up Mum and Dad's marriage.' Her voice was harsh as she stared at me. 'And it ruined our childhood, don't forget … William needs to sort himself out. But don't you get dragged into it.'

Becky is always so impatient of weakness.

'Does he like taking a chance on things?' Becky asked.

William – climbing up the cliff-face, with no rope. Taking a risk for the thrill of it.

'Maybe …' I admitted. 'But I feel sorry for William. As a friend, I think I should try to encourage him to seek help.'

'Keep away from him,' she said. 'He might try and

borrow money from you – or pressurise you into borrowing money for him, if he's desperate.'

I remembered the hard edge in William's voice as he spoke to Mr Locksley; I hadn't mentioned his faintly menacing words to Becky: '*You'd better help me now or -*'.

'He's probably got loan sharks tracking him down,' Becky continued. 'Things could turn nasty, Alice.' She sighed. 'I wish I could be here to look after you.'

'I don't need looking after! We're not kids any more.'

'Well, all I'm saying is – Keep your distance from him!' Her voice was urgent.

'But I love him.'

Becky sighed in exasperation. 'It's just infatuation. He holds a sort of mystique for you just because he's a professional actor. What do you actually know of love? You've spent your life buried in books and only been out with a few guys – and then for two weeks, if they're lucky. You live in your head all the time. I've been saying it for years. See what's out there! …'

I took a deep breath. Why did she always try to control me? Things hadn't changed between us. Becky was exactly the same. She really pissed me off. This was one of the reasons why I'd decided to leave London. To get away from Becky.

'…Plenty of other fish in the sea, as they say.'

'But people aren't fish! You really like to reduce everything and everyone to the same level, don't you?' My voice was icy.

'I don't know what you mean. I just meant go out with loads of guys.'

'What? Like you, you mean?'

'Yes, I suppose so.'

I just couldn't resist it and I snapped out the words, 'Ah, but I'd rather have quality than quantity!'

But as soon as I said it, I regretted it. She breathed in sharply.

'I'm sorry, Becks,' I said. 'I didn't mean it to come out like that. I just wish you'd let me make my own decisions.'

In silence, Becky returned to her file at the table. She turned the pages noisily.

I was sorry I'd upset her – but she was always so sure she was right. It had always been like this between us. Her self-confidence bordered on arrogance. Here she was, at it again, telling me what to do. She was bloody annoying. And why did she always make everything seem so *mundane*? I knew a lot of the time she spoke sense, but surely I knew love when I found it?

Anyway, it wasn't infatuation. Infatuation was Romeo *before* he met Juliet. Infatuation was just loving the idea of being in love, playing around with words. "O heavy lightness…" Words filled with ridiculous ideas … "Love is a fume filled with lovers' sighs."

Yes, there was the heady thrill of attraction. But a profound passion stirred beneath between William and me. Of that I was sure. But Becky simply wouldn't accept it.

Some of her words had struck home though. *Gambling's an addiction. Just like alcoholism. It's the same thing.* Becky always seemed to have the weight of factual certainty and conviction behind her. And William hadn't really opened up to me about his problem. He must be in denial; he'd never be completely honest with me.

Did I want the relationship between William and me to

follow the same path as that of Mum and Dad? With the flame of passion suffocated by the problems of addiction – until finally it was snuffed out. Maybe life was not a case of branching off onto different paths in the wood but rather going round and round in a circle. A vicious circle. Making the same mistakes as the previous generation, over and over again.

Perhaps Becks was right. I should avoid William. But I loved him so much.

'I'm going to bed,' I said heavily. I couldn't face any more work tonight.

'But it's only early.' Becky said.

'I can rest my leg better in bed. Goodnight.'

She shrugged and grunted, 'Night.'

The poultice on my knee had now gone cold and clammy but I mustn't take it off till tomorrow. I hobbled to the kitchen to make myself a hot drink to take to bed and I glanced out of the back window. A bee was wandering from rose to rose in the gathering twilight. As usual, lines from literature rose to the surface from the depths of my memory, this time Keats' 'Ode to Autumn' – when he writes of the:

"later flowers of the bees

Until they think warm days will never cease

For Summer has o'erbrimmed their

clammy cells …"

So beautiful but also rather gloomy. This place would be very different when winter came. The loose windows wouldn't be much defence in February against the howling winds, even after John's attempts at draught proofing them. And, as Becky said, it wouldn't be much fun digging myself out of metre-high drifts of snow either. Mr Locksley seemed too frail to do much digging himself. So I'd be digging us both out with frozen feet and cold, stiff fingers. And then what about struggling down the frozen track to get to school half a mile away on time?

I limped up the stairs to my bedroom. Romanticism. My way of coping. I'd browse through my latest copy of *Countryside* next to my bed to cheer myself up. I loved looking at the glossy pages, the beautiful cottages.

There were instructions on growing a hawthorn hedge in the gardening section. It sounded a great way to encourage the wild birds and it might help to provide a windbreak when the winter gales were whistling down the dale.

I found an interesting article about keeping hens. Yes, I could just picture them in the corner of my garden, with a dear little hen house painted sage green. I couldn't keep a dog, as did so many of the people featured in *Countryside*. I'd have loved a beautiful cream Labrador. They were such gentle dogs. But it would be cruel to keep a dog indoors when I was out at work all day. But hens, that was a different matter. I could give them names – like Henny Penny, of course.

There were some lovely breeds of chicken photographed in the magazine. The Sicilian Buttercup hen looked beautiful with glowing orange neck feathers and speckly black and white wing feathers. But they were noisy apparently; Mr Locksley wouldn't appreciate being disturbed in his reading by loud cackling, I was sure. Or maybe the lovely Amber White with beautiful cream feathers. They lay well too. No, it would have to be Buff chickens, which were quite happy to be petted. They'd be lovely to cuddle and stroke. Mum would love them when she came to stay.

The chickens would all come bustling around me in the morning, clucking excitedly, feathers fluffed up at the thought of breakfast. The sounds of the farmyard. And every afternoon, after school, they'd rush up to greet me, squawking as I scattered their feed ... Mustn't give them too much feed though, as apparently that'd attract pests. Have to watch out for foxes, too. And make sure the chickens didn't fall in my stream. Maybe Dad could help me put up a wire fence around their enclosure when he came up at the end of the month. Yes, chickens were a great idea. Then I'd have fresh eggs for breakfast every morning. I love scrambled eggs. And poached. Couldn't kill a chicken for my Sunday roast though. No way. They'd just have to die of old age.

I heard Becky closing the back door downstairs. She was probably locking it. Typical Londoner – so aware of possible burglars. I hadn't bothered to lock up every night since I'd arrived, I must admit- we seemed so far from town.

I returned to my magazine. Maybe get a couple of potbellied pigs, too. They don't need taking for walks ... Wouldn't they be tasty with a sprig of mint from another of the herbs I'd found hidden near the back door. And apple sauce from my apple trees – No! How could I even think such a thing? I'd have to have them killed. I'd only keep them for their cuteness. Don't suppose Mr Locksley would like the smell of pig manure wafting next door much though.

I flipped through the rest of the magazine's pages. I could always buy a lovely copper kettle to sit beside the hearth to go with my copper bucket. That would look lovely, glinting in the blaze of the fire.

It didn't take long before my spirits started to rise a little. I lit a couple of candles and placed them on the side table by my bed. The delicate fragrance of vanilla filled the air and I sniffed appreciatively. My escape from reality.

But I was to escape reality for only a little while longer.

Chapter 9

The sunlight, diffused through my curtains, beamed into my bedroom next morning. I bent my knee experimentally and it bent with ease. No pain, not even an ache. I unwound the bandage and removed the poultice. My knee no longer looked swollen; in fact, it looked just the same as the other knee. William's herbal remedy had worked! My spirits lifted. Good. We could go to Haworth and have a bit more time together. And I'd try to make it up with Becks. She was going back to London in a couple of days anyway so I didn't have to put up with her for much longer.

The other good thing was that I was finally on the internet. I checked the computer screen – and found, in my email account, a lovely message from Liz!

'Welcome to your New Home, Alice,' she'd written, 'Hope all is well with you and that you are happy in the Yorkshire Dales. We'd love to come and see you – maybe in a couple of months' time?

Thought you'd like to know I've got *another* item for the National Scapegoats Society's first meeting! Somebody hid Peter's glasses again today – and guess who the Number One suspect was?! I said to him that I would never hide his glasses, as I'd look like a *Picasso* painting if he kissed me

179

without his glasses on; I pointed at my face – one eye here and one up there, my nose off to the left! Can you imagine! But Peter still wouldn't believe me.

So, as I say, another item to be put on the NSS Agenda; I'm definitely "the wictim o' connubiality", as Mr Weller says in "Pickwick Papers"!

Anyway, looking forward to visiting you soon in a lovely part of the country; I'm sure we'll all have some fun … What larks, eh, Pip?'

Much love, Liz and Peter x

I smiled. Dear old Liz and Peter. They were always making fun of themselves and each other, but only in a teasing way – not taunting. And they were always so cheerful. The same interests. Their marriage was perfect; they were like role models. You could feel their love for each other. They were soul-mates if anybody was. It *was* possible.

Liz had had a tough time, she'd said, with Peter a few years ago. But then she'd helped Peter through it by finding professional help for him. Because she loved him so much …

Perhaps some time today I could persuade William to admit he was a problem gambler and seek counselling for *his* problem. Maybe I could change him. Help him overcome his problem, as Liz had helped Peter. And maybe William would tell me he loved me passionately and that he wanted us to go on seeing each other.

I went downstairs, ready to smooth over the cracks with Becky. She was already sitting at the table, eating some muesli. As she looked up, she looked wary, with dark shadows under her eyes, as though she hadn't slept.

'Look! My leg's much better!' I said. 'So I can go to Haworth … Why don't you come too? We could all have a nice day out together.'

There was a pause. Then she said,' No, I don't think so. Thanks.'

'But you could see meet William and see for yourself how – lovely – he is.'

She looked at me again with a strange expression, unreadable.

'I've already met William.'

'What?! When?'

'Last night.'

My brow cleared. 'Oh, did he come round after I'd gone to bed? To check on my leg?'

'No.' She stopped. 'I went round there last night.'

Oh, yes. I'd heard her shut the back door.

'Why?'

She looked at me. 'I did it for you, Alice.'

'What? What did you do for me?'

'You're my little sister. You need looking after, Alice. You always have.'

I stared at her. 'What did you say to William?'

'You shouldn't encourage him, you know. He could be a real danger to you …'

'What did you say to him?!'

She licked her lips. 'When he came to the door, I – I said that my leg wasn't too good and that we shouldn't go to Haworth today. I said it quite coolly – to put him off.'

I gasped. I stared at Becky's long blonde hair, her blue eyes, her face – my mirror image. 'You – you *impersonated* me? I don't believe it!'

'It was for your own good, Alice,' she said but her voice wavered. She knew she'd gone too far this time.

I took a deep breath. 'You had no right! Whatever makes you think you have the *right* to do something like that? Why do you always think it's okay to interfere in my life?' I could hardly speak in my rage. 'How can you be so arrogant? How *dare* you!'

All my resentment at her domineering ways, boiling beneath the surface for years, suddenly erupted. Before I knew what I was doing, my hand had shot out and I'd slapped her face. I'd never hit anyone before in my life.

She gasped and put her hand to her cheek. 'B- But he's got an addiction, Alice. William is Trouble with a capital T!'

'I don't care. I'll help him sort it … You don't understand at all, do you? I love him. Do you even know what that word means?'

Now her eyes were filling. 'I just wanted to protect you.'

'Possess me, more like.'

'I'm sorry.' She knew she had done wrong. A tear trickled down her cheek. But I felt nothing but cold hardness.

'Please leave, Now,'I said.

'But, Alice. You don't mean that. ' She looked at me, stunned. Her cheek glowed a dull red.

'Pack your bag and go.'

She stood stock still for a moment with a look of anguish on her face, then she turned and ran upstairs.

I stood there, smouldering. How could she do it? What *temerity*! When we'd impersonated each other as kids – and that had been her idea too – it had been a joke, although I'd felt uncomfortable about it then. But for her to pretend to be me now, as adults! Not only was it probably a crime, it was also surely the ultimate deceit. And it showed such contempt for my ability to look after myself. I never wanted to see her again.

I'd definitely see William today. I didn't care if he was a gambler being chased by loan sharks. I wanted, I *needed* to see him again.

Alice came downstairs carrying her overnight bag. She looked contrite. 'I'm sorry, Alice. I shouldn't have interfered. Please forgive me.'

I sighed. 'Just go.'

As soon as she had disappeared down the track, I went next door.

As William opened the door, he looked surprised to see me. I shrugged, smiling up at him. 'I'm *so* sorry about last night, William. My leg was really hurting and I didn't feel I could face a trip today.'

He still looked confused. 'But you seemed quite set against the idea.'

I shook my head. 'The nagging pain was really getting to me. I thought maybe I'd done lasting damage and I was worrying about how I'd cope at school when term started.' He nodded in understanding. 'But − I couldn't believe it this morning when I woke up − good old Culpepper has worked a miracle! I didn't have much faith in him last night, I must admit, but he's proved me wrong.'

William's face radiated relief as I lifted my leg to show him how I could bend it fully.

'Oh, I'm so glad ... Are you sure you're okay − to come out with me?' He still looked rather puzzled and concerned.

I nodded vigorously. 'I'd love to come out with you. I'll just go and get the picnic ready.'

'Great.' he beamed. 'Is your sister coming? I'd like to meet her.'

I looked at him. 'Oh, sorry. Not this time. She's had to go back to London early. An important meeting at her school she'd thought was next week.'

'Oh, right. What a shame.'

'Give me half an hour and I'll be ready.'

I packed the wicker hamper which Becky had bought me for our birthday. She'd bought it just before the summer holidays. 'A hamper is *de riguer* for a country dweller!' she'd written in my card; I'd bought Becky a new pair of very expensive trainers.

It was a lovely hamper, lined with yellow gingham and including two plates decorated in yellow and blue flowers, two dishes, two wine glasses clipped inside the lid, knives and forks. I packed a small bottle of red wine, a small loaf of my homemade bread, cheese, tomatoes and slices of salami and covered the sealed box of food with a tartan rug.

As we loaded the boot of the car, Becky's words from last night echoed in my head and I must admit I did glance down the track and up at the cliffs above. But no sharp-suited, thick-necked loan sharks were to be seen lurking in the bracken. Anyway, I was going to forget all about Becky now and enjoy what was left of my time with William.

We drove along the valley floor, passing green pastures, divided up into fields by storm-worn grey stone walls, where Friesian cows grazed peacefully. The country smell of dung wafted across our faces. Further along, a farmer and his dog were driving a flock of sheep up to rough grazing land on the moors.

Haworth looked just as I had imagined it. A main street

of grey cobbles leading up the steep hill to the old church at the top. Above the church was the graveyard, beyond which stood the Bronte Parsonage. Just like in Stratford, the shops lining the High Street made the most of their famous inhabitants, with names like 'Heathcliff Cafe' and 'Bronte Tea Shoppe'. There were hundreds of tourists wandering in and out of the shops, buying Bronte buns and striped sticks of Rochester rock. A sign hung over the old Apothecary shop informing us that this was where Branwell Bronte, the only son of the Reverend Bronte, bought opium regularly.

We followed the road up to the Parsonage, the rooks cawing overhead from the tall elm trees high above the gravestones. After parking the car, we joined the queue waiting to enter the Bronte family home. A big fuschia bush, its flowers hanging line tiny scarlet lanterns, grew beside the front steps.

We shuffled into the front hall and I gazed reverently into the dining room where the Bronte sisters had paced round the original mahogany table and where their tales had unfolded, teeming with tender love or potent with thwarted passion.

'Emily read from her novel "Wuthering Heights" as she was in the process of writing it in this room,' the guide told us. 'And Charlotte told her friend, Mrs Gaskell, that it caused her many sleepless nights. Emily died in 1848 and Anne passed away six months later on that sofa over on the right,' she went on. 'The family servant ached to hear Charlotte Bronte 'walking, walking on alone' around the dining table here every night. Mrs Gaskell said that she could imagine the souls of the departed following her round and round in their nightly ritual.'

Indeed, the house did seem haunted by the Brontes, their ghosts almost palpable. To think that they'd grown up here from infancy, lost their mother early in their lives, crossed the flag-stoned hall to the back kitchen numerous times, gazed out of the front windows – as we did – at the graveyard below, and devised their famous stories within these walls.

Upstairs, we peeped into Patrick Bronte's bedroom, which he had to share with his son, Branwell, to keep an eye on him as Branwell's drink and drugs problem grew worse.

Branwell. He'd be a good lead into William's own addiction problems. I just needed to find the right moment.

I pored, along with many other tourists, over relics such as the Reverend Bronte's spectacles or Charlotte's narrow shoe until I looked up to see William surveying me with wry amusement. 'They're almost mystical objects in your eyes, aren't they,' he murmured. 'A true devotee.'

'I suppose so,' I admitted, half shamefaced. 'I felt the same in Stratford-on-Avon, at Shakespeare's birthplace. I actually read the letter there that Quiney wrote to Shakespeare, as well as seeing the portrait of Shakespeare – and, possibly, his second best bed. In the place where his creative genius began!'

We examined the tiny books created by the Bronte children filled with stories set in the fictional worlds of Gondal and Angria. Then we spent twenty minutes in the gift shop, where I bought various postcards and visual aids for my 'A' Level lessons. At last, we were ready to have some lunch and we collected the hamper from the car. William slung it over his shoulder and we climbed up the fields leading to the moors above. I walked gingerly at first; I had put a supporting bandage on my knee but I wasn't taking any chances.

We picked our way up the muddy path alongside the narrow gully to the Bronte Falls where, it was said, Emily would sit and muse, pondering her ideas. A curlew warbled overhead and a cock crowed faintly from a distant farm somewhere over the bristling moors. Bright furze bushes shone yellow in the sunshine. I placed my feet carefully on the tussocky path as I walked. My knee seemed to be standing up to the challenge, thank goodness, although there was the odd twinge if my foot bent sideways a little. At the Bronte Falls, the breeze drumming in my ears, I took some photo's to show my students the stream tumbling under the slender Bronte Bridge.

A signpost to 'Top Withens' was written in English – and Japanese, which, for some reason, we both found hilarious.

'Why on earth *Japanese*?!' We shook our heads, nonplussed, as we climbed up the gulley to the ruin of a farmhouse on the skyline. According to Ellen Nussey, Charlotte Bronte's friend, this was the original Wuthering Heights. I took a photo of it, stark on the skyline.

I was determined to broach the subject of Branwell Bronte's problems.

'It's poor old Branwell I feel sorry for,' I said.

'The brother?' William picked a blade of grass and chewed it.

I nodded. 'He must have felt such a failure compared to his brilliant sisters. I can understand a bit how he felt. Becky's always been so much better at stuff than me. I really felt it at school – she was excellent at Maths – and, of course, in Games. I was crap at both. But she's so skilful.'

'But Alice, you have amazing skills, too,' William assured me. He looked at me seriously.

'What? At reading books?' I laughed.

'Yes, why not? You'll be a great teacher and you've got such enthusiasm for literature, which I know you'll pass onto your students. That's really important.'

'Thank you.' William made me feel so good about myself. I smiled into his eyes. 'Anyway, Branwell wasn't quite good enough to be a successful artist ... so he took to drink and opium. Always down at the Black Bull pub below the Parsonage. His father and sisters despaired of him. He must have felt such a failure. D'you know he painted a picture of himself and his three sisters – and later he painted himself out of the picture! What a thing to do – to *erase* himself because he was so ashamed, I suppose ... I think he drank himself to death.'

William shook his head sadly. 'What a pity. Such a waste,' he murmured. He threw the blade of grass to the ground.

I gazed at the ruin in front of us. The wind raked through the rough grass around the old farmhouse. 'I suppose Branwell needed help. But, of course, those days there wasn't such a thing as counselling or self-help groups,' I glanced at William. 'I was the one who managed to persuade Dad to go to AA, you know. He could be quite aggressive about his problem ... defensive, you know ...'

William nodded sympathetically.

'Becky and Mum just criticised him – but I could see he

needed help, not blame. He was in the grip of an addiction. I managed to convince him it was beyond his control.'

I looked at William expectantly. Now perhaps he would open up. But he just looked at me admiringly.

'Good for you,' he said.

I gave up. I approached the square-built farmhouse standing in front of us and surveyed it critically.

'Seems too small to fit the description Emily Bronte gives of it in "Wuthering Heights",' I remarked. A dog barked down in the valley.

'Artistic licence?' suggested William.

'Maybe.' The wind whipped my hair into my eyes and I brushed my hair away, laughing. 'Although the bracing wind up here is certainly "wuthering"!'

As we went closer to the ruined farmhouse, I studied the stonework. 'No. Can't see any sign of the carvings of crumbling griffins over the door either. I think you're right. Emily Bronte used artistic licence.'

I took a couple more pictures. 'That'll do for my students,' I said. 'Now could you stand in front of the door?' I said. 'I'll take a photo.'

William obliged, smiling. 'This wild place is the perfect setting for Heathcliff's brooding love.'

'Yes, it's not what you might call picturesque. But these swells of heath do have their own beauty, don't they. ' I opened the hamper and we spread out the rug on the rough grass in front of the farmhouse. 'This heath land is certainly an integral part of the book. Emily Bronte saw people in terms of landscape ...'

I poured out two glasses of wine and we drank the tangy red wine, gazing dreamily at the glowing heather stretching for miles around us. 'Think about the name "Heath – cliff".' I said. 'Through that *name*, she has created the man from the moorland. Language can have such power ...'

'But Heathcliff was pretty ruthless and cruel, wasn't he?' said William, cutting my homemade bread into slices and buttering them. He placed layers of salami and salad on the slices. 'Not really the romantic hero at all – or the rough diamond people like to imagine ... Didn't he hang Isabella's dog in crazed revenge? '

'Yes, when his love for Cathy was thwarted.'

'A terrible man, really.'

'I suppose so. He was the Byronic hero – handsome, moody, passionate ... I think I just love the idea of Cathy and Heathcliff being soul-mates. It sounds *wonderful*.'

William looked at me. 'I think you're wonderful.'

Then he put his arm round me and drew me close to him. My lips sought his. His kiss was so tender, my nerves jangled with need of him. Gambling problems or not, I loved him.

We sat there, enclosed in our own world, and he gathered me closer in his arms. But the spell was suddenly broken by a babble of voices. Climbing up the footpath towards us was a huge group of – Japanese tourists! Chattering excitedly to each other, they were pointing at the farmhouse. William released me abruptly. Then they gathered all around us to take photographs from different angles of the Top Withens and the surrounding fells. One man even thrust a camera into my hands.

'Please? You take?' he asked. So I smiled, nodding, and held the camera to my eye. I took a photo of him and his wife standing in front of the front door of Top Withens.

The man nodded his thanks. Just when we thought we were alone, the whole world seemed to be there. William burst out laughing. 'And now we know why the signs are in Japanese!' he said.

Giggling, much to the puzzlement of the Japanese tourists, we gathered together the debris of our picnic.

My phone rang as we set off back down the track to Haworth.

'Alice?' Mum's voice was strange. She sounded distressed.

'Hi, Mum. How are you doing?' I said. I picked my way carefully round a big boulder in the middle of the path.

'Alice. Becky's just told me. About you and that young man ...'

'Oh, she has, has she?' My voice hardened. They were at it again. Mum and Becks, trying to get me to do things I didn't want to do. Ganging up on me, even when they were hundreds of miles away. But I bet Becky hadn't told Mum about impersonating me.

'Yes. She told me about his gambling problem.'

I glanced at William who was walking just in front of me.

'Mum, this is hardly the time ...'

'No, but Becks is right.' Her voice sounded anguished. 'I'd avoid him like the plague.'

'I think I know what I'm doing,' I said frostily.

'Listen, Alice. I've never told you this – but that's what happened between my Mum and Dad.'

I was stunned. 'You mean -?'

'My Dad was a gambler – yes. I never told you the truth about him. I suppose I was – ashamed of him. He spent all their housekeeping money at the bookies. They had no money left. Mum tried to make him stop. But he couldn't. She just couldn't trust him. In the end, Mum threw him out. I was only a little girl at the time but I can still remember Dad crying as he left the house. He didn't want to go. They still loved each other but he couldn't control his addiction to gambling. We never saw him again.' Mum's voice was urgent. 'Just don't go down the same route, dear.'

'Look,' I said pointedly. We were approaching the town. 'It's difficult to talk now. I'm out in Haworth at the moment … But I'll think about what you've said, I promise.'

'Everything okay?' William asked as I switched off my phone.

I smiled at him. 'Oh, yes. Just some family problems. Needs a bit of thinking about.'

I was quiet as we drove back to Inkley. My mind kept churning over what Mum had said … That explained her crying all those years ago as we watched 'Brief Encounter'. The sad scene when Alec left Laura. She must have remembered Dad leaving Mum. Because of the gambling.

William seemed to become lost in the maze of his own thoughts too. His eyes had a veiled expression. Something was preoccupying him. After this lovely trip to Haworth, a brief idyllic interlude, he must be facing grim reality again, forced to confront his huge financial problems – somehow. If I was him, I wouldn't be able to think of much else. He obviously didn't feel he could confide in me though. I felt a pang of disappointment.

I rubbed my poor knee which was aching. Perhaps I shouldn't have walked on it quite so far after damaging it…

I know that Mum meant well but – just because Mum's

mum and dad's life together had ended so disastrously, it didn't mean that William and I would end in the same way. All I knew was – I *so* wanted to go on seeing William. But somehow I couldn't tell him how I felt. Because he hadn't said anything to me about the future. I suppose pride prevented me.

William had to finish decorating his uncle's spare room before he left for Edinburgh the following day, so we parted at my front gate. He was going to gloss the bedroom door, he said.

It reminded me that I had a bit of painting that needed doing. I went to the little tool shed near the stream in my back garden to get out the sandpaper and wooden block from amongst the DIY materials John had bought me. He said he'd put them in there somewhere. I needed to sand down and paint the frames of the French windows before the wood started rotting. But the shed was a jumble of old earthenware pots, bags of fuller's earth, wire netting, a hoe, a hedge trimmer and other garden tools belonging to George Lawson. It took me a little while to tidy it out and find the sandpaper and wooden block. All the time I could hear the burbling, bubbling stream in the background.

As I was closing the shed door, a female voice said, 'Good afternoon.'

I looked round. It was Annie, carrying a large canvas shoulder bag. 'Beautiful day.'

'I'm just about to tackle my peeling window frames,' I said. 'Makes a change from gardening.'

She smiled. 'Enjoy!'

She made her way up the side of the moor, the sky eggshell blue above the rugged crags on the skyline.

I went back into my sitting room and started to rub down the peeling wood. A slight movement outside caught my eye.

I stared out of the window. Two figures were climbing the zigzag path up to the moor top. I recognised Mr Locksley's light beige jacket and his slightly stooping figure. Yes, that was William beside him, his tall figure in dark blue sweater and jeans. William must have glossed the door quicker than he thought. And maybe they'd sorted out their disagreement. Perhaps Mr Locksley had agreed to help William out financially. Now they had nearly reached the rocky outcrop above.

No, the view was still glorious, with the tangled but colourful flowers now visible and filling my garden, which led to the back fence. Beyond the fence, the moors curved upwards. The two figures were now surrounded by glowing heather and a couple of flaming gorse bushes. What a view I would have every time I came home from school! I would sling a hammock between the two apple trees in my back garden – yes, the distance was about right, approximately seven or eight feet. I'd lie there for a couple of hours, look at the view, gaze at my chickens pecking at their feed and recover from an exhausting day at school. I was so lucky.

The two figures disappeared round the back of the huge rocks. Then they emerged shortly after on the skyline. It was definitely them. There was no-one else about on the moor anyway. One figure, tall and lean but with broad shoulders, the other shorter and rather portly. The sun was overhead so I blinked to try and clear my slightly watering eyes.

As I watched, what happened next seemed to take place

in slow motion ... The shorter figure seemed to stumble. William jerked forward, arm outstretched, touching Mr Locksley, who swayed – then he – he p*lunged* headfirst down the face of the rock. There was a streak of beige plummeting down the dark rock surface. A faint cry drifted across to me almost simultaneously.

I blinked again. I must have imagined what I'd just seen. Some sort of weird optical illusion. A hideous, monstrous trick of the light. But I could see William, a frozen figure on the cliff top. He didn't seem to move for ages. But then he seemed to step back from the edge and disappeared from view. It can't have been an optical illusion; there'd been that faint cry as well. A terror-stricken cry.

Oh, God, please don't let it be true. *Please* let me have imagined it. I couldn't, I wouldn't believe what I'd seen.

I felt sick. No, it couldn't be real. Suddenly I seemed to have left the normal, everyday world of normality and been thrust into the realm of nightmares.

I looked up again, trying to make out what was happening up there. There was no-one on top of the rocky outcrop now. Then, from round the side of the rocks, raced a tall figure, stumbling over the rough ground in his haste to reach the base of the cliff. I just couldn't move. I stood in a chill of sweat, muttering over and over, 'Oh, my God. This can't be happening.' My mind was too numb to think clearly.

Nobody could have survived a fall from that height.

A fly crawled up the windowpane in front of my eyes and I could hear the grandfather clock's slow tick in the sitting room. The rough sandpaper was still clutched in my clammy hand. Normal, everyday things still going on indifferently whilst other unimaginable horrors took place close by. Mr Locksley must be dead. How could I even notice such ordinary things at a time like this?

I suppose I just couldn't really grasp what had just happened.

But then I could imagine the sickening crack of his bones as he smashed into the ground. Mr Locksley with his pointed nose and silver half- moon spectacles. His body was lying up there, broken, at the foot of the cliff. I should rush up there to see if I could help.

But the thought of what I would see struck chill to my soul. I couldn't go up there and see what had happened for myself. I was such a coward. If I went up there, the scene would stay with me for months afterwards, I knew it, recurring in terrible nightmares. I put my head into my hands.

If only this were some cosy detective story. The kind of thing I sometimes watch on the telly. In detective stories, the body is discreetly covered in a sheet. And the murder takes place in a pretty village, giving it the lustre of glamour. The melancholic sleuth detects wrong and always restores justice. Then death is diminished to syllogistic logic. And so we ward off the horror of death through abstract deliberations.

But this was a real grisly, *hideous* death. Stark reality.

Truly I couldn't move. I just stood there shaking at my French windows and in a little while there came a plaintive wail of an ambulance. It came slowly up the track leading to the cottage and stopped a bit further along. Two paramedics jumped out of the ambulance and pulled a stretcher on wheels out of the back. They trundled it up to the footpath, accompanied by a policeman, and it bumped up the zigzag path to the rocks at the top.

I staggered into the kitchen, filled the kettle and put it on the hob. A strong cup of coffee should help. I kept seeing the terrible scene over and over again in my mind … the two figures standing side by side on the cliff … the lurching stumble of the shorter figure … his plunge to the ground beneath. The image was burnt into my retina.

But at the back of my mind, a darker fear was haunting me.

William – he'd lunged forward, stretching out his arm – was he trying to grab Mr Locksley and pull him back from the edge but Mr Locksley had slipped from his grasp? *Or had William lunged forward to push Mr Locksley over?*

Chapter 10

William had jerked forward – but why?

I tried to recall the scene moment by moment, like rewinding a film, frame by frame – but it was impossible. Anyway, my eyes had watered because of the bright sky, so my vision was a little blurred. So how could I be sure? And William was a kind man; I couldn't possibly suspect him of anything so awful. But there had been real tension between them; I'd felt it. And there'd just been that terrible row … No, I was being ridiculous.

I sat, hunched and shaking in the window seat for a few minutes. Suddenly I realised that my phone was ringing. I fumbled for it in my bag. 'Alice, something's wrong, isn't it. I'm sitting on the London train, approaching Birmingham.'

I couldn't speak for a minute and Becky continued,' Please speak to me. I promise I'll never interfere in your life again … Alice?'

'Becky,' I croaked. I sounded like a zombie. I rocked backwards and forwards in the window seat. My arms were covered in goose bumps.

'Alice, are you okay?'

'No, not really.' My voice was weak.

'I thought so. I knew straight away.' Her voice was urgent. 'What is it?'

'Something terrible's just happened …' I cleared my throat. 'My next door neighbour – you know, the elderly gentleman I was telling you about? – Well – he's just – fallen off the cliff above my cottage.'

'Oh, no. How dreadful.' Becky sounded anguished. 'Is he – ?'

'I think he must be. That cliff is at least a hundred feet high – and he fell head first.'

Becky gasped. 'Did you see it happen?'

'Yes. I was sanding down my window frames. You remember I said I had to paint them?'

'Yes.'

'Well, they … Mr Locksley and William – went for a walk about half an hour ago – up to the huge cliff above here. And I saw him fall. He just plunged to the ground below. He won't have stood a chance.'

'Have you called an ambulance?'

'I think William must have called it. It's up there now. I just couldn't go up there, Becky. This is just awful …'

'Accidents happen so easily…' Becky tried to comfort me.

'Oh, Becky -'

'Yes?'

'I think they're bringing him back to the ambulance now. I'd better go and see if I can help in any way. Speak to you later.'

'Yes, of course. 'Bye.'

The paramedics were pushing the stretcher down the last part of the path. I watched, in a sweat of fear. The stretcher was covered in a blanket. My heart sank. The paramedics followed the path which wound round the side of my cottage, over the little stone bridge which arched over the stream, to the rough track at the front. William was following them, staring at the ground. They lifted the stretcher into the ambulance.

I went out into the front garden.

'William?'

William turned round from speaking to the paramedics. He looked shocked and pale, his eyes wide and staring.

He was a bloody good actor.

'I'm so sorry, William,' I said. 'It would have been over very quickly.'

He looked at me, his eyes searching mine.

Was there a flicker in his eyes, a subtle change in his face at my words? A strange look … of apprehension?

'Did you see him fall?' His voice was sharp.

'Yes,' I nodded. 'Through my French windows. I phoned for an ambulance. I wasn't sure if you had your phone with you. I'm so sorry.'

He took a deep breath. 'We just thought we'd go for a stroll, the weather was so nice. I'd gloss the door later on, I said. So we went up to the cliff, onto the top …' he said, slowly. Utter disbelief was written across his face.

But was it a mask? Had he prepared these words like a sort of script?

'… We were looking at the view – and –' The effort was visible as he struggled to speak, 'I think he must have caught his foot – it's so uneven up there – then he lurched forward … I tried to grab his arm but the sleeve of his jacket slipped from my fingers. Oh, God.'

His eyes grew bright and wet and I put my arms round him, trying to comfort him. 'I'm really so sorry,' I murmured.

I felt him nod, then draw away from me. 'I'm alright. I've got to go to the police station to give an account of what happened ... But I ought to let Aunty Annie know what's happened. Do you know where she is?'

'I'm here.' Annie appeared from behind the cottage, staring at William. Her eyes were wide with horror. 'I saw what happened,' she babbled, her voice filled with shock. 'This is terrible. Poor Joe. I can't believe it.'

William shook his head. 'It all happened so quickly.' He clasped his hands together. 'Oh, my God.'

'I was up on the moor and I saw what happened,' Annie said again, staring at William. He looked at her. She began, 'I saw something unbelievable and − '

She broke off as my phone started ringing in my pocket. I pulled it out, held it in my sweating palm and looked at the screen. 'Sorry,' I said. 'It's my sister.'

As I walked down the flagged mossy path back to the cottage to speak to Becky, I heard Annie saying, 'As a witness, I'd better come to the police station too.'

'I'll see you later,' I called back to them.

William nodded bleakly, then he and Annie climbed into Annie's camper van. Annie started up the engine and they headed off down the track. A sheep stood staring at me blankly through the bars of my garden gate − but this moorland sight no longer had the power to fill me with delight. I couldn't bear to lift my eyes to the massed battalion of crags above my head. They seemed louring, ugly monsters now, no longer beautiful natural outcrops of rock.

'Alice. I just thought − shall I come up. To be with you? I could catch a return train at Birmingham.'

'No. You were planning to head back to London anyway, tomorrow. And you've got enough to do, getting ready for school. I'll be alright. But thanks, Becky.'

'Are you sure? … I really am truly sorry for what I did, you know.'

'I know. And I'm sorry I slapped you. Something terrible like this puts our row into perspective. Honestly, Becks. I'll be fine. It's just been such a shock.' I stared at the yellow gingham curtains above the kitchen sink. The hem of one of them was hanging down, the thread dangling. Something lurking at the back of my mind made me add, 'I just need time to think.'

'Oh,' Becky sounded faintly surprised. 'Okay, if you're sure.'

'I'll give you a call in a little while.'

Why did I need time to think? What was there to think about? A terrible accident had occurred and my neighbour had died. Very sad – but not thought-provoking. But something was bothering me about all this – the row between Mr Locksley and William. The money William owed … 'You won't get a penny till I die'…

Surely he wouldn't? But he'd sounded *desperate*. And he hated his uncle – I thought I'd detected a ruthless note in his voice – and maybe the opportunity presented itself on the cliff.

Or perhaps he'd planned it from the beginning, pretending to make it up with his uncle, then persuading him to go up to the cliffs on a walk together. It would have been so easy – one quick push …

No – William couldn't contemplate *murder*! He was such a warm, kind, sensitive guy. And I loved him.

I pulled at the thread of cotton hanging from the curtain and the entire hem was pulled away.

There'd been real pain in William's eyes as he told me what had happened. His eyes had filled with tears. And his face was so strained and white. Surely he couldn't feign that.

But do you ever *really* know someone? 'Prepare a face to meet a face,' said T S Eliot. And, as always, unprompted words filled my mind: "There's no art to find the mind in the face"; Duncan's observation to Malcolm in 'Macbeth'.

And Cathy's parting shot had been: 'Don't trust William, Alice.'

Who was the real William?

In the past, I've read in the newspaper about some convicted murderer and then I've studied the accompanying photograph – and wondered whether I could detect any murderous qualities in the face. Often there seemed to be a deadness about the eyes in the face of a murderer, I've thought. But William's kind, lively face showed nothing of this. He had appeared truly grief-stricken, betraying nothing wicked within. But what about his performance in the cave? Playing Iago? The malice he'd shown in his face …

Maybe William has a fatal flaw. Just as Othello's fatal flaw was jealousy and Macbeth's was ambition, perhaps William's is greed.

Stop! William's a real person. Remember what Becky said…

But perhaps William's a superlative actor. And acting is itself a lie.

Or maybe, even … acting had *affected* him. Maybe

literature had influenced him even more pervasively than it had me! Perhaps he had a sort of … negative capability. He'd been playing such villains during the last few months – Iago, Dracula, Squire Corder. Iago is so terribly malign, without any real motive for his evil behaviour. Squire Corder, driven through debts from gambling, to commit murder. And then he played Dracula, totally inhumane, able to adopt many forms – again a manifestation of pure evil … What *effect* must this have? Suspension of moral judgement at the very least – like reading a dramatic monologue. Is that healthy? …

When an actor performs a role, does he merely don the part, like a mask? But acting isn't merely emulative, William said that. You actually inhabit the character. It all comes from within. But maybe performing evil roles leaves stains, like bruises, on his soul? Had he been corrupted, tainted to the point of pushing his own uncle off a cliff to satisfy his greed for money, his craving to gamble … How much did I really know of this man? … Was William a monster?

I was going mad. I'd be tilting at windmills next! Unable to distinguish between reality and fantasy. I needed to gain a sensible perspective on this. I had two different versions of William in my head both at the same time. What – what had really happened on the cliff?

I had to talk to Becky again. I needed her – to give me … stability. I still needed Becky, whether I wanted it or not. She was always so clear-sighted – if blunt – unclouded by emotion or wild speculation. Always so rational and objective in her view of things. And able to identify the empirical truth. Holding my mobile in my sweating hand, I told her everything.

'What you're saying is really serious, Alice.'

'I know that, for God's sake.'

'You need to think very hard about what you actually *saw*. Any accusation must be based upon evidence.'

I nodded. 'Ocular proof.'

'What?'

'Sorry – I mean you're right. That's what I keep trying to do, over and over and over again. But the distance was too great for me to be sure.'

'I suppose it's not so much a "whodunnit" as a "didhedoit?"' she mused. '… There's seems to be a motive, an opportunity and a sort of murder weapon …'

I controlled my impatience. Talk about pots and kettles! Becky was doing what she told me never to do – drawing on her knowledge of fiction. But I suppose at least the detective novels she likes to read do have a certain cool, clear-headed logic.

'… But ultimately I think it all boils down to this …' Her voice was calm and practical, as I had hoped. 'Could you have definitely seen William trying to push Mr Locksley over the edge of the cliff? '

I considered. 'No … I don't know.'

'In that case, your alternative 'memory' is not – what is it they say? – "beyond all reasonable doubt." No, I wouldn't go to the police.'

I breathed a sigh of relief; that was what I was really wanting to hear.

'But do steer clear of him, Alice.' She sounded really concerned.

Maybe Becky was right after all.

'Perhaps we ought to tell Mum what's happened.'

'No. There's no point worrying her.' I paused. 'Anyway, I think you've told Mum enough about me and William as it is.'

Becky tried to interrupt but I carried on talking. 'I suppose you thought you were acting for the best but I really think it's best not to mention to Mum what's happened. There's nothing she can do. Anyway, I'm pretty sure it must have been an accident.'

The kettle was whistling. I said goodbye to Becky and made a cup of coffee and a sandwich.

But the bread tasted of cardboard. The ham had gone dry and I couldn't eat it. My heart was beating in a strange, jerky way. I could see Marmalade through the window stretched out on my grass, rolling around in that luxurious, abandoned way cats do. He stopped and stared up at me with an inscrutable expression for a few seconds, and then he sat up and began washing his thick fur. Poor old Marmalade. Who would look after him now, when Annie had gone off on her travels again? And William had left for Edinburgh. I suppose I could offer to adopt him. Have to keep him away from my chickens though. And the pigs.

I tried to do some more work on "Macbeth" to try and take my mind off what had happened; Mr Locksley's notes were very useful, structured and clear. But it was difficult to concentrate. I ended up watching TV till two in the morning.

But still I couldn't sleep. I lay there, semiconscious, overshadowed by a sense of unease, of dread, nerves jangling.

When I finally fell asleep, I had the weirdest of dreams. A nightmare.

I was rock-climbing up on the cliff high above my cottage again, with William. Three quarters of the way up a rock face, but this cliff was hundreds of feet high - with no rope on. But I didn't seem to be panicking at the thought of falling off. I was scanning the rock face for a ledge or fissure and I finally found a crack over to my left. I wedged my fingers in the crack and clambered up a couple of metres, glancing up occasionally at William's encouraging smile above.

As I neared the top of the cliff, William stretched out his hand, still smiling. But then the phrase: "smile and smile and be a villain" echoed round and round my head and I tensed.

I glanced at his outstretched hand and was about to take it, when I saw that it was quite dark in colour, hairy and knuckly. Not William's finely tapered fingers. I looked up at his face – his features were contorting, twisting hideously into a malevolent grin. This wasn't William. This was Dr Jekyll, transforming into Mr Hyde. A shape shifter! A man who could tramp calmly over a child's body.

My hand froze in mid-air, and then my arm jerked down. Nothing would induce me to take William's hand. William's smile vanished.

"Then all smiles stopped together." Again the words resounded in my head, unbidden.

I tried to scream but I could hardly breathe. I dug my fingernails into the gritty rock, and peeped down. The rock face beneath my feet dropped dizzyingly down to the ground, hundreds of feet below. I pressed my body against the rough surface and shut my eyes, nerves on edge.

Then I heard William's voice, high-pitched and thin: "'Look like the innocent flower…'

I forced my eyes open and peeped up. William was staring down at me, his lips twisted into an evil sneer. His face was filled with all the hatred in the whole world as he spat venomously:

'But be the serpent under 't".'

Suspended by a rope round his waist, he lunged down at me, shoving my shoulder violently. I could feel my fingernails rip as I was flung out into empty space. That was when I screamed.

And I jerked upright in my bed.

I was panting, drenched in sweat. I scanned my bedroom, my heart racing in the half light of dawn. I could see something yellow glittering. Where was the cliff face? … Where was William?

No, I wasn't on the cliff face at all; the yellow I'd seen glittering was my brass bedstead shining in the early morning sunlight. I was here, safe in bed. My head was thick and my mouth tasted stale. It took me several seconds to realise that I'd had a nightmare.

Gradually my breathing returned to normal. The slanted rays of the early sun were filling my bedroom, filtered through the pink rose pattern of my curtains. I went to the bathroom to clean my teeth. I glanced into the mirror. My face was pale with dark smudges of exhaustion under my eyes.

Maybe this dream was an omen, maybe it betokened some kind of supernatural sign that William had indeed committed murder … But what would Becky make of it? I couldn't phone her at this time in the morning but I could guess her response.

She would criticise me for not dismissing my nightmare

out of hand. 'Nightmares are due to an overactive imagination. Nothing more.' That's what she'd say.

She'd never had much time for my imagination. When I'd seen the face of a bearded old man in the wood grain of our old wardrobe as kids, she'd made fun of me: 'Don't be so silly, Alice. It looks a bit like a face but it's just wood. ' She'd react to my dream in exactly the same way. Fanciful nonsense. And I suppose she could be right. I'd been overwrought by the accidental death of Mr Locksley. And my imagination, always pretty heated, had been overstimulated, *inflamed* by all the books I'd been studying recently – Macbeth, Jekyll and Hyde, Browning's monologues…

I was like Catherine Morland in 'Northanger Abbey', with her passion for gothic novels. As a result of her reading, she had become wrongly convinced that General Tilney had murdered his wife …

I was doing it again. No more literature!

To try and recover from the terrible dream, I rose wearily from my bed, made myself a cup of camomile tea and took it outside. Wearing my dressing gown, I sat in the wicker chair in the front garden, breathing out clouds into the sharp, early air. I smelt the damp-dew earth and the sweet, fresh grass. There *was* something magical about this place, something of Wordsworth's "sense sublime" here. I gazed at the exquisite gossamer webs stretching between the spindly branches of the rose bush next to the front door. Their lacy structures sparkled with the early morning dew, sparks of brilliance glittering like diamonds in the dawn sunshine, graceful and enchanting. This place was lovelier than I'd ever dreamed. Down in the valley, a wispy layer of soft mist rested like flock over the sleeping houses …

I wasn't sorry I'd decided to come to live in this beautiful place, despite this terrible tragedy. Poor Mr Locksley. But it had been a ghastly accident. He had stumbled and fallen. I wished I could have got to know him even better; maybe we didn't have a lot in common but he was a very interesting and erudite man. I could have learned so much from him. He might even have become a friend.

Mum, John and I had gone for a "Yorkshire Tea" at an old farmhouse up the dale the day I moved in. An old farmer, in checked waistcoat and wellingtons, assured us, as we ate the scones and cream on our plates, that this was "God's own country." As the rain was drizzling down the old mullioned windows when he uttered those words, we had gazed at the grey mist outside rather incredulously. But now I knew that he was right.

But then it suddenly struck me that presumably Mr Locksley's cottage would be sold. Or maybe Annie and William would let it and a stranger would move in. And William would have no reason for coming back to Inkley at all in the future. I might never see him again. I felt sick at heart.

I finished my tea, shivering. It was so depressing. My feet were freezing; the temperatures were distinctly lower here than they were in London. I went back to bed and slept for another six hours.

There seemed to be quite a bit of coming and going next door for the rest of that day. I suppose William and his aunt were dealing with all the practical business that has to be done when a relative dies. I felt that I shouldn't intrude on their grief. I emptied the rest of my clothes from my second and third suitcase into the old mahogany wardrobe in my bedroom.

As I tried to put the suitcases on top of the wardrobe, something stopped me from sliding them back against the wall. What was it? I put the old wooden chair in the corner in front of the wardrobe and peered over the wardrobe door. A small pile of books lay on top of the wardrobe against the back wall. I pulled them towards me. Three of them were very dull-looking accountancy books. They must belong to George Lawson.

The fourth book was light grey in colour with the picture of a man on the cover, staring seriously at me, dressed in dark sombre grey. He had long, curling hair and moustachios, beneath a large nose. He was clutching a small book in both hands under the title 'The English Physitian. Being a Compleat Method of Physick.'

This was, I gathered, a modern reprint of the book originally published in 1652 by Culpepper. The one William had borrowed and knew so well. I glanced inside the covers of the book. It would be interesting to read this sometime. The comfrey leaves poultice William made had healed my swollen knee so well. All sorts of medieval herbs were catalogued inside the book. One was a herb called Wood Betony, which was supposed to help cure 'falling sickness', whatever that was, as well as headaches, cramps, convulsions, bruises and sour belching.

I could do with finding some remedy to give me energy. I felt so weary with all the emotional upheaval of the last few days. Still, no time to browse through it now. I must just keep going. Give myself targets each day and work hard to achieve them. Take a leaf from Becky's book. First on the list was to finish sanding down the French windows and then paint them.

I remembered the bag of Yorkshire Mix I'd bought from Matt lying on the dresser in the kitchen. I opened the paper bag, the distinctive smell of nail varnish wafting up from the pear drops. The sweets gleamed like jewels but had stuck together in a bright solid mass. I broke a humbug off and popped it in my mouth and sucked it as I finished work on the French windows. Afterwards, I removed the masking tape from the glass.

Then I painted the rather battered old bedroom furniture in the spare bedroom white. While I waited for it to dry, I worked at my lesson preparation. I was due to meet my Head of English, Jessica, the following day to discuss my schemes of work. Once the furniture was dry, I decorated the old chest of drawers and dressing table with stencils of lilac flowers. Finally, after washing the brushes in white spirit, I stopped for some tea.

I hadn't been out for a while. It felt stuffy in the cottage. The smell of paint was making me feel a bit sick and I desperately needed some fresh air. I'd get some outdoor exercise for a couple of hours by strolling across the moors to White Wells to buy a nice Yorkshire cake for Jessica when she visited.

I set off up the footpath leading to the moor tops; it was a blustery day, the damson-coloured clouds scudding across the sky and creating blooms of shade across the green fields on the other side of the valley. The almond scent of gorse pervaded the air.

As I approached White Wells, I looked over at the wooden table and chairs where William and I had sat the other day. We'd shared that moment together, looking at the emerging butterfly. A special moment, gone forever. Sometimes a sad sense of loss seems to haunt me as time marches on relentlessly.

'Stop wallowing in self-pity,' I told myself sternly. I know I'm too emotional at times.

It was quiet inside the café, with only two elderly ladies with curly white hair sitting at a table, sipping cups of tea.

Matt greeted me warmly when he saw me. 'I 'eard about poor old Joe Locksley,' he said, his bulging pale blue eyes protruding even more than usual with sympathy. He *did* look like Joe Gargery. 'Stop that,' I told myself sternly. But I couldn't. The habit was so engrained in my brain. 'William must be devastated.' He clasped my hand in his huge paws and shook his head.

'Yes, he is,' I said.

My mobile rang. It was Mum. I told her about Mr Locksley's terrible accident but I didn't tell her about my suspicions. Mum was horrified.

'Mind you, he did seem a bit shaky on his legs when we met him,' she said. 'Poor old gentleman.'

I told Mum I was visiting a friend of the Locksley family so our conversation was brief. She didn't mention William at all and I didn't either.

'I know William and 'is uncle've 'ad their differences in t'past,' Matt said reflectively. 'But 'e were very fond of 'is uncle Joe.'

I nodded.

'When's t'funeral?'

'A week on Saturday, I think,' I said. 'William's coming down for the day from Edinburgh.'

'Well, I'll try and make it. I'll close t'café for t'day.'

'That's nice,' I said. 'I'll be going along to the funeral too, although I didn't get much chance to get to know him very well. I wish I had. He was an interesting man, and very well educated. It's such a shame.'

'Still, at least it was over with very quickly,' said Matt. "E wouldn't 've known much about what was 'appening.'

His words sparked the memory of the streak of beige plummeting down the rock face, the terror-stricken cry. I took a deep breath, then I nodded. 'I suppose you're right.'

"e was getting very doddery.' Matt went on reflectively. He shook his head. 'Only a few weeks ago, 'e came 'ere on 'is own for a cuppa. And 'e nearly came a cropper, tripping on t'corner of me old rug in t'café. I just caught 'is arm in t'nick of time.' He pointed at the flag stones on the floor in the cafe. 'I've got rid of t'rug that was down there since. Too much of an 'ealth 'azard.'

'Good idea. You can't be too careful … I just wondered whether I could buy a whole cake off you,' I said. 'I've got my Head of Department coming tomorrow and I thought it'd be nice to welcome her. We'll be working quite closely together for the next few years, I expect.'

'Of course. I've got a nice Yorkshire fruit cake in t' freezer I made meself. Would that do thee?'

'That'll be lovely,' I said.

A family consisting of a mother, father and two little girls had come into the café and were standing behind me. They were followed almost immediately by three men in climbing gear, with ropes wound round their shoulders.

'Can I have some some Bonfire Toffee and Yorkshire

214

Mix, as well as a Cola?' the younger girl was asking her mum. '*Please?*'

Her mother sighed exasperatedly. 'Just this once then, our Kylie. But you're taking most of the sweets home – and they're to last you all week.'

A queue was starting to form behind me so I quickly handed over the money and took the cake.

'Give me regards to William. Tell 'im I'll be in touch about booking t'sherpas,' said Matt. 'And tell 'im to start getting as fit as possible up in t' Cairngorms. It won't be a picnic up there in them 'imalayas.'

'No, you're right. I'll tell him.'

'But 'e isn't to do any free climbing, remind 'im. If 'is foot slips,' Matt shook his head, 'it'll be lethal – and they won't allow free climbing in t'expedition party we're going with anyway.'

'I know. He does seem to like to take chances,' I said.

'Yes, 'e likes taking risks, does William. Allus 'as. But not anymore,' said Matt firmly.

'I'll tell him,' I said. 'No more risk-taking.'

Chapter 11

I was making a mug of lemon green tea when I got home, when my eye fell upon the poems William had given me. I stared at his handwriting. It was a mature hand, graceful with gentle loops, yet powerful. Years ago, I'd gone to a talk by a graphologist at my local library in London. She'd analysed several pieces of anonymous writing and mine had been amongst them. She'd described me as being quite academic and someone who read a lot, judging by my small script and other features. It was a pretty accurate portrait of me and I'd been very impressed; she was even employed by the police to create character sketches of criminals they were seeking.

When I marked the kids' work during my teaching practices, some of their essays had been handwritten and I had noticed their individual style of handwriting. And I'd always wondered. Did bubbles drawn over the 'i's reflect an effervescent extrovert or perhaps flamboyant flourishes and curls suggested a vain disposition?

What would the graphologist make of William's writing? Would she detect an impetuous streak in his sweeping loops and bold dashes? Did his writing reflect his love of risk-taking – on the cliffs or in other ways? ... Someone who might impulsively kill his own uncle to save his own skin? Or should it have been scrawled and messy to indicate some criminal traits in his soul? Someone who had planned a murder in advance?

I cast my eye over William's James Bond poem written out on the page; was it only a couple of days since I'd laughed so light heartedly as he performed it in the underground cave? It seemed like centuries ago. I browsed through the other poems. Maybe in his writing he might reveal some hint of callousness, a certain ruthlessness. The sort of ruthlessness he'd displayed when he was 'acting', performing the role of Iago. One poem was an attack upon our celebrity culture with which I certainly could identify:

"Please welcome ...
A figure in society,
The focus of idolatry,
Because of his virility
Or maybe her banality.
These symbols of vacuity,
Of very small longevity
With nothing like sagacity,
Are really an absurdity.

And so with some temerity,
May I present this entity –
Or dare I say, nonentity? –
Which we call a celebrity!"

So often I had watched so-called 'celebrities' on some inane Saturday night TV programme – and switched it off in disgust. William and I shared the same thoughts. Shakespeare's marriage of true minds.

There were other poems focusing on nature – one describing a fox's feelings as it was being hunted, another concerned with a tiger in a zoo. They were as good as the poems in Annie's campervan. William seemed to engage as fully with the natural world as his aunt. My heart was touched as I remembered how compassionately he had cared for the starving bee in Mr Locksley's dining room, his face suffused with kindness.

I gazed at the photo I had taken of William smiling in front of Top Withens; his features looked so warm, open and gentle ... I couldn't help it. I was still in love with William.

Matt had said how fond William was of his uncle, hadn't he. He seemed to know William really well, known him for years. And he seemed so down- to-earth and honest, a good judge of character. And he'd said how Mr Locksley had been getting really doddery. He'd nearly taken a tumble on Matt's old rug in the café.

Mr Locksley *could* just have stumbled and fallen off the cliff. Had I just imagined that supposed push? It was perfectly possible, with my inflamed imagination and my blurred view of the scene. My ideas could be entirely without foundation. In which case, William was an innocent victim, grief-stricken and bereaved of his uncle of whom he was so fond.

Another poem simply titled 'A Marriage of True Minds' brought me up short. I think it had been the uppermost poem when William handed the pile of poems to me, before I had dropped them and they scattered all over the floor. I had noticed it because, of course, the title was a quote from a Shakespeare sonnet – Sonnet 116. It was a love poem written by William, beginning, 'My Darling,' and it was so passionate, it brought tears to my eye. There was no date at the bottom of the page, as there had been with the others, so I didn't know if he was writing about a past love affair or a recent passion. It was profoundly and unbearably tender, a beautiful poem.

There was a knock at my front door and William was standing there in a bright blue cagoule with white stripes down the arms. He looked pale and hollow-eyed. The bereaved victim. My heart went out to him.

'How are you?' I asked him sympathetically. 'There must be so much to do.'

'Yes. We haven't stopped.' His voice sounded flat. 'I should have gone to Edinburgh yesterday but rehearsals have been postponed for a couple of days. Aunty Annie can't do it all on her own.' He looked at me. 'To be honest, I could do with a bit of a break from it all. I need a change of scene for a couple of hours ... I was wondering whether you'd come with me. I've really missed your company. And there's one more place I want you to see, not far away. A major Yorkshire attraction. We can walk there from here.'

I looked up at the sky behind him. 'Are you sure that's a good idea? Have you seen the sky?' I said.

He looked up at the dark, bruise-coloured clouds ominously massing over in the west. 'Oh, I think that'll soon clear. Anyway bring your cagoule too, just in case there is a bit of rain.'

'What is it that's so special?' I asked.

'You'll have to wait and see ... Will you come?'

Becky's warning words were ringing in my ears: '*Steer clear of him, Alice*'. But I looked up into his warm brown eyes and nodded. William occupied my heart and soul. Reason had no place here. My feelings meant everything to me, as vital to me as the earth upon which I stood.

What a fool I was.

I put on my cagoule and we went down to the river in the centre of town and started walking upriver beside the footpath. The river curved up the dale and round the moorland. Blue dragonflies darted about above the river bank. The light seemed harsher, more austere. There was hardly a breath of air and my t-shirt stuck to my body. William seemed to be lost in the maze of his thoughts. What was he thinking? Not the brooding Mr Rochester but an enigmatic young man. I didn't really know him.

At first, the river was quite wide, sweeping over the stony bed, splashing and rippling as it glittered in the sunlight. Two swans flapped languidly up into the air ... Yeats' wild swans at Coole with their 'clamorous wings'. At the edges of the river, clumps of fawn-coloured foam eddied in the little pools in the rocks. Gnats whined as they hovered in a grey mist over the water. A clump of trees cast dappled shadows over us as we walked upstream. The entire sky had now turned a slate grey but it was very hot; the air was oppressive.

We followed the path, which led away from the river towards some dense woods. The leaves on the trees were starting to look tired, a dull green. It wouldn't be long before they started to curl at the edges and turn yellow as autumn advanced. A sharp smell of wild garlic hung heavily in the still air and the leafy branches above arched over our heads. The plaintive bleating of lots of sheep floated across the river. There seemed to be a distressed, agitated note to their calls somehow.

'They've just had their full-grown lambs taken from them,' commented William.

I gazed at the forlorn-looking sheep, still calling for their young and felt sad for them. The sheep seemed to know they had lost something very special.

'What are your plans after Edinburgh?' I asked. I wondered whether he might talk about us. 'Got any more acting contracts?'

'Yep. Hopefully some panto work in Blackpool. Not definite yet though. As a jobbing actor, you're never sure where the next pay-packet is coming from,' William said.

Was he hinting at his financial problems? Although now, of course, his money problems would be solved with his inheritance from his uncle.

'Then I've got the Everest trip next May, of course. I'm glad we're doing that. That should raise quite a bit of money for UNICEF.'

Yes – or would he vanish after the trip, taking the UNICEF money raised with him to fund his gambling habit?

No, stop these niggling thoughts.

'As I said before, maybe I've inherited my parents' philanthropic gene,' he mused. 'Perhaps it's Nature working on me – or Nurture. Who knows? Anyway, I'd like to give something back.'

I nodded. 'Good for you.' I felt a sense of guilt, mingled with relief; I shouldn't be so suspicious. How could an altruistic person so concerned for others possibly murder his own uncle?

We were approaching a clearing in the woods, where a café lay. The heat was coming up at me in waves from the ground. Rooks flew up from the trees in a raucous, flapping flock. Every so often, one reeled about, cawing in the leaden sky. A heated wind was blowing through the wood.

'So what is this place you're going to show me?' I said.

'In a minute,' he said. He looked at me inscrutably; he was hiding some secret, I was sure. I'd only known him for such a short time. And he'd never talked much about his feelings. Lots about ideas, theories, yes – but he'd never confided in me. William was really a stranger to me. He paused. 'Did you enjoy my poems?

'They were very good,' I said. 'I loved the one about the fox being hunted; I felt so sorry for it … You've obviously inherited your aunt's love of nature. It reminded me how *caring* you were when you helped that bee the other day. Your uncle was all for finishing it off with a newspaper.'

He smiled. 'Yes, I love nature. I used to go off with Aunty Annie sometimes during the summer holidays in her campervan, you know. We had some wonderful trips. I'd explore the rock pools whilst she painted … Once we found a grass snake in the sand dunes in the Devon. We brought it back here and called him Sammy. He was a beautiful creature. A delicate pale brown with fine black markings. I liked to coil him round my neck. But unfortunately I left him in the garden alone for an hour, and he escaped …' He looked at me. 'Did you enjoy my poem, "A Marriage of True Minds"?' he asked.

I nodded vigorously. 'It was beautiful.'

'Did you look on the back? ' He asked.

I stared at him; I'd never thought of turning the poem over.

But then his mobile rang. 'Hello? … Hi, Aunty Annie. Everything OK?'

222

There was a silence as he listened. His expression changed to one of concern.

'Oh, dear. How bad are the pains? ... I bet it's this stomach bug that's going around. Right. Listen, I'll come back straightaway ... Are you sure? If it's that stomach bug they were talking about at the town hall, they said the doctor recommended going to bed and drinking plenty of water? Alright ... Well, let me know what they say. Yes, I'll find the key, don't worry. See you later.'

He switched off, looking worried. 'It's Aunty Annie ... she has stomach pains and vomiting ... It does sounds just like that bug that's going around. Poor Aunty. I was all set to rush back but she's called an ambulance. She's so independent – never likes any fuss.'

As he spoke, I watched his face. Again, my brain was turning over his words. Annie ... she had told William that she'd seen what had happened on the cliff – that she'd seen something *incredible*. Maybe she'd seen *the push* – and had been threatening to tell the police what she'd seen. Now William was attempting to shut her up for good. 'Dead men tell no tales.' Where on earth had I dredged that up from? And he'd used poison ... The sickness and the stomach pains! Yes, Annie was like Ambrose in 'My Cousin Rachel'. But how had William poisoned her?

Chapter 12

The plants in my garden! William knew all about plants and their remedies from George, my landlord! His knowledge of herbs was amazing. But were there any plants that could *kill* in my garden?

My heart was beating strangely, jerkily. The birds were hushed now in the trees above. I passed my tongue over my dry lips.

'I just need to pop into the Ladies,' I said and plunged into the café. The man behind the counter was stacking chairs on top of the tables. They were clearly closing but he waved me through to the toilets.

'Won't be a minute,' I said.

As soon as I was in a cubicle, I phoned Becky. The reception was poor and her voice was faint. Oh, no – I'd forgotten to charge the battery last night.

'I was just about to phone you. There's something wrong, isn't there?'

'I need you to look something up on the internet right now …. I wish I had a Smartphone. Then I could find out for myself.'

'What on earth do you need to know that's so urgent?'

When I told her what had happened, she gasped. 'Oh, no. I told you to keep away from him … Tell me what plants you have in your garden and I'll check them out on Google.'

I tried to recall the names of the different plants William had identified for me. 'There's some plants called fluellen, red-hemp nettle, geraniums and daphne – oh, and some foxgloves.'

'I'll call you back.'

The mirror in the Ladies reflected my pale face back at me, my hair lank and hanging round my face, dampened by the humid atmosphere.

I went out of the darkened café. William was standing just outside the door, waiting for me. Anxiety just beneath the surface rose in me, making my heart beat faster. Mustn't let him know I'm suspicious.

'Come on. Let's go and have a look at The Strid.' He took my hand firmly and led me down another path which curved down towards the river. I followed him as though in a dream. I couldn't speak. What was going on? … What on earth was The Strid?

'You won't see it at first, you'll *hear* it.'

We stepped over the gnarled old roots of trees which coiled and twisted like skeletal claws across the muddy path. The canopy of black tree trunks created an eerie half-light and the footpath gleamed faintly through the pallid gloom. The white stripes down the arms of William's blue cagoule gleamed in the gloom. The earth smelt bitter and mossy. A faint rumbling emanated from the river further down and the ground vibrated slightly under our feet. Round the bend in the path, the ground started trembling and the rumbling increased in volume to a roar. We followed the path around another bend …

Then I see it! The *entire volume* of river water is being funnelled into a narrow gap between two huge boulders. The distance between the huge stones is only about seven feet wide. The water thunders as it rushes downwards, hammering against the moss-covered rocks before slamming into the boiling cauldron below. The whirlpool is churning and heaving violently; the power of this huge cauldron is *terrifying*. With a missed heartbeat, I stare at this horrifying phenomenon. The air is damp and chill and my skin prickles. I shiver uncontrollably.

'Isn't it fascinating … *mesmerising?*' William yells over the roar. 'Did you know that nobody has ever survived falling into that water? It *sucks* its victims under. The force of that pounding water has carved deep underwater caves beneath the waterfall.

Hardly breathing, my heart lurches crazily within me. I stare at the churning water.

'There's a famous legend associated with The Strid, you know,' he continues. 'Apparently, in the twelfth century, the "boy of Egremont" met his tragic and untimely death here. He was the son of William Fitzduncan, the nephew of King David 1, who at that time occupied the whole of Cumberland and claiming it for the Scots. Anyway, whilst he was on holiday at the home of his Aunt Cecily at Bolton in Craven, the "Boy of Egremont" used to like going out walking with his two hounds. He loved to come to The Strid and jump it with the two dogs. However, unfortunately one day, one of the dogs refused to jump but the other dog did jump – and so the boy was caught between them – and plunged to his death.'

He seems to speak with such relish. I feel deadly sick. Still I can't speak. Fear tastes like metal in my mouth. "If it be now, 'tis not to come.' No, I'm not ready. It can't be now.

'It's so wild and wonderful. Can you guess which poem this makes me think of?' William shouts, his teeth gleaming through the gloom. My throat feels dry and tight. I shake my head, so he starts to bellow the lines:

"'This darksome burn, horseback brown
His rollrock highroad roaring down
In coop and in comb the fleece of his foam
Flutes and low to the lake falls home ...

A windpuff bonnet of fawn-froth
Turns and twindles over the broth
Of a pool so pitchblack fell frowning
It rounds and rounds Despair to drowning ..."
He speaks the last line with great relish and grins. 'Hey, we're back to Hopkins again! We've come full circle.'

He studies my face, noting but misinterpreting, my look of horror. 'Don't worry. I'm not going to try and jump The Strid!' He says. 'I only take risks when I think the odds are in my favour.' I glance around. There is nobody else about. It is getting quite late in the afternoon by now and the sky has turned as dark as night.

He comes closer to me, smiling at me. A villain with a smiling cheek. His face looks pale in the weird twilight glow.

My mobile rings. Mechanically, I switch it on.

'Yes?' I shout. My voice sounds high-pitched and unnatural. Sweat is trickling down my sides, and it's not because of the clammy, oppressive day.

'Alice? I know there's something very wrong. Are you

227

OK? I can hardly hear you.' Her voice over the phone is crackling. 'What's that terrible noise?'

'Sorry,' I try to sound normal. 'I'm standing next to a waterfall.' My heart is thumping inside me.

'What are you doing near a waterfall? It sounds *huge* … Can you hear me?'

'Yes. Just. The signal's bad.'

'I've checked them out, the plants. I've found it – foxgloves!' I can just make out her words. 'They're very poisonous – causing stomach pain and vomiting. Are you with William?'

'Yes.' A chill trickles up my spine. My hand moves to my throat.

'Get away from him, Al – '

The phone dies, run out of power.

I take a deep breath. There is the sound of a beating drum in my head 'OK,' I shout, 'I'll think about solar panels but, to be honest, I don't think I can afford it at the moment.'

William takes me by the shoulders and leads me closer to The Strid; I can't resist, in the grip of a terrible fear. My blood trickles icily through my veins. The ground is shaking under my feet with the force of the water, the air filled with a cold mist. William has a strange expression on his face, unreadable. We stare at each other. His eyes look deadly black in the twilight and they give nothing away … "A grin wrinkled his cheek … he seemed to jeer as with his fiendish finger he pointed at me … Great God! The malignity of the fiend."

No, William is not Frankenstein's monster! But what is he thinking? … Of course! He *knows* that I saw Mr Locksley fall. I might tell the police about my suspicions at any time …

I dig my nails into my hands, rigid with fear. The Strid is below my feet. Its roar is deafening. There is a flash of lightning some distance away through the trees. Illuminated for a second by its brilliance, the trunks and branches look stark and sinister.

A cold mist sprays over my face, stinging my eyes as he stares at me. He's definitely hiding a secret. A deadly secret. The face of a killer. Fear slices into me. I can't move, trembling violently. It'll only take a sharp shove from him….

Hideously afraid, I open my mouth to scream – but no sound comes out. … I can already feel how it will be – my body flailing in empty space, the threshing waters closing over my head as they suck me in, somersaulting crazily, spinning over and over. Water flooding my nose, my mouth – my lungs. Writhing convulsively, fighting for breath as it drags me down, down into its terrible black depths …

This can't be the end. The conclusion to my story. We've reached the climax. But if this is the climax of my life-story, where's the twist, where's the twist at the end?

Suddenly I jolt into action. I pull myself from his grasp, shouting, 'Need the loo again. Must have your aunt's stomach bug!' I pelt up the path towards the café. William calls out something and comes pounding after me. Then I hear him curse; I glance round to see him lying sprawled on the ground. He's tripped over a tree root.

I stumble blindly around the second bend in the path and up to the cafe door. But the cafe is in darkness. I pull uselessly at the front door. It's locked. Sobbing, I run round the back of the café. A spot of rain falls on my head. I stumble, gasping for breath, up the rough path that leads to the lane.

Lightning forks across the sky and more drops of rain sting my face. I turn round to see if William is in hot pursuit – but there is no sign of him. I stare down the lane which leads back to Inkley. Must think clearly. I could run along that – but William's so fit, he'll catch me before I get back. Or I could take the track over the moor. I noticed it on the walkers' map I'd bought when I arrived. It's much quicker – straight across over the top to Inkley Moor, rather than going back twisting round the contours of the moor, parallel to the river. It should lead me straight to my cottage without having to go down into town at all. Hopefully William won't expect me to go that way either. He'll probably follow the lane back to Inkley and it'll take him far longer to get back. He doesn't even know I have a map of the Dales.

I rush up a slippery grassy bank, nearly slipping but just keeping my balance. I cut across to the footpath sign I can see sticking up on the other side of a dry stone wall. I clamber over the stile, red-faced and heaving, the sweat trickling down my sides. The rain is falling thick and fast, driving into my face. Thunder cracks ominously overhead and lightning flashes round me lighting up the grass a livid green. Perhaps not the best idea to go onto the tops in a storm but I don't have much choice. The sign indicates 'Inkley Moor'. I climb the steep moorland path, half-blinded by the lashing rain. My jeans are soaked through and cold rain trickles down my back.

Maybe Annie is dead by now. Another of William's victims. I need to call the police as soon as I get back.

The thunder roars and lightning strikes around me simultaneously, lighting up the soaking moorland brilliantly; the storm is right overhead, crackling with tension. I duck instinctively, struggling up the moor side.

Blow, winds, and crack your cheeks! Rage! Blow!

You cataracts and hurricanoes,

I reach the top of the moor, exposed to the full force of the wind and the rain. I *must* get home. I want to escape into my country cottage, safe, protected from this violent, hostile world, and curl up, just as I did as a child ...

I struggle across wild and rugged landscape. Must be careful to avoid the bumpy ruts in the path. My knee still isn't right, racked by occasional jabs of pain as I rush along. Cold air sweeps across my face and the bitter smell of fern and earth fill my nostrils. The rough grass is flattened in the blasts of wind and long green rushes shiver. I keep glancing round to check that a tall, lean figure isn't pursuing me. No, hopefully he's gone back along the lane. I can't be sure though. I try to walk faster, my breath coming in starts and sobs.

My face is drenched by the cold rain and the stony path is running with streams. The cold water seeps through my trainers into my socks. Lightning is flashing all around now and the storm is *raging* ....

No, I *won't* use language like that anymore. The storm isn't a person and it doesn't rage; neither does its violence reflect my agitation.

Cloud Cuckoo Land, to use a cliché – that's where I've been living all these years. Becky is right; I *am* Alice in Wonderland, believing in soul-mates, bonding with the landscape, a marriage of true minds – all that romantic

231

crap, those phantom conceits of the brain. I've been blind to reality, perpetually escaping into a fantasy world. That fantasy has led to me falling in love with a murderer. My judgement has been distorted. Fancy following my heart and going with William to The Strid! I should have kept away from him, as Becky said. What a fool.

I climb down from the moor top towards the path leading to my cottage. The granite crags look sinister and austere though the driving rain, buttresses of grim rock … what a load of crap, thinking I could find books in brooks and sermons in stones!

The thunder is fainter now, the flashes of lightning moving up the valley. I can see my cottage down there. Just got to keep going. Get into my cottage.

The thunderstorm is moving away but now wind is sweeping down the dale, bringing thick veils of more mist and rain. The air smells damp and mossy. Trying to dodge the deep, rippling puddles that are forming on the moor path, I mentally prepare the statement that I'll make to the police. Rain is trickling into my eyes; I can hardly see my feet crunching on the gritty path. I rub away the water from my eyes.

I can see below me the two streams that converge just above the little bridge, before entering my garden. They are swollen by the storm, boiling over the paths they have carved through the landscape. The water is in full spate as the streams surge together to form a torrent pouring through my garden. The water has spread over onto the lawn but it's nowhere near the cottage. I stare at the boiling water …

My life isn't flashing before my eyes, as you might expect; it's more as if I've gained the long view. Detached myself for a moment from the present. The water seems somehow symbolic, its two sources intermingling to form the narrative flow of my life. One tributary springing from my desire to be Me, my self. The other deriving from my Romantic dreams of a rural idyll. These driving forces have shaped the course of my life, precipitating me here – at its disastrous climax.

I look behind me to check that there is no sign of William. Oh, my God. A man is striding down the bleak curving moor side towards me, wearing a light blue cagoule. His hood is up so I can't see his face. Oh, God, just let me get into the cottage and lock the door.

The ground is uneven on the rough moorland path leading down towards the little stone bridge. My foot jars against a jagged stone and I stumble. My injured knee suddenly gives way and I fall to the ground. My cheek is scraped on the gritty ground as I fall and it stings. I can hear footsteps some distance away. He is running up behind me. I must get away!

I try to scramble to my feet but a pain shoots up the inside of my leg. I can't move. I can't get away. The footsteps ring out on the stony path behind me, closer now. I lift my head up from the gritty path, every nerve alive with fear. My cheek burns from the fall.

This is it. The end of my life. This is the way to dusty death. The footsteps are a few metres away now.

Out, brief candle.

No, it's too bloody brief – I'm only twenty two.

I can hear his breath over my shoulder, panting menacingly.

'Are you okay?' a light, high-pitched voice enquires. I

look up, expecting to see William towering above me. It's a teenage girl staring at me in concern from under the hood of her bright blue cagoule. She's quite tall and slim and auburn curls peep out from under her dripping cagoule hood. 'I saw you fall. You've cut your face.'

I nod, unable to speak.

'I got lost up there on the top of the moor and was caught in the storm. It was terrifying. I was so relieved to find the footpath down towards the town. I couldn't get down fast enough … You haven't broken anything, have you?'

'No, it's my knee. An old injury. It just gave way,' I whisper.

'Are you sure you can get up?'

I nod and she helps me to my feet.

'That's my home just there,' I mutter feebly. 'I'll be alright in a minute. I must get inside.'

'You need to rest that leg. And you must wash that cut.'

The girl holds my arm and I limp over the little bridge, the roaring water beneath surging over the stone sides. Then I head towards my front door. 'Yes, I will,' I croak. 'I must get inside.'

'Ok. If you're sure.' She looks at her watch, wiping away the rainwater. 'I need to catch my bus back to Leeds in twenty minutes.'

'No, off you go. I'll go inside and sit down for a while. Thanks.'

The girl heads off down the track.

All is dark and still next door.

I fumble with the key to my front door, hand shaking. The door is flung open by the wind. I enter my cottage.

I lock the door and lean against it. It's so gloomy inside because of the dark sky that I can hardly see in the rusty darkness. But I won't put the light on. I don't want him to know I'm here. As the rain lashes down on the slate roof, I feel the cottage rock slightly, battered by the blasts of wind …

The casements rattle and the wind howls like a banshee down the chimney. Oh, God, now I'm straying into Victorian gothic.

My sitting room has lost its lustre, stripped of its pretty patina of romantic nostalgia and now all I see is a dreary, old room. The old grandfather clock. It's not ticking. I must have forgotten to wind it up last night with the big heavy brass key … Everything looks drab and grey. The dusty piano. Nothing of D H Lawrence's soft life in the glowing lovely things any more.

Literature breeds such fatuous lies.

The air seems stagnant and shadowy in the dim light. Rain pours down the window panes outside and clatters on the roof tiles. I've been living in Never Never Land. I should have appreciated Becky's brisk scepticism as she tried to keep me grounded in the real world. And what a world it really is. This place is cold, stark and dank. A ghastly blankness has crept into my life. I lock the front door and slump onto the sagging sofa…

I don't know how long I have been sitting here, huddled on the sofa. The storm has died down. I must call the police. He could be here soon. But I seem to be paralysed – frozen with fear. And chilled to the marrow. I can't stop shaking, shivering as my soaked clothes chill my rapidly cooling body. I *must* get warm. The cottage is dark, desolate and silent.

I pick up the matchbox on the coffee table with a

trembling hand. I fumble to open it. My knee aches. I stretch over awkwardly to put the tiny flame to the kindling in the grate. The twigs catch and crackle. The draught from the wind down the chimney makes the flames waver. A faint warmth starts to creep into my bones. I reach for a clean tissue to wipe my bleeding cheek. I hold the tissue against my cheek to stem the flow.

Suddenly I jump. What am I doing? He'll be here soon! He might try to break my door down. I must phone the police. But the mobile's run out of power.

There is a movement outside. Gripping the chair arm, my skin goes into goose bumps. I stare through my front window, in a sweat of anxiety. My vision is blurred by the rain-distorted glass. My body jerks upright in sudden alarm as a figure appears at the gate. High above him, the cliffs swim. My heart pounding, I try to focus my eyes...

Chapter 13

It's Annie! She looks pale and weak. Thank God. She must have got to the hospital in time and been treated for the poison. She mustn't go into the house! If William finds that she's survived when he gets back from The Strid ... I limp over to my front window and knock on the pane. She pauses at the gate and looks over at me. I beckon her urgently to come to my door.

I open the front door and she is on the doorstep. The rain is falling more softly now and there is a faint breeze caressing my face with the smell of fresh, sweet grass from the lawn. The mist is lifting slightly; I can see across to the bedraggled- looking bracken on the other side of the track.

'Are you alright?' I ask. She smiles, a little sadly. 'Not really. No ... What have you done to your cheek?'

'Oh, it's nothing. I fell. Come in.'

I help her to the rocking chair by the fireplace and she sinks into it. She begins to rock gently, to and fro.

'What do you mean? ... Haven't they managed to treat you?' I stretch out my aching leg on the sofa and wrap my arms around myself. 'Has the poison left lasting damage?'

She looks puzzled. 'What poison?'

'The foxgloves,' I babble. 'You don't need to protect him, Annie. I know what he's done. He's tried to kill me too ...'

The startled shock that comes into her eyes silences

me. She looks mystified – and alarmed. 'Who's tried to kill you?'

'William,' I say falteringly. 'Didn't they didn't detect the poison at the hospital?'

She looks up at me. 'Alice. I haven't been poisoned.'

'B-but what's wrong with you?' I stare at her stupidly. 'How do you know you haven't been poisoned?'

Again, that sad smile. 'Because I've got cancer, Alice. Stomach cancer. I've already started the chemotherapy and it's working – but the pain got too great today.' She rocks gently backwards and forwards in the rocking chair. 'So I went to hospital and they've given me some pain killers. I feel much better now.'

I look at her horrified. 'I'm so sorry, Annie. I didn't realise ... Does Will ...'

'No. I didn't want him to know. He'd only worry himself sick ... But I had to let him know I'd gone to hospital because he'd left his door key at home and I knew he wouldn't be able to get in. I didn't know how long I'd be ...' She stares at me. 'What do you mean – William tried to kill you?'

I speak but my voice wavers as I play the scene again over in my mind. 'At The Strid. He was going to push me into that terrible whirlpool ...' But my memory now is as uncertain as my voice. Why *did* he hold me by the shoulders like that?

'But why?' Annie's voice breaks into my thoughts. Again I see the horror, the disbelief in her eyes. 'Why on *earth* would he do that?'

I try again. 'He pushed Mr Locksley off the cliff ...'

'No, he didn't.' She looks stunned. 'I was nearby when it happened. I saw everything.'

238

'But – but you said you'd seen something *incredible*,' I say accusingly.

'Yes, I'd just found a Corn Buttercup, a critically endangered plant! I couldn't believe it. It's incredibly *rare*.' I stare at her. 'On the edge of the moor, only a few hundred yards away from Joe and William. Then I looked up – and saw William grabbing at Joe's sleeve.' She looks down, shaking her head. 'But his sleeve slipped out of his hand. I told the police what I saw. William couldn't hold onto him, despite his best efforts.'

The vision I have constructed of this evil madman, ruthlessly killing any witnesses to his crime, is disintegrating, crumbling away before my eyes.

Annie looks at me incredulously. 'How could you think that of William?'

'But …' I persist, 'what about William's gambling debts? All the money he owes?'

'*Does* he? Surely not. I'd know about anything like that; William and I have always been so close.'

I feel I am on more solid ground now. 'But I overheard him telling Mr Locksley … in the garden. He owes thousands of pounds. He's addicted to gambling … It's like a disease, he says.'

Annie ponders, then her brow clears. 'I think I know what's happened.'

'What? *Please* tell me.'

'William mentioned to me that in one of the one act plays he's performing in Edinburgh, he plays the part of an inveterate gambler; the drama shows the impact it has on his family. William was very impressed by the writing … He must have been going over his lines with Joe.'

239

I stare at her. 'But they both read so well. It seemed so *real*. Mr Locksley isn't – wasn't – an actor.'

'Not professionally, no. But he was an excellent amateur. He and I were regular members of the Inkley Playhouse years ago.'

'Oh, yes. I remember you saying. He played Antony in "Antony and Cleopatra, didn't he. He did it really well.'

Annie nods. 'As a professional actor, William doesn't normally put feeling into his line bashing unless he's at a professional rehearsal but he knew his uncle enjoyed doing a bit of performing again. So he indulged him.'

Water drips from the gutter outside the front window. The rain has stopped.

'But,' I continue, still puzzled, '… there definitely seemed to be some tension between William and his uncle?'

Annie nods. 'You're right. Sometimes William and his uncle have had spats in the past.'

'What did they argue about?'

She pauses and sighs. 'Joe was a very old-fashioned, traditional sort of man. Especially in recent years – after Jane. You probably noticed. He didn't really approve of people behaving in an unconventional way.' She shakes her head. 'He never really liked me travelling round in my campervan. Thought I should be married and living in a house, not going around the country like a gypsy. And as my older brother, he told me so in no uncertain terms. Like some sort of Victorian patriarch!' She smiles. 'I think he would have liked to live in Victorian times – or preferably earlier. Probably the ancient Roman times. He wanted things always to stay the same. To keep the old traditions and customs, he said. But he wasn't going to control me. I loved being a bit of a bohemian.

'We lived here together when I was in my twenties. I was an art teacher, working in Bradford. But I was restless. I wanted to travel, live in different places. And I felt that art was my true vocation. I wanted to paint scenes of hope and love ... couples, families, beautiful places. So the campervan seemed the ideal option. But Joe went mad. Thought I, as his sister, should be here, looking after him! As unmarried sisters did in Victorian times. We had a real row. I flung back his classical arguments in his face. He said that we should do things as people did in the past. Stick to tradition. Keep things as they were. So I quoted Herodotus back at him. He's not the only one who knows something of the classics. Herodotus stated that life is, by definition, a state of flux! And he didn't know what to say to that. You can't make people stick to old customs forever ...

'But even so, Joe had such self-assurance, he could be quite overbearing. Maybe teaching gave him that air of certainty. A certain moral authority that fewer and fewer people seem to have these days. And I know it sounds ridiculous but I found it difficult to defy him. Do you know what I mean?'

I nodded.

'Sorry. I digress. Well, anyway, I fought Joe for my right to live freely. And finally Joe had to accept it.' Annie smiles. 'Him and his puzzles. He did enjoy them. Everything in its place, I suppose. And every problem had an answer. And his garden, so symmetrical and perfect. For him, there had to be a structure, an order to things ... But neither Will nor I accepted our jigsaw pieces or the way we were supposed to fit into his vision of things.

'Joe didn't want William to be an actor either. He thought it a risky profession …'

Mr Locksley's words come back to me, *'You like taking risks, William, don't you?'*

' … He would have preferred William to have had a steady job,' continues Annie, 'as an accountant or something well-paid and reliable like that. As his guardian, he thought he had the right to forbid William from going into acting. I know Joe only had William's best interests at heart. And William's always known that too. He was fond of his uncle.' She sighs. 'But William knew what he wanted to do. He wanted to follow his dream. And I supported him in that. You've got to let young people do what they want to do.

'And William is doing well in his chosen profession – but not earning anything like what he could have done as an accountant. Joe's idea of "success" has always been financial.' She shakes her head. 'A clash of values, I suppose. Of course, he thought Cathy's change of career direction made her into Superwoman or something. But that's not William's view of success, of doing well – nor mine. But it's been a source of friction between William, and Joe and me for years. Joe grudgingly accepted William's career choice – but sometimes their different outlooks caused tension. They've had a few arguments over the years.'

'B-but Cathy said William was not to be trusted.'

Annie gives me a shrewd look. 'Cathy was very possessive – she was *furious* at William's rejection of her. Hell hath no fury and all that. And William had told her about his feelings for you. She couldn't bear the thought of you two being together – so I think she was trying to warn you off. If she couldn't have him, neither would you.'

The case for the prosecution has collapsed.

Realisation floods through me, and *at last* my vision is truly clear. I am the original unreliable narrator! My vision of William has been skewed by misunderstandings, misconceptions. My 'evidence', my attempts at logic and reason were false arguments based on an error of judgement. I've had some sort of delusional disorder – and the delusions don't lie so much in literature as within me.

I'm such a dreamer, the tissues of my brain infiltrated by books, and my imagination has truly excelled itself, bodying forth the forms of things unknown, "imagining some fear,

How easy is a bush suppos'd a bear!"

William is not the grotesque caricature I have created of a gambling- addicted killer – but a loving, caring man. I cling to this thought and take a deep breath. Waves of relief wash over me.

Outside, the clouds have been slowly parting as we've been talking and a golden shaft of evening sun streams across the flagstones inside my cottage. The rosewood grandfather clock glows warmly in its dim beams. Outside the clouds are faintly rosy as the sun starts to set. The heavens seem to be smiling on me.

Maybe there is something in pathetic fallacy, after all.

'But where's William now?' Annie asks. 'He said he was a few miles up the dale but that was ages ago.'

I smile wryly. 'I think he might be looking for me ... He took me to The Strid.'

'The Strid!' Annie's eyes widen and she stares at me, a smile playing round her lips. 'Wow, just like his dad … That place has great significance for our family, you know. He must have made up his mind, then.'

'How do you mean?'

'About you.'

I stare at her.

'He wasn't sure how you felt about him, you know. We've always been very close and he opened his heart to me. It was love at first sight for him. He loves your rather eccentric ideas.' I started. 'And he thinks you're really attractive.' She smiled as she leant forward confidentially. 'He told me he thinks you're lovely! … But he felt you were blowing hot and cold towards him, holding something back. He thought maybe you had feelings for your friend – Alex, was it?'

'But Alex is a girl friend!'

'Ah. Well, you seem reserved, even distant at times towards him. And he wasn't sure why.' She raised her eyebrows, with a wry smile. 'I think I can see why now.'

'I really have totally misunderstood everything,' I said. 'God, I feel a stupid fool.'

'Well, no, I can see how it's happened,' she said. 'But imagine thinking that a sweetie like William was a gambler – and a murderer!'

'I must go and find him,' I said suddenly.

'Where is he at the moment?'

'I'm not sure. He may still be at the Strid.'

'Well, you'd better get back to him. I can take you there. He wants you there for a particular reason, you know. He can be quite impulsive – and he's decided to take the bull by the horns, so to speak. I think I know what he is planning to do.'

I stare at her, mystified. 'What is he planning to do?'

'Well, I suppose you could say that a certain tradition surrounds the Strid, as a result of certain family – customs …' She smiles mysteriously.

'It's where my great grandfather and my grandfather took their girlfriends – to propose … And it's where Alfred, William's dad, proposed to his mum a week after they met; I told you he was an impetuous man!'

My eyes widen. Surely not. A proposal must take place in a beautiful garden or maybe in a lamp lit restaurant … But then, why not the wild, phenomenal Strid to seal our love?

'Now William isn't a traditional man, as you know, unlike his uncle. But maybe in this case he makes an exception. And he does believe in one particular Latin tag, I know for a fact.'

'What's that?'

'Carpe Diem. Seize the day!'

A butterfly dances past the window. Okay, I suppose that, strictly speaking, it just fluttered but, for me, it *danced*! Long live anthropomorphism!

'Oh, dear,' I say slowly. 'I think William may be panicking, searching for me everywhere, as I did rather vanish … Maybe he thinks I've fallen or collapsed in the woods – or something.'

'Oh, dear. You'd better let him know straightaway that you're here, hale and hearty. He'll be languishing there. Put him out of his misery.'

'Come, I will have thee: but by this light, I take thee for pity,' I say.

'Pardon?'

'Sorry,' I say. 'It's Beatrice's excuse for marrying Benedick in "Much Ado About Nothing". Because she feels sorry for him! … I'm afraid I've always had this irrepressible urge to quote literature. '

Annie smiles.

The clouds in the sky outside are turning crimson and gold as the sun starts to set. The future suddenly takes on a warm, hazy glow.

'It's delightful when your imagination comes true:' the words of Anne of Green Gables, when she learns that Gilbert Blythe loves her, float into my mind. As I dial William's mobile using Annie's phone, suffused with happiness, my glance falls upon the pile of his poems lying on the sofa. Holding the phone to my ear, I find the poem titled 'A Marriage of True Minds', a line from Shakespeare's Sonnet 116, and I turn the sheet of paper over. The poem, full of rapturous love and tenderness, is addressed to me in William's sloping, graceful handwriting. He concludes by quoting the clinching final couplet of Shakespeare's Sonnet 116 :

"If this be error and upon me proved,

I never writ, nor no man ever loved."

What a gloriously conclusive affirmation of true love….

Epilogue

And so my story ends with a complete volte-face for, I unashamedly admit, my belief in Romantic literature has once more been totally restored – much to Becky's disgust. The pastoral and romantic traditions are joyously and firmly re-established within me. I remain a defiant dreamer – after all, as Shakespeare himself declares: "We are such stuff as dreams are made of".

I have learned the value of reason, seeing now the dangers that can lurk in fantasy, thanks to Becky. "All power of fancy over reason is a degree of madness", said Dr Johnson and I can see his point too.

But hey, I'm not just an animal capable of reason, which seems to be Becky's modus operandi. I do believe in souls – and in soul-mates (but certainly not in Becky and I being soul-mates). Catherine Earnshaw's suggestion that there is "an existence of yours beyond you" has been given validation for me. Like Jay Gatsby, I have a faith in an inner vision, in "a promise that the rock of the world was founded securely on a fairy's wing." And don't worry, I do know that Catherine Earnshaw and Gatsby are fictional – but surely their ideas reflect *real* possibilities?

Indeed, time has moved on a little and all illusions, delusions and misconceptions cleared up. I have spoken on Annie's phone to a bewildered, incredulous William. I have explained, elaborated, apologised to him profusely. He has shown understanding and forgiveness, bless him.

And, as I walk down the track from my cottage to meet William, a rainbow arches over the valley behind him, as colourful as a stained-glass window. The bracken around him stirs in the breeze. William greets me, his face warm and loving. The face of my soul-mate. He buries his face in my hair, holding me so close I can feel the beating of his heart…

And time has once again moved on, and I have just sent my sister a card for our joint 23rd birthday. I want to thank her for being there, for caring for me, for supporting me – despite the fact she drives me mad. I want to move beyond the conflict between us and express my love for her. There will always be a special kind of closeness between us, even though I can't live with her. My solution is to send her a birthday card. It's not the usual birthday card with the plain simple message 'Happy Birthday' on the front, typical of the ones I usually give her. It is a card entitled 'To My Sister' and is decorated in colourful flowers with butterflies fluttering about. The words inside about my sister are sentimental and rhyming and Becky will be horrified. But I think that sometimes sentimental words can be the best at expressing genuine feelings and I hope she will sense in them the love I feel for her.

Again, time has moved on and my story can conclude with two phrases I've *always* wanted to use. Phrases which are disgracefully, exuberantly, and outrageously cheesy.

Two phrases to defy all the cynics of this world!

Two of the most famous phrases in English Literature.

The first: "Reader, I married him".

So I suppose that this, the story of my life so far, has been a comedy, not a tragedy as I had imagined – for Shakespeare's comedies always end with a marriage, a good ending. And some of my delusions have indeed been farcical, I'm afraid. But, of course, a marriage is not an ending but a significant beginning.

So the second phrase is one that requires a wild leap of faith to fulfil – the hope, but *not* the illusory, delusional hope – that William and I will indeed live "Happily ever after."